THE PROVING OF ROSE ALLEYN

Copyright © Vivien Freeman 2023

All rights reserved

The right of Vivien Freeman to be identified as the author of this work has been asserted in accordance with Section 77 of the UK Copyright, Designs and Patents Act 1988.

The characters and events portrayed in this book are fictitious. Any similarity to any real person, living or deceased, is coincidental and is not intended by the author.

No part of this book may be circulated or stored (or otherwise retained) or lent, resold or hired out in any other format without the explicit written consent of the Publisher.

A CIP catalogue record for this book is available from the British Library

ISBN 978-1-7397814-5-3

Published by 186 Publishing Limited 2023

www.186publishing.co.uk

The Proving of Rose Alleyn

Vivien Freeman

186 Publishing

Chapter One

I am not looking forward to this evening. While Leonard was away, I let my attendance lapse. I didn't have time anyway, what with running two shops and hospital visiting. Or that was my excuse. But really, I could not bring myself to go, for I always thought - still think - that if The Fabian Society had made a statement condemning the World War, then my dearest Leonard might not have gone, might have acted on his initial surge of revulsion at the prospect of killing fellow human beings who were essentially no different from ourselves. Men who also had families or, even if they did not, were still someone's son. Whatever their nationality, they were, as Leonard always said, 'cannon-fodder', victims sent out to fuel the great death-machine of Empire.

But the Society made no public statement until January 1916, and then only to say that 'in accordance with the rule that forbids it to speak unless it has something of value to say, it has made no pronouncement and adopted no policy'. In the first two years of the War, before conscription, years which in hindsight seem to have about them an inevitability of outcome, my husband, for all his love of foreign countries, discovered in himself what it was and is to feel English, with a touch of Welsh and anything else which might be in the ancestral mix that makes British. Not only this but, as he said after one of those endless nights awake, why should he be any different from every other man who bowed his head and accepted what he had to do? What gave him the right to place himself above them and step aside to let another die in his place? I still feel sick at the thought of how I felt, selfish me, while he talked into the early hours.

A sense of having been let down is not the only reason for my lack of enthusiasm about this evening. I know I should feel some sympathy for our speaker. Fred Rawlins had made a name for himself as editor of a local newspaper in a big town nearer to London than Widdock but, during the War, his job was taken over by a woman and has not, apparently, been restored to him. I can't help supposing that this is because he was a Conscientious Objector. He wasted no time, however, in founding a radical newspaper which already has a healthy circulation. He is here tonight in Widdock to give a talk taking its title from the popular campaign, 'Hands Off Russia', a defence of the Bolshevik system. The subject does not fill my heart with joy.

Leonard, on the other hand, is looking forward to the debate. He is almost his former, pre-war self, a self I feared I might never see again after his return last year, shattered, from the front in Egypt and Palestine. So I should thank Mr. Rawlins for bringing the old Leonard to the fore, and indeed I could not be more thankful for that. I have only met Fred Rawlins a handful of times since first encountering him in 1900. Leonard seems to have forgotten a certain event which will stay forever branded on my mind – or if he does remember, he chooses not to mention it.

'Oh, the light this time of year!' he exclaims, voicing my thoughts as we walk arm in arm through the quiet streets.

Behind the silhouetted cowl of Britannia Malting the sky is almost turquoise, flushed with striations of the gentlest peach. We turn into the courtyard of the Quaker Meeting House, its fine, plain glass windows lit by welcoming lamplight. In the dense foliage surrounding the darkening garden, a blackbird begins his evening peroration, and I wish, not for the first time tonight, that we were free simply to walk around the town we love, our home, one which we made here and that, thank God, we still share together.

This and much else plays on my mind. We walk through the door and are immediately greeted by the Chairman as if we had never been away. The warmth of the place, the gentle hum of conversation help me to relax. These are my friends.

It is from respect and, I dare say, love that neither the Chairman nor his wife asks Leonard how he is, simply telling him how good it is to have him back. 'And you, Rose.' They mean it, too. 'Allow me to introduce tonight's speaker.'

I have of course spotted him, together with his wife, Gladys, two figures linked by an exclusive intimacy, an invisible circle which they seem to cast around them as they stand, heads inclined towards each other as if in urgent colloquy.

Leonard greets both, and my husband's generosity of nature lights a reciprocal smile, if on a lesser scale, in Fred Rawlins's face. 'It's good to see you again, Pritchard,' he says with what looks like genuine pleasure. They have enough in common to be kindred spirits – except in that great gulf where one made a fundamentally different decision from the other.

'Mrs. Pritchard, Rose.' Now, he's taking my hand, and I remember how his eyes, like dark wells, seem to mesmerise me against my will. 'How's business these days?'

This could be a perfectly innocuous question and yet, coming from Mr. Rawlins, it appears to brand me as an arch-capitalist. I search for the words to frame an answer neither apologetic nor complacent. Before I can speak, someone taps his arm, his attention is diverted, and my 'Not too bad, thank you,' coincides with his 'Will you excuse me?' as he and Leonard turn towards a Labour councillor, eager to greet them both and speak to them.

I am left with Gladys Rawlins's disquieting gaze, and it comes to me, as I attempt the mental adjustment to make some form of conversation with her, how physically alike they are. I had forgotten this. Indeed, they could be brother and sister. This insight does not help me.

'I'm so glad your husband has made such a success of his new job,' I say, hearing the note of desperation in my voice.

As I speak, her eyebrows knit slightly in puzzlement. 'New job...?' Then, she smiles in a tight, comprehending way. 'Another one who thinks he's been replaced,' she says almost as an aside, spoken in a weary undertone, yet one which slaps me in the face.

I try not to bridle. 'But, he's now the editor –'

She cuts across me. 'Yes, yes, but that's a side-line – though it shows they couldn't smash him!' This is almost a snarl, her dark eyes snapping fire, but she re-orders her composure. 'Kit Jeavons has done a reasonable job as editor of The Greenfield Argus. So she should with our M.P. behind her! But her man returned and now he's recovered, so she's leaving to get married. Fred will resume his position on the first of June.'

'Oh... good...' The ineffectuality of my comment passes unnoticed, as she continues her own train of thought.

'I expect you had your husband back for Christmas - 1918,' she says in the measured voice of one about to dispense enlightenment.

'Actually -'

'I didn't get mine back till nearly this time last year. Yes, that's right - six months after The Armistice.' She cannot conceal the hard ring of anger in her voice.

'I'm so sorry, but why...?'

'Why do you think?' She says.

I am thinking, but before I can find any form of words which will do justice to the extremity of both our feelings, she says it plainly. 'They had to pay the Conchies back, didn't they?' She takes my blank shock as misunderstanding. 'When the shooting match was over, they weren't going to send C.O.s home first as an act of kindness, were they?'

'Where was Mr. Rawlins...?' An image of prison flashes before me. I wish I hadn't asked.

'The Western Front,' says his wife, 'as far as I know,' she adds, darkly.

'I'm so sorry,' I repeat, and mean it. Leonard, usually keen to share his thoughts with me, has hardly told me anything about his experiences at Gaza, and not much about Jerusalem. Although I thank God every day that he's alive and has come back to me in one piece physically, I know that mentally he has suffered. I cannot help but draw the conclusion, therefore, that he wants to shield me from those terrors which still wake him in the night. I forbear to mention any of this to Gladys Rawlins. Nor do I tell her that it has taken till now for Leonard to be in any way able to do more than go to work and come home in the evening, ready to eat his meal and go to bed. I try not to allow my thoughts expression even in my face, for this is not a competition about whose husband has been punished more. And how could I begin to tell this woman, emanating righteous fury, of the anguish which preceded Leonard's final decision to enlist? This doesn't mean that I'm not motivated to try to frame an unapologetic but tactful account of it all. I am spared the attempt by the Chairman, asking us to be seated so that the meeting can begin.

Although I am aware of Mr. Rawlins making his case, it is as if I am listening from a great distance. I am re-living my conversation with his wife and thinking of what I should have said which might have shown her that we had not simply swallowed official propaganda and become lackeys of Empire, but had taken a principled stand.

Preoccupied though I am, when questions are taken I notice that our speaker doesn't have it all his own way. The words 'partial,' 'partisan,' and even 'blinkered' are used about Bolshevik supporters such as H.G. Wells. Leonard suggests that, given the criticism voiced by the recent independent T.U.C./Labour Party Delegation to Russia, perhaps it would be wise to suspend judgement until after publication of their report. There are murmurs of 'hear, hear' to this intervention.

I realise that the meeting's ended, the speaker's being thanked and we all clap. I glance anxiously at Leonard. His expression is abstracted and, I can't help thinking, slightly strained. His face clears as the applause ends and people start to move. 'Yes, good to be back,' he replies cheerfully to well-wishers, as we move towards the door. 'Enough excitement for one evening,' he responds to others. And now we're outside in the cool, starry night.

We cross the little garden, through the gate and turn for home. Two dark figures in front of us are the Rawlinses. My heart gives an involuntary dip. Their route is ours, for they will be on their way to Widdock East railway station. Before we can be presented with the dilemma of whether or not to strike up a conversation, Fred Rawlins pulls a watch on a chain from his pocket. 'Better get a move on, Glad,' he says, and the couple quicken their step, trotting away from us like a pair of carriage ponies.

Leonard remarks, when they are out of earshot, 'Bit of a misnomer – Glad.'

I look at him. He is giving me what I can only describe as an impish smile. 'I won you, and he had to settle for –'

'Shh...' I tap his arm with the hand threaded through it, and we walk on in companionable silence, each of us no doubt reliving the evening of the Fabian Society Summer Party twenty years ago, when we appeared together walking just as we are now, in order to deceive Fred Rawlins into thinking that, rather than being merely employer and employee, we were an engaged couple. I shall never forget what led to this ruse, the horrified realisation that what my naïve sixteen-year-old self had taken for friendship was something more – or at least other - than that. Nor shall I forget my sense of shame when Fred, as he'd introduced himself to me at his first Fabian meeting, left the party early, his final words spoken with eyes burning into me and reverting to formality to make his point, 'I don't fit in, Miss Alleyn, I've had enough.' I did not see him again for many years after that. How I wish there could have been another way to disabuse him of my feelings, rather than Mr. Pritchard's, Leonard's, cunning strategy. Perhaps this residual trace of guilt explains my unease whenever I have to encounter the man. Thank God it is not often.

Tomorrow, Tuesday, will be a working day for both of us but I am not surprised, somehow, once we are both upstairs and in our night clothes, that Leonard catches me in his arms. I run my fingers through his lovely hair, grown more luxuriant again since he came home. We sink under the turned back sheet.

The muffled thud of the church door closing behind me and the thump of a hymn book, dislodged as I try to slide inconspicuously into a pew at the back, manages to fill that still moment in which the choir has concluded the introit and the service is about to start. My brother-in-law, Gerald, turns to address his flock. From her seat at the front of the choir his wife, my sister Hilda, turns for a moment to direct, from eyes of startling blue, a look which if I did not know her to be short-sighted I would interpret as meant for me, a searing admonition for my lateness. I put aside any sense of shame, finding solace in the prayers and responses, known by heart, and pleasure in the singing of hymns.

As we all file out afterwards, greeted by Gerald in the porch, Hilda takes my arm and steers me into the churchyard away from other parishioners. 'Is everything all right? It's not like you to be late, Rose.'

So she had spotted me. What can I say to her? It is my husband's birthday. The light coming in through the curtains woke us both at an early hour. I lay in his arms, listening to the thrush's clarion call to his friends to 'Get up! Get up!' and how all the other songbirds joined in that joyous Maytime chorus. And then, Hilda, how we found ourselves stirred by that springtime song into the most wonderful, I might say archetypal, celebration of our love. And that is why I was late for church. 'We overslept,' I say which, in its way, is true.

Hilda nods, with a little inward smile. Having satisfied her low expectations of us, it is as if we with all our shortcomings can now be dismissed. 'We'll call round for tea at three,' she says, in a cheery voice, already preparing to greet someone else.

They actually arrive at quarter to. Hearing their knock, we leave our newspapers and deckchairs under the apple tree, and let them in. Gerald, bearing a large cake tin, is full of apologies for being early. He has a christening at four o'clock.

'We didn't want to let you down by not coming at all,' says Hilda.

'Very thoughtful,' says Leonard, not catching my eye. 'Come through.'

In the kitchen, Hilda takes the tin, presenting it to Leonard, 'Happy Birthday!' Gerald echoes her. 'Your favourite,' Hilda says, 'Victoria Sponge Sandwich!' (I cannot parallel her lightness of touch, nor would I try. My contribution to this marvel, graciously accepted after some prevarication, was half of my last week's sugar ration.)

'You spoil me,' says Leonard. 'Thank you so much.'

Hilda dimples with pleasure.

I glance at Gerald to see how he is taking this little pantomime, but I should have guessed he would be wearing that expression of benign acceptance he must have honed in his twenty years of ministry. Added to that, I honestly believe he is as much in love with Hilda, whose prettiness has blossomed into stately beauty, and whose loving care and innate expertise in homemaking is second to none, as the day he set eyes on her when he was a curate in our little town of Markly, twelve miles away from here.

'We thought we'd go in the garden, as it's so lovely,' I say. 'We can't seat everyone anyway if they all turn up, and it'll be nicer out there.'

'I'll put the little trestle up for the tea things,' says Leonard. 'Can you take this, please?'

So, Gerald gets the cake tin back. Leonard takes the picnic table from its hook in the broom cupboard and they wander outside. As I fill the kettle at the sink, I watch the two men, atheist and believer, heads inclined in conversation as they make for the dappled shade by the deckchairs, both no doubt enjoying the chance to flex their intellectual muscles in an easy, years-old friendship. Behind me, Hilda has put milk in four cups, and filled the sugar bowl. At a knock on the door, which opens with a 'Coo-ee,' she adds milk to two more.

And here comes my favourite sister, Phyllis, walking straight in with Jenny, her special friend – and my friend, too, from when we were resident twenty years ago at the house named after its own apple tree, where they still live in a cowshed they have converted in the garden, with a workshop for Phyllis' carpentry. 'Do we wait for everyone else before we give him his presents?' She asks, after we've all exchanged fond greetings. She is carrying a large canvas bag. I know what it contains.

'I should think so,' I say, 'but go on out. He'll be pleased to see you.'

Leonard loves to talk to Phyllis because she is his equal in being abreast of political events. Hilda follows Phyllis with a large plate and cake slice.

The front door opens again and in steps Lettie, with whom I shared a room all those years ago in Apple Tree House. She is followed by her husband, my brother Hubert, and Tom, their eighteen-year-old son.

'You set a pace, you two,' says Hubert to Jenny.

'I called out, but you didn't hear,' says Tom.

Jenny simply smiles and carries the tray of tea plates and assorted forks outside.

Lettie's gaze follows her into the garden. 'Hilda's here already, I see. Puffed sleeves don't suit her.'

Lettie is the manageress of Ladies' Fashions and Haberdashery at Giffords, our local department store. Surprised at her uncharitable tone, I remember that if the War had dragged on any longer Tom would have been called up, and in fact he only just escaped it; whereas Hilda and Gerald's son Ambrose, of similar age, is an ordinand in the Church of England, so would never have been sent to the Front Line as a combatant.

'How's Alex?' I ask Lettie, as we take the tray and tea pot outside. This is my niece, Hubert and Lettie's daughter of nearly thirteen.

'Covered in calamine. It's all in her hair!'

'She looks disgusting,' says Tom.

'You looked as bad when you had chickenpox,' says his father.

'They're both in the vicarage garden,' says Hilda, meaning Alex and her daughter of the same age, my other niece, Dee. She lifts the cake by its greaseproof paper wrapping. Jenny helps her to coax it onto the plate.

'At least they both went down together, but they're ever so disappointed not to be here, aren't they?' says Lettie.

Hilda straightens up. 'They're concocting some piece of writing to give to Leonard, but I said we couldn't bring it now, it might be contagious.'

'Tell them, I'll appreciate it all the more for having waited,' Leonard calls across. He, Phyllis and Gerald have acknowledged the arrival of the others, but don't break off from their discussion.

'Meg and Winnie not here yet?' asks Hubert. 'It isn't like them to be late.'

These are the final members of our old residency, two sisters who started as juniors and are now respected scientists at the big pharmaceutical company in Widdock.

'No, not with that special clock – what is it?' Lettie says.

'Sidereal,' I say, 'based on atomic time.'

I've almost seen the joke coming before Tom starts, with a giggle, 'I've got a backside-ereal clock. It chimes – '

'That's enough!' says Hubert.

'Was that a knock?' I run back indoors. It occurs to me as I lead Meg and Winnie through, and they tell me how they bumped into the genial Chairman of their company and couldn't politely get away, that this afternoon we've had apologies for being both early and late.

Leonard, Gerald and Phyllis greet Meg and Winnie with warm smiles. They start moving towards the table while Phyllis is still talking. 'So, do you reckon they've given this warning about higher food and coal prices to take our minds off how they're handling the Irish problem?' She looks inquiringly from one to the other of the two men.

'Now, now,' says Hilda, clapping her hands, 'no politics, please, this is a birthday party. Leonard – you must cut the cake and make a wish but don't tell us.'

'It's all right, Hilda, I know the ropes,' says Leonard, affably. He places the serrated edge of the slice to make the first cut, and as he presses down, closes his eyes. Opening them again, he says, 'That's done.'

We all clap and chorus, 'Happy Birthday!'

For a moment, Leonard looks slightly perturbed. I know the signs – loud noises – of course, the clapping – I should have thought. Unlike when we applauded Fred Rawlins's talk, this time Leonard was taken by surprise. But before I can speak he recovers himself. 'Thank you, thank you.' He turns to the task of apportioning the cake. 'Thirteen's impossible.'

'And unlucky!' Hilda and Lettie speak as one.

'Actually,' Leonard pauses, slice raised, 'in pre-Christian times thirteen was a lucky number.'

'Well, we're in Christian times now,' says Hilda.

'Don't fret, I'm cutting twelve.'

'Make mine a sliver,' I say, 'then you can take a piece back for the girls to share.' This to Hilda, and Lettie agrees that this might cheer them up.

'Would anyone like to share a ground sheet?' Winnie asks in a business-like way, as Meg produces one from her rucksack, and they both unfold the thin rubber cloth. It turns out they use it when they go camping. (Camping? What have I been missing?) They are so resourceful, these sisters. I say I'll sit with them when I've passed round the cake. Lettie helps me, and Hilda pours the tea, everyone to take their own cup. The men say they'll risk the grass despite dire warnings from Lettie, 'stains' and Hilda, 'you know what!' 'Piles?' Tom grins, encouraged, surprisingly, by Winnie, keeping a straight face, 'Don't worry, we've got cream for those,' and Meg, barely managing to, 'haemorrhoids, if you want their anatomical name.' 'Room for another small bottom on here,' I say, the level of humour rather infectious, and Jenny joins us, followed by Phyllis, 'budge up', the two friends giggling in their close proximity, which I love, too, as Phyllis winks at me and Jenny gives her flame-like smile. We're in a lovely triangle of friendship. This arrangement leaves Hilda and Lettie sitting in the deckchairs, above us like two queens.

Hubert taps his spoon on the side of his cup. 'Just a few words of appreciation,' he clears his throat. 'We're a funny lot we Alleyns – ' 'You can say that again!' from Lettie, and similar expressions of mock-agreement from the other non-Alleyns, 'we don't make much of our birthdays because they're mainly all so close together – and it wouldn't be fair on those of us who can't celebrate – ' sympathetic agreement from Phyllis, Hilda and me as we think of the three who are in service in big country houses – 'so, I'd like to thank Leonard on behalf of the Alleyn family for allowing his birthday to be the birthday of the year.' Leonard makes a gracious gesture. 'And the fact that it fell on a Sunday meant it was convenient – well, not for everyone –' It's Gerald's turn to be magnanimous, 'part of the job.' He smiles and nods at Hubert to continue, but Hubert seems to be finding it difficult, and his face is wobbling slightly. 'The other thing I'd like to say,' he swallows, 'on behalf of those of us who weren't called upon to make –' he swallows again, 'what might have been the ult...' his voice wavers.

'The ultimate sacrifice,' Gerald takes over as naturally as if it had been Hubert going on speaking, 'yes, indeed. From the bottom of our hearts, thank you, Leonard.' Gerald was, of course, exempted from conscription but so, too, were my brothers Hubert and Joe, both station masters who, when they presented themselves at the recruitment office, were told that their positions were far too responsible to be undertaken by women or any other untrained person. 'And may I say, it's good to have you back – truly back, as you now are.'

I blink away tears.

'I have to thank dearest Rose for that,' says Leonard, quickly, before any more clapping can break out, 'but I'm very touched by what you have just said.'

And I am touched by that tribute, dear Leonard, I want to say but I can't speak.

'And now,' he stands up in a business-like way, 'I think we'd better get on with those things you've been concealing.'

Hilda explains that the sponge we have been eating with so much appreciation was their present. With regret, they say that they must go before the other gifts are revealed: a new straw boater from Lettie and Hubert, from Gifford's; an outdoors thermometer from Winnie and Meg ('you can't take your temperature with it,' says Winnie to Tom, in such a way that has him giggling again); and a stylish wooden footstool worked by Phyllis and covered by Jenny with a contemporary patterned fabric. Leonard is overwhelmed, and thanks them all profusely. No one needs to ask what I gave Leonard. It is the same gift which he gives me, a token both practical and beautiful: a notebook of the finest quality paper whose cover is a lovely marbled card. This arrangement entirely suits us.

Once satisfied they are not needed to clear up, Meg and Winnie leave. Lettie is collecting the rest of the dirty crockery from the garden. I catch Phyllis alone with Jenny in the kitchen, Phyllis washing, Jenny drying. I start putting away.

'How's things?' I ask them, meaning the situation with our dear Mrs. Fuller, owner and one-time landlady of Apple Tree House.

'So-so,' says Phyllis.

'She sent her apologies,' Jenny adds.

'Of course. Neither of us thought for a moment that she would come today. Give her our love, though. I'll be up in the week.' Not that she needs telling of that fact.

'She did say,' Phyllis lowers her voice, glancing out of the window, 'she'd like to see you in the afternoon on the tenth, even though there's nothing to celebrate.'

The sadness we all share cloaks us for a moment, each of us still reliving the shock of that day when the telegram came to Apple Tree House. Phyllis, who never cries, hurried round to the shop with tears streaming down her cheeks to tell me that Miles, whom I'd known since he was a toddler arriving with his mother Beatrice, Mrs Fuller's daughter, one autumn evening twenty years ago, because she was fleeing from an unfaithful marriage in Italy – Miles, whom I'd treated as another nephew, whom I'd watched grow into a fine young man, was dead.

The others return from the garden. 'Gerald's not the only one who has to go back to work,' says Hubert, 'come on lad.' Tom is a Controller at Widdock East, where Hubert is Station Master.

'And I'd better go and collect Alex before Hilda thinks she's got her for the night,' says Lettie.

'Tell Spotty I'll see her later,' says Tom.

We stand at the door. Lettie turns and waves as they pass under the arch. Then they are gone.

Phyllis and Jenny look as if they are about to follow suit.

'Can we tempt you to linger?' Leonard says. 'Rose is going to make her delicious scrambled eggs with smoked salmon for supper.'

'You know you're both very welcome,' I add.

'It's a lovely offer,' says Phyllis, 'but we'd better get back and make sure they're all right.'

We both make understanding noises. Phyllis took over my unofficial job as cook when I left to get married, a role which she has retained all these years, and one which puts her at the forefront of caring for Mrs. Fuller and Beatrice. She looks tired herself now, and I suspect that once she and Jenny have satisfied themselves that all is as well as it could be in the circumstances, they will retire to the quiet haven of 'The Byre', the name they gave their home, and conclude reading the Sunday papers.

We finish tidying up, by which time my sliver of Hilda's sponge seems a distant memory. While I make scrambled eggs and toast, Leonard lays out the salmon and slices a lemon, just as Mrs. Fuller did one evening in 1900 when she and I were alone and making something of the occasion. I had never tasted smoked salmon before. I learnt that this dish was one she and her late husband used to have for breakfast. Truly, she was a mother to me in that year which started with my own mother's death. 'In the midst of life, we are in death' – never more so than these last few years, but tonight is a celebration of the triumph of life in the form of my dear Leonard. During the meal we talk over the success of his party. Everyone, sensing the emblematic importance of it, had maintained a tone of harmony.

'I've had a wonderful day from beginning to end,' he says and, after we've cleared everything away, 'there's something I'd like to read to you.'

I stay seated at the kitchen table, where we ate the meal in the evening sunshine. He comes back with a book by a poet whose name, Ezra Pound, I do remember as being a new voice.

'I won't say anything about this poem, I'll just read it,' Leonard says. I can hardly believe the beauty of the images, and the way the ardour in the poem is unspoken yet unmistakable. This is the kind of writing which accords with Leonard's, which he developed especially in the rare moments he had to himself on the Front. He found this intense, condensed form of words a lifeline to his spirituality – though he wouldn't call it that. I feel uplifted – almost forget that I, too, have something to contribute. I pick Mother's dear anthology of poetry from the shelf because, throughout the meal, although I had been concentrating perfectly, and have been transported by the poem Leonard just read, Christina Rossetti's lines have been playing through my mind again and again and, despite the fact that 'A Birthday' is not one of Leonard's favourite poems, I have to read it to him. By the time I come to the two lines closing the final stanza, '...Because the birthday of my life/ Is come, my love is come to me' I am speaking through my tears. 'But they're tears of joy,' I manage to say, looking up from the book into his eyes, which are wet too. The next moment we are tight in each other's arms.

Chapter Two

When I first came to Widdock as a sixteen-year-old I had imagined that Pritchard's Bookshop, where I was to work, would look, on the outside, like this one which I now own, with its two generous bay windows sweeping round on either side of the path to the door. I recall the fleeting pang of disappointment at first sight of Pritchard's. It's true it also has a window on each side of the door, but that door and both windows are flush with the brick frontage, making a much less imposing picture than my daydream. Or so I had thought, but only for one moment. How my perception changed as soon as I stepped inside and felt the energy that my employer, Mr. Pritchard, gave the place even before its official opening. With its enticing window displays, in which I played a part right from the beginning, and the scent of new books begging to be read, the next time I walked towards the building, on my second morning, my view had entirely changed.

Life has the strangest way of turning out, though. Years after that instant when my brief whimsy became swiftly reconciled with a far more interesting reality, I was to be granted a version of that wish. I shall never cease to be astonished at how I came into possession of this shop. What a mixed blessing it was then compared to the haven of enrichment I sit in now, quietly going through my records during this half hour before early closing.

Brisk footsteps make me look up as the door opens with a peremptory abruptness.

'Good day to you, Mrs. Pritchard,' says Mr. Vance, one of a trio of Leonard's stalwart friends and supporters. 'Would you be good enough to tell your confounded husband that he has no business to be 'having a meeting at the training college',' this spoken in a higher pitch, 'according to young what's-her-name.'

'Miss Briggs.' Leonard's assistant, whom I took on while he was away.

'As you wish – when I have come hot-foot as an envoy from Cotteringbury School, no less, with an invitation for a poetry reading which he might care to share with me?'

I take a deep breath. 'If you would like to give me the details, Mr. Vance, I'm sure Leonard will be interested, and if he possibly can attend – '

'I thought of all this,' says Mr. Vance, waving a hand to encompass retail trade, 'that's why I suggested they have it on a Thursday afternoon.'

'You're very kind,' I say, taking the sheet of paper he thrusts at me.

'I'm not, and you well know it.' He gives me his crooked smile, 'but when old Wilkers, the headmaster, button-holed me in Cottering High Street and started asking me whether I would be prepared to inspire the dear boys with some verses from my hoary tome, I couldn't help thinking that it was about time Pritchard sought an audience again.'

He stomps out before I can adequately thank him.

It's one of those cool June days which belie the name of summer, rain a possibility at any time in the dull wash of grey overhead. I take the passage beside Apple Tree House, where the coalman brings his sacks to tip their contents down into the cellar, and the fishman comes to the kitchen door every Friday to show his tray of catch to Phyllis for her to choose from what is in season something which will be both tasty and refined – two lemon sole, perhaps, or a couple of skate wings. With these she'll try to tempt her two employers, more her two patients now, to forget for one moment their overwhelming grief and become like children, simply relishing the savour of well-cooked food invitingly presented.

Out of habit, as I pass the corner of the house, I cast a glance at the French windows of the dining room, which once Winnie and Meg shared as their bedroom when we were all young women living in the house together. Today, as expected, the room is in darkness. Mother and daughter never entertain now, but take all their meals in the kitchen, much as was the custom when we all lived here. I knock on the back door and Phyllis lets me in.

'They're on their way down,' she says and, as I follow her through the scullery to the kitchen, I can hear voices on the stairs, my dear Mrs. Fuller's, a shadow of its former sonorous authority, Beatrice's with a slightly higher, diffused note. I carefully unpack from its cardboard box the cake which I have brought, and set it onto a gilt-edged plate which Phyllis has provided in the centre of the table.

'Hello, Rose,' says Mrs. Fuller, entering first.

For one who was as brightly coloured as an artistic peacock she is now, in her plain lilac dress, as muted as a dove. My heart weeps, but at least I am no longer shocked by the hair, drawn up into an elegant French pleat, which once was red-gold but which, by Phyllis's account, turned white after she'd collapsed at seeing the telegram in Beatrice's stricken hand.

'You sit here, Florence,' Phyllis says, guiding the elderly lady, queen for the day, into her place at the head of the table. I so admire my sister for the ease with which she accepted the familiar mode of address that this remarkable woman wants us all to share. For me, she will always be Mrs. Fuller, Mother.

Beatrice sinks into her chair at the other end, the various layers of her black silk dress susurrating into compliance. Her tow hair, which in her younger days seemed to have a life of its own, has been caught up with a brutal twist into a jet comb on top of her head. Truly, I regret to say, these two grieving women could be sisters.

I sit down between them, Phyllis standing on the other side pouring tea. It feels warm, harmonious, just the four of us. Jenny, who would be the other natural participant, does not, in her position as Personal Assistant to the Managing Director of a local factory, have Thursday afternoon off. 'Don't save me any,' she said, when the three of us discussed the cake last week. 'You can't cut it easily into five, and if you did six, that leftover slice...'

Our eyes met in silent acknowledgement of whom that slice would symbolically represent.

'A mille-feuilles gateau!' exclaims Mrs. Fuller, 'I don't know how the Askeys do it in such restricted circumstances.'

'And I don't know that we should be entertaining something so frivolous,' says Beatrice, eyeing the cake, which consists of delicate layers of pastry, sandwiching strawberries and whipped cream and dusted with icing sugar. It is just the right size for four people to eat.

'We honour what it represents,' says her mother, with a flicker of her old spirit.

As Phyllis serves, I pass round the plates and we each begin to tease our slice with a pastry fork. We are all no doubt reflecting upon the drama which occasioned the eternal gratitude of Mr. Askey Senior and, indeed, his son. Mrs. Fuller was first off the mark to write to The Widdock Courier, we others close behind, saying how important it was that none of us should sink into brutality and xenophobia. Her letter appeared next to that of Mr. Askey Junior, addressed to: 'Whoever threw a brick through our window and caused my father's seizure. I should like you to know that though he worked for some years learning his trade in Berlin, my father is Polish. His name was Aszkielowicz. He left Germany because he suffered persecution there, and came here where he was made welcome. I was born here. I am a British citizen. I was about to serve my country but have been granted leave to run my father's business while, it is hoped, he recovers. Paul Askey.'

'I guessed a cake might be on the cards,' says Mrs. Fuller, when we've all finished, 'So, I've started a note of appreciation to Michal Askey.' Her eyes stray to the dresser. Phyllis slides out of her seat and brings the notepaper and pen beside it. 'All I need to do is add a line about the particular qualities of the one we've just enjoyed. What do you think - 'your delightful strawberry gateau?''

'Or 'your superb strawberry gateau?'' I suggest.

'Yes, yes, I like 'superb' - the alliteration. Very good.'

She flashes me a smile which nearly breaks my heart. It is so redolent of her former, vital self, I have to glance away for a moment to allow my tears to subside.

'Perhaps you would be kind enough to take the note with you, Rose, when you go,' says Beatrice.

'Of course.'

'But don't go yet,' says Mrs. Fuller. 'I want you to tell me your news. Are your nieces over their illness now?'

'They are, thank you, and have been round to read Leonard's birthday poem to him – all about a perfect day in May.'

'How charming! Was it any good?'

'Yes, it was, if...' I choose my words carefully, 'somewhat reminiscent of his style of writing.'

'Oh well, you know what they say,' this from Phyllis, 'imitation – the sincerest form of flattery.'

'You will tell Leonard, I was so sorry not to attend his birthday tea. I'm afraid all those people would have been too much,' says Mrs. Fuller.

'I've already told him. He understands completely,' I say. I give her a sketch of the party and my week at work. She takes it all in with interest.

'Mother, I think we should...' Beatrice intervenes.

'Yes, dear, I know. We must rest. Did I say, it's the inaugural meeting of the War Memorial Committee tonight, of all nights?'

'You did,' I begin.

'And it's our duty to attend,' says Beatrice, helping her mother to rise.

'Poached egg at six-thirty, then?' Phyllis asks in a cheerful, business-like voice.

'That would be perfect,' says Mrs. Fuller, 'and thank you all for everything. That's all I can say.'

'Yes, thank you for making Mother's day a true consolation,' says Beatrice, as she lets Mrs. Fuller pass first into the hall corridor. Her strained, white face reminds us how much this afternoon's attempt at normal behaviour has cost her.

When they've gone I move to help Phyllis clear the crocks. 'No, leave it. I can do it in no time when I come back. Let's go down to The Byre.'

I pick up the note to Mr. Askey, and we walk down through the formal garden, recently a pageant of bright tulips and cherry blossom but now suffering a gap in flowering. With columbines over and the lovely profusion of roses yet to bloom, the empty green seems almost desolate.

At the end of the lawn, beyond the border backed by a line of cherry and damson trees, is the vegetable garden, neatly planted up by Phyllis and Jenny with rows of runner bean poles and drills of broccoli. To one side of this, north-facing, is the former stable housing Mrs. Fuller's studio, unvisited since Miles's death. Next door is what was once a cowshed, now called The Byre. Outside the front door are pots overflowing with scarlet geraniums - pelargoniums by their proper name - descendants of the ones which Meg and Winnie grew outside the French windows of their bedroom in the sun-trap well of the house, twenty years ago.

Phyllis reaches to unbolt the lower half of the stable door. I follow her inside The Byre, fragrant with the lingering scent of last autumn's apples stored in most of the loft space, a small part of which, directly above us, is also Phyllis and Jenny's bedroom. I am always pleased to be here in this white-washed room with its simple pine table and two chairs made by Phyllis, and glad fabrics - warm, brick-red curtains, the colour picked up by the rug, these being Jenny's contribution to this lovely place which is both restful yet full of life. Her knitting needles protrude from a bag beside the enveloping sofa. On a shelf three green glass bottles catch my eye, labelled in Phyllis's neat yet vigorous hand: Elderflower Cordial.

'Would you like some?'

She must have followed my gaze, and bats aside my protestations that she and Jenny should keep it for themselves. Disinclined to argue, I sink into the sofa, disturbing a trace of last year's lavender from one or more of its bright cushions. Behind me is a pine partition made by Phyllis. Its sliding doors stand open in their summer mode, revealing a larger, light-filled space which is Beatrice's painting studio. Like her mother, she has not ventured there since her son's death.

Phyllis hands me a v-shaped glass of fragrant cordial. 'Well, what did you think?' I see the lines of strain behind the anticipation in her strong face.

'I thought she seemed... well... a lot better,' I say, tempering my optimism. We both know who I mean, our primary concern being Mrs. Fuller, my older friend.

'That's what I thought,' says Phyllis, 'but I wanted to make sure I wasn't imagining it because it's what I've wished for so much.'

'When she was talking about the wording for the thank you letter –' I am re-running the last hour in my mind – 'she seemed almost to be humorous.'

Phyllis nods. 'Perhaps this War Memorial business has given her a purpose.'

'It's certainly galvanised Beatrice.'

We each know what the other is thinking: it's a good cause but will it help or hinder these two women in trying to overcome their grief?

Since we cannot know the answer, further speculation would be pointless, so we move on to our own topics: how work is – steady; any news from the family – nothing to speak of. I leave well before Jenny is due home, for I know how precious is that time of the evening when a couple, apart at work for eight hours or more, comes together to mull over the day.

Walking home to enact our version of that situation, I can't help feeling, unspoken reservations aside, light-hearted.

As I carry my tray downstairs, I think of that afternoon briefly, and of the following Thursday afternoon when I called at Apple Tree House and also found Mrs. Fuller in better spirits. These two cheering memories fuse with the pleasurable surprise of being woken gently with a cup of tea, followed shortly by a boiled egg with fingers of toast and more tea. When Leonard said that he would cook today, I didn't realise that this would include breakfast. As I dip toast into a perfectly-cooked egg I wonder, a shade ruefully, what my favourite brother Jack, who works as groom and chauffeur at Sawdons Hall, will be doing on this special day we share, he being my senior by exactly one year.

Although wash days have no respect for birthdays, and Lizzie Munns will soon be here to help me with our laundry, this sunny, longest day of the year spreads a beneficence which even the austere surroundings of the wash house and the rigours of lighting and filling the copper cannot quite dispel.

Just as her mother-in-law, our dear, redoubtable Mrs. Munns always used to arrive early at Apple Tree House to help Mrs. Fuller with all our washing, Lizzie, with her bright smile and birthday greetings, joins me before time. She is waving an envelope which must have arrived while I was out here communing with the god of cleanliness, this squat metal tub on legs. She takes the washing-dolly from me, pressing the envelope into my hand. 'Go and open your card.' I thank her and take it through to the light-filled sitting room, puzzling who could have sent it given that, being ten of us, most with birthdays close together, we Alleyns never observe them.

I have so seldom seen it that it takes me a moment to recognise my sister Dot's handwriting. Although she is Cook at Sawdons Hall, correspondence by or with those in service was always frowned upon by the family upstairs – until the cruel necessities of the War wrought a lasting change. Dot has never been one for writing letters, though, so I am surprised and touched that she should choose to remember the date in this way. I slit the envelope, my questing finger discerning not a card but a letter – goodness me, how lovely! I see Dot's sweet smile, her comfortable figure all rolled up with the lightest of pastries, the heartiest of broths. I feel all this as I draw the sheet of ruled paper out and read:

Dearest Rose,

I write in haste. Firstly, I'm truly sorry to spoil your birthday – I hope you are still able to enjoy it – but I have to tell you that Jack is not at all well. He talks about you all the time. I seem to think you have early closing in Widdock on Thursday. Might you be able to find a way to get here then? If you can, let me know, preferably by return. I'm so sorry. I hope to see you on Thursday.
Your loving sister,
Dot

I sink into my armchair, mind reeling. I'm still holding the letter when Lizzie comes to find out what has detained me. From all her experience of families (her mother-in-law had seven sons) she understands. 'Bad news?' I tell her. 'Leave the wash to me,' she says, but I tell her, no. For one thing, going through the mechanical process of laundering might calm me and help me to think, for another, I shall be glad to talk it over with her. She is a good-hearted woman, already trying to think of ways she might coerce one of the extensive family of Munnses to help me.

Fortunately, I haven't a moment to indulge in the least pang of self-pity either for the time I would have had to myself after Lizzie's departure or for the fact that anxiety over the challenge I am about to face has robbed me of the pleasure I was looking forward to of cycling gently across the parkland on this fine afternoon observing any subtle changes to the landscape's picture which this longest day might present from that of last week's traverse.

My bicycle is a route to freedom. Sometimes, in the darkest days when my mind had me bound to a treadmill of despair about what was happening to Leonard – if he was still alive – I would have to put the 'Closed – back soon' sign on the shop door and slip into the saddle, just as if I were to go for a ride on dear Iolo, the old Welsh cob Jack saved from a certain fate by striking a bargain with his master, the heir of Sawdons Hall, to buy him for a penny. Both horse and former owner are now gone, Iolo to an eternal pastureland, Master Greville, for all his faults, and they were legion, to the place where God will be the judge of them against the fact that he gave his life for all of us.

Oh, how I loved to ride Iolo, that hot summer of 1900 when I was on holiday at home, rising at dawn, riding in my nightdress, bareback.

And now, such reveries have brought me to St. Ann's, a small convent part of which, at the outbreak of war, was converted into a hospital for those men no longer on the critical list. My mouth is dry as sawdust, as I leave my friend to chat to other bicycles in the rack next to the arched porch.

By some grapevine - for I'm sure I haven't mentioned it - our four remaining patients from the War have grasped the significance of the date. By winks and nods from the men I, in turn, have understood that there will be a modest celebration, a cake with afternoon tea, Cook tells me. This meeting would also have been a valediction, since they leave for the convalescent home on Thursday, an appropriate occasion to wish them well from the bottom of my heart. I cannot be at peace, though, till I've carried out my mission.

I enter the stone-flagged hall, so familiar now. On another day, I might have paused to take in, for the last time, its graceful panelling and vaulting, but I see Sister in the corridor to the refectory-turned-ward. She hears me out but directs me to Matron. I guessed she would.

Matron has a small reception room leading off the entrance hall. Her door is partially ajar. I take deep breaths to calm my pounding heart, rehearse for the hundredth time what I have to say. Then I knock - not too loudly, but not feebly either.

'Enter.'

I open the door and walk in, halting some feet from the desk.

'Mrs. Pritchard.' She disregards my courteous greeting. 'You have something to say to me.'

My cheeks are flaming. 'Yes, Matron.'

'Well, you'd better spit it out.' She looks inscrutable.

I swallow. 'My brother Jack is ill again.'

'I'm very sorry to hear that.' She manages, without saying it, to weigh Jack's suffering in the scale of all those suffering men not least, of course, our own patients. I feel dreadful.

'Is that all?'

'I'm very worried about him. He works - when he's well, that is - at Sawdons and - '

'You wondered whether you might accompany our last patients there on Thursday.' Her neutral tone gives nothing away.

I can't speak, but nod furiously. I manage a hoarse whisper. 'Yes, Matron.'

The silence is deafening. Is there something in her eyes, the glint of a smile, or am I imagining it? 'I have no personal objection to the arrangement, and you can quote me on that, but you know the person who must give the ultimate sanction.'

We both speak the name together.

In my two years of visiting at this impromptu hospital, I have exchanged only the most perfunctory of pleasantries with the Commandant, a formidable figure, busy and elusive.

Widdock Auxiliary Hospital H.Q. is the convent's post room, situated on the other side of the entrance hall and thus easily accessible for the installation of a telephone. The door stands open. I peep inside but, as expected, find the room empty. At a slight loss, I step outside the building.

And there, as if by magic, is the Commandant leaning against the end wall of the bike shed smoking a cigarette in the sunshine.

'Good afternoon,' I say, 'I'm Rose Pritchard.'

'I know who you are,' she says. She's probably younger than me, with pale hair parted at the side and pulled back into a tight chignon behind her ears so that, from the front, she looks not unlike a boy. Her eyes are a penetrating blue.

I explain my mission. My voice sounds like that of a schoolchild trying to curry favour with a teacher.

'Of course you can come,' she says, stubbing out her cigarette with her boot, then picking it up in her strong, cupped hand. 'You can keep me company in the cab.' She starts to walk towards the stables where the ambulance is parked. Over her shoulder, she says, 'Oh, and Happy Birthday, Rose.'

Throughout the years of Leonard's absence, my bicycle and I have led what one might think of as a charmed life. Now, it is as if the discussion Lizzie Munns and I had this morning has acted like an evil spell making what was dreaded happen. We ruled out my cycling to Sawdons, a good three miles beyond my old home town of Markly, because the risk was too great that whilst I was crossing some lonely stretch of countryside I, or rather the bike, might suffer a puncture which I would be unable adequately to repair. Perhaps the bicycle is angry with me for being a doubting Thomas after ten years of staunch service. At least it has the compassion to wait to act until I'm entering the High Street. But I was right in my decision, confirmed by the brief period as I try to lift it and push it on its unaffected wheel. The landlord of The Bull, sunning himself before opening time and seeing my painful progress, hastens to my aid, telling me my dear old companion may stay locked up in his still till we come to fix and collect it.

I am just home with the kettle on before Alex arrives, followed minutes later, with the scrunch of tyres on gravel, by Dee. It's a day of two bicycles. For about three years now, the girls have called by after school on a Monday. At first, this was probably inspired by duty, a suggestion made by their busy mothers to make sure that Auntie Rose was getting along in Uncle Leonard's absence.

When I realised that it was to become a regular event, I decided to abolish the polite awkwardness of such an occasion and let them do what clearly they wanted: catch up with each other. Alex attends the girls' school in town, Dee cycles a mile outside Widdock to a small school for parsons' daughters. At weekends, Lettie co-opts Alex into work related to Gifford's department store, just as Hilda marshals Dee into parish duties. Although my nieces have their own friends, they do like spending their limited free time together. But they couldn't always remember every detail of their respective week apart. 'Oh, I wish I'd written it down – exactly what she said.' Alex had clutched the air, as if it would yield a faithful record. This was the point at which I'd intervened. 'Yes, write it down, both of you. Keep diaries or notebooks. Every day, if you only write one thing, try to find the precise words which will make the subject real to your audience.' 'Audience?' Dee had questioned. Alex was smiling already. 'We can read it out here, can't we, Auntie Rose?' 'You certainly can. I'm sure we'd all enjoy that and, if you like, you can sit at the table where I like to write and see if anything else comes to you.' And so a tradition began.

'We've got these,' Alex proffers a white cardboard box. Her brow furrows. 'But there were only three, so we couldn't get one for Uncle Leonard.'

I open the lid to reveal three Swiss buns. The moment the thought occurs – that I could save mine and divide it to have later with Leonard – I know from my nieces' eager faces that this would be the wrong move. Although I'm partial to these trusty staples of all our celebrations at Apple Tree House this bun, on top of the slice of sponge I ate with those four men who have become as dear in their way as friends, will take the edge off my hunger for the meal prepared by Leonard. Never mind. Besides, these buns are a shadow of their pre-rationing selves, smaller, with only a lick of icing. 'Uncle Leonard had his lovely birthday cake made by your mother,' I say to Dee. 'We'll enjoy these now.'

I pour some lemonade, by which stage the girls have produced an envelope which I open to reveal a card depicting a deep-red rose. I pause to take this in and make a suitably appreciative comment, but I sense their impatience, so I open it. Under the conventional message, there is a handwritten verse:

Really, you are our favourite aunt
Of all because you are so kind,
So good to us. We always find
Ease to express ourselves, you grant.

I am, of course, immensely touched, and tell them so, but I think the girls rather shot their bolt in writing the poem for Leonard's birthday, free of all constraints of rhyme and metre, concentrating on the theme of nature and one glorious, credibly-imagined day walking along by the Blaken, following the river's course past the old mill, which is the factory where Meg and Winnie work, and on across the water meadows.

'Please don't show Uncle Leonard,' says Dee. 'He won't like the last line being the wrong way round to get the rhyme.'

'But we made the first line flow into the second quite well...' Alex tails off.

'He'll be as proud of you both as I am,' I say.

He is, of course, but he does give a wry chuckle, as he returns the card to the mantelpiece to stand next to one with a pink rose signed by the nurses and patients. It is, however, by no means the first thing he does as he steps across the threshold and I close the door behind him having, fortunately, glanced out of the window and seen him coming laden with two bouquets, the first of which, a dozen red roses, he presents to me.

'Happy Birthday, dearest Rose.'

'They're beautiful, thank you, thank you.' I find my eyes filling. Leonard is so nearly restored to his former vital self. I realise too, as our lips touch over the heavenly scent, how utterly exhausted I am by the physical and emotional upheaval of the day.

While we have been kissing, he has been holding the other bunch of six creamy-pink roses to one side. Now he proffers them with a flourish. 'And these are from your gentlemen friends.'

'Oh, my goodness!'

'You didn't think you'd get away with a birthday unacknowledged, just because Quinn-Harper's was closed?'

This name, the two words run together as the gentry say it, Quinnapers, belonged to the former owner of my bookshop who, to my utter consternation, willed the shop to me - with the proviso that I should retain his name for it which, in deference to his extraordinary generosity, I do - even if I'd like to change this awkward appellation either to Pritchard or to my maiden name Alleyn. This I own, however, would probably be a bad idea since every tongue in Widdock knows its way around what every brain conceives by 'Quinnapers'. My gentlemen friends, as Leonard always delights in calling them, are the backbone of that elderly, established clientele inherited from Auberon Quinn-Harper's day. I shake my head but can't help smiling at the gallantry embodied in this bunch of flowers.

While I find vases, Leonard puts new potatoes and peas to boil, each with a sprig of mint, all three fresh from the garden. He lays a generous slice of ham upon our dinner plates.

'Only one for me, please.'

He looks up, letting the remaining ham, in its grease-poof paper, rest on the table. Almost as a statement, he says, 'You're not quite right, are you?' His eyes are so dark-blue, like a swallow's wing, and however I try to stop it, I feel my face beginning to break up.

The next moment, I am in his arms, telling him all about Jack being ill, my trip to the hospital, the puncture.

'No wonder you're all in,' he says, stroking my hair. 'I can deal with the bike, that's easy. But you've done so well, charming the battle-axes into your proposal. And it's just what Jack needs. His favourite sister. Think what a tonic seeing you will be!'

I have to smile. It's true. I know I can raise his spirits.

Chapter Three

During the War, many servants left Sawdons Hall. If they were men, they went to fight; if they were women, to work for better pay in munitions factories or to follow their patriotic calling as nurses. In such altered circumstances, Dot became both head cook and housekeeper, a dual role which she has retained. In my brief acquaintance with this place, I had never been above stairs, so I took Dot's word for the fact that Sawdons remains much reduced from what it was in its heyday which feels like a lifetime ago, when I turned down a job here with such youthful determination. To me, though, looking about this large, ornate drawing-room whose French windows stand open, it seems pretty grand. Behind me, the Commandant, today wearing her uniform jacket with gold braid, is seated next to the lady of the house, quietly handing over our patients' financial papers and records of any equipment issued, such as crutches or artificial limbs. Coffee spoons clink against bone china.

I have a patient on either arm, as does Blanche Fawcett, the last V.A.D. on duty at St. Ann's, who rode in the ambulance as medical supervision. She and I help the four men into comfortable basket chairs out on the terrace with its view of the formal garden and parkland beyond. The lawn is still given over to the war-time requirement to grow vegetables, but the herbaceous borders are rich with the favourite flowers of summer, those self-set annuals or perennials which can be relied upon, more or less, to look after themselves – spires of purple foxgloves, blue Canterbury bells, bushes festooned with roses drifting from the purest white to the warmest yellow, from a dozen shades of pink to the deepest red. I think for a moment of my brother, Ralph, who worked at Sawdons twenty years ago and is now Head Gardener at a great estate far from here.

Private Reed, Percy, touches my sleeve with the hand he taught to write his name on my birthday card. He is a sweet boy, little more than sixteen. I immediately turn my attention to him.

'If you come to visit yer brother regular, you know, you could pop in on us, Mrs. P.'

He is an orphan, miles from the home he shares with an elderly uncle. I can't bring myself, however gently, to disillusion him. This excursion from the hospital today gives my presence at Sawdons a thin legitimacy but my brother, ill or not, is in service and, as such, forbidden visitors - especially, if it came out, one who refused a servant's job here.

'I think we'd better say good-bye as if it really is,' I say, trying hard not to let the tears I see standing in young Percy's eyes prompt my own to fall.

Nurse Fawcett and I go round all four men, clasping their hands and wishing them well. Then Blanche starts to retrace her steps to join the other two women for coffee. Before anyone can divert me, I walk swiftly along the terrace and round the side of the house to the courtyard which I recognise, with a slight chill.

I see again that winter's afternoon, light failing, my father waiting with the horse and cart after I'd let them know here that I would not become a tweeny. I see a youthful Leonard, black hair untouched by silver, smiling with joy that Father had added his consent to my acceptance of the post as bookshop assistant. I was to take that post up only a few days later, after the end of Leonard's role as tutor to the second son of the house who, now deemed strong enough after great illness, would be sent to boarding school and grow up just in time - I stop these thoughts.

There is no sign of Jack, but the sweet smell of hay and horse stands in for him. The back door, I recall, opens on a corridor with rooms on either side - laundry - still room - pantry, at the end of which is the kitchen.

I see Dot, organising lunch, before she sees me. I am shocked at how drawn her once sweetly cheerful face looks. She claps eyes on me, and it is as if, somehow, all the lines of tension have dropped in a moment of unguarded relief. 'Rose!' She recovers her authority immediately and comes forward, smiling her old smile, but my arrhythmic heart misses another beat.

'We'll take our tea in my room,' she instructs one of her staff, and walks back down the gloomy corridor expecting me to follow, which I do, but am beset with dismay. Hers is the very sitting room I stood in twenty years ago, loaned me by the then housekeeper for the purpose of telling my brothers and sisters, working here, the sad news of Mother's death. Dot may have come to terms with this memory, as she has had to come to terms with everything else the War has wrought upon her, but this is the first time I have set foot in here since that day. I am deep in my painful thoughts, when she turns and says over her shoulder, 'Cousin Grace is here.'

My spirits lift straightaway. 'Oh, lovely.'

Dot's brows knit, momentarily. She turns and opens the door.

I'm feeling dreadful. What a trite remark! This is probably one of their regular meetings to talk about Dot's son, poor George.

'Hello Rose, dear.' Cousin Grace rises and clasps me to her, and I remember that lovely wholesome scent she has of fresh linen. 'This is so good of you.'

I'm slightly at a loss. 'It's good of you, too,' I falter. 'After all, he's my brother.'

'Well, that's it...' Dot looks as if she would say more, but there's a knock, and a young maid brings our tea things in.

During the flurry of activity which results in the girl's departure, Dot taking up the pot and Cousin Grace distributing tea plates for parkin, I find myself anxious anew. 'Where is Jack? I'd like to see him.' I voice my thoughts rather more abruptly than intended.

Dot shakes her head. 'He's still trying to carry out his duties. But it's beyond him. They've told him – well, Madam has to be exact, the Squire and Master Hector wouldn't be so – oh, no – talk of angels...'

While she has been speaking, we have become aware of an uneven tread approaching along the corridor, the sound of footsteps accompanied by the thump of a stick. There is a pause on the other side of the door.

'Everything's all right, Master Hector, everything's all right,' Dot calls with a practised air.

The young man who will one day own this house and land gives an audible, groaning sigh. We wait. Then we hear him stomping away.

Cousin Grace looks ashen. 'I can't stay long.' Her eyes implore Dot, whose own anguish is clear to see, firstly for the son she had to relinquish to be raised by this woman, however dear, our father's wife, then for the other young man just encountered, whose life has been shattered, one whom she has known longer and more closely than her own son.

The brief silence brings me to resolution. 'I must see Jack.'

At that moment, the reverberation of a motor car engine fills the courtyard. I hurry from the room, Dot's words ringing in my ears, 'But what are we going to do about him, Rose?'

Outside in the fresh air, I witness my brother's pain as he extricates himself from the driver's seat.

'Jack,' I cry out.

Jack straightens up, his face lit by joy. 'Rose.' He tries to hasten towards me. 'You've talked to Dot and Cousin Grace, then?'

'Er... yes...' I am bewildered, but he doesn't seem to notice.

'So, you've come to take me home with you?'

My silence on the return journey goes unnoticed, thank goodness, for both my companions are absorbed in talking about the estates, in other parts of the country, to which they will return and the presumption, on the part of family, that each will slip back into the role of dutiful daughter. My mood matches the darkening, muttering sky.

'This do?' The Commandant pulls up in the High Street.

I thank her and seem to find coherent words to wish her and Nurse Fawcett the very best for their future lives. Once on the ground, I even manage to smile and lift my arm to wave good-bye, though I could have spared myself the trouble since, understandably, once divested of her final responsibility, the Commandant's piercing gaze is firmly fixed upon the road.

Unless something has cropped up to detain him at the shop, Leonard will be home. My thoughts swirl back into the dark chaos of anger, remorse and, ultimately, anguish in which they have been tossing ever since Jack's question, which turned my day – my world – upside down. I nearly get myself run over by the first of a fleet of Hallambury's smartly-liveried freight motor vehicles on the way to their London depot. The blare of their horns rings in my ears as I gain the far kerb, slip across East Street, an alley full of shops, and go on under the arch which leads to our yard, fat rain drops falling as I run to our door. I fling myself inside as the shadowy room leaps into garish light. Thunder cracks overhead.

'My love!' Leonard calls from the kitchen, rising as I hang up my jacket and hat. I go through. His radiant smile drains away. 'Oh. What happened?' He slips an arm round my shoulder, takes my hands with his free hand.

'I walked into a foregone conclusion,' I say in a tight voice, scarcely my own. 'Not that I agreed to it, especially without consulting you.' Instantly, the spark of anger cools, like the storm which seems to be rolling away. 'But I felt – feel – awful about it.'

I let myself be pulled into a hug. Above my head, Leonard says, 'So you and I have got to have a serious talk, and I imagine it involves Jack.'

I give a great involuntary sigh. 'Yes.'

'Well, I think you should sit down there, let me make you a restorative cup of tea, and you can start telling me from the beginning while I'm doing it.'

'But you were – ' A half-eaten cheese sandwich lies next to a cooling cup of tea.

'Never mind. I'll eat in a minute.'

So, I tell him everything up to the point where I had to disappoint Jack. 'When I said I'd just come to visit.. oh...' A low moan escapes me.

'I can imagine,' says Leonard, standing up. His face looks pained. 'Let's go and sit next door.'

On our little sofa, he puts an arm round my shoulder and I lean into the comfort of him. Outside, rain falls, soft and persistent. I know he's thinking the same as me, the one thing we don't talk about. The thing we've managed, in our separate ways, to come to terms with. So, I start with something else.

'You see, you can understand how Dot and Cousin Grace had to consider everything.'

'Of course. They're in no position themselves to care for Jack so, naturally, it falls to his other sisters.' He pauses before he goes on, and I bless him for that, squeeze his hand. 'Phyllis has more than enough on her plate with Florence and Beatrice. Hilda...'

A vision rises before my eyes. We both speak at once. 'He can't go there.'

'She has too many duties,' Leonard says.

'And she's still got Dee at home, and Ambrose when he's not at Cambridge.' I don't need to say this, but I'm steeling myself for what I'll say next.

'No, Jack must come here,' Leonard says.

I take a deep breath, let it out slowly. 'I know this isn't the person you'd have wanted - expected -'

'Rose, Rose...' He pulls me into his arms as my tears threaten to spill. 'That's no one's fault. It's just one of those things. And we've had - we have - an enriching life, don't we?'

He looks deep into my eyes, and I'm gone just as I was when I first met him. I have to smile and agree.

'We'll get him better,' says Leonard. 'And it'll be jolly. Remember how much we enjoyed having the Janssens?'

This was a family of four Belgian refugees allocated to Widdock during the War. All of the houses the Council had built were occupied, so somewhere else had to be found. The family came early. The ear-marked cottage wasn't fit to be seen, let alone house people who'd lived through hell. We stepped forward. 'They come from a place called, let's see,' said the Clerk, 'Malign, well it would be, poor souls.' Malines. 'You speak French,' said the Clerk. But my clever husband followed his hunch. Oh, those long discussions with his friend the Librarian, looking at maps. 'We think this is Mechelen.' So he polished up his rusty Dutch. And he was right. They were lovely people – a mother, father and two little boys. What times we had getting to know them, their favourite dishes – she insisted on cooking sometimes, Anneke, and the things we learned – what they'd been through. Even after the fortnight they stayed with us, when they'd moved into the cottage, we still remained friends. But after the War, a one-way ticket paid for by our government could not be ignored, and their country wanted them back. I still miss the Janssens.

Leonard's quite right, though, about how we can help Jack.

'Thank you so much for feeling like that,' I begin to say, before we move into a loving embrace.

3, Blessings Yard
Widdock
24th June 1920

Dear Cousin Grace,

Leonard and I are in complete agreement that Jack must come here, where he can rest and get well again in his own time. I hope this will ease your anxiety about him. We will take as our example the loving care which you and Father give George.

I assume that Will Sturgess and Son are still unresolved about retiring Sable the Second in favour of the 'daylight-robbery' motor hearse, so I am hoping Father may borrow her and bring Jack on the cart – unless someone can offer a more comfortable conveyance, though I know Father wouldn't like to ask for such a favour. A Sunday might be the most convenient day, mightn't it? We have made no plans for a holiday, so any Sunday in July would suit us. From Jack's point of view, sooner rather than later would be preferable, though I don't know how much notice he has to give of leaving. If it's a week, would the 11th be possible, do you think?

Of course, you'll read this letter to Father, so I'll be glad to hear what he has to say. I'll now write to Dot in similar terms as this. She can tell Jack.

We both hope that George comes through this latest bad patch quickly, and that the inhalations will ease his lungs and give him some relief.

With much love from us both,

Rose
xxx

I am sitting on the bench under the apple tree, just placing the two letters in their envelopes, when our back gate from the alley swings open and Gerald steps into the garden.

'Ah, that's what I like to see, honest labour,' he says, addressing Leonard, who has straightened up from hoeing his potager, as he calls it.

Leonard grins. 'That's right – man of the soil, that's me.'

They both laugh.

It is Gerald's custom to come round to us on a Monday evening, a quiet time for all of us unless he has an unexpected call upon his pastoral duties. He and Leonard, though sometimes diametrically opposed, enjoy the cut and thrust of intellectual debate. Leonard is lucky. He has abundant opportunity to exercise his mind, given the varied clientele of Pritchard's Bookshop, some of whom come for precisely this, and never buy one book. But Gerald, I suspect, does not have such easy access to mental stimulation. Out of deference to my birthday, he had said he would not visit us this Monday. Now he comes to check that next Monday is back to normal. It is.

'I've started looking at that book on the German Peace Treaty,' he says. 'I'll be interested in your views. I expect you have some.'

'I do,' says Leonard.

I stand up.

'Oh, Rose, I didn't see you behind the tree. I don't want to interrupt –'

'It's all right, I'm just going,' I say. 'I'd like to catch the post. Jack's not well.'

'I'm so sorry,' Gerald says.

'He's coming here.' Leonard joins him on the path. 'If you have a moment –' he ushers Gerald towards the bench. 'I can tell him, can't I, Rose?'

'Please do. I'll say good-bye.'

They both sit down, relaxing into each other's company.

I start to walk away, then a thought occurs to me, 'Is Hilda at home, do you know? I really should tell her about Jack myself.'

An equivocal look flits across Gerald's face in the split-second before he answers, 'Er, yes, I believe so.'

Of course, the person I'd really like to talk to about Jack is Phyllis. I called in briefly on Tuesday evening to let her know I was visiting Jack today, and might not be back in time to go on up to The Byre. As I turn into the High Street, who should I see ahead of me, clearly making for the same destination, but my dearest sister. I call her name, and she turns with a bright smile.

We post our letters. Phyllis's, she tells me, is her regular invoice to the firm of Liberty for the wooden tableware and bookends she works for them. I tell her briefly what has occasioned my two letters, and where I'm heading.

'I'll come, if you like,' she says, knowing my glad answer.

As we walk on down the High Street, I give Phyllis my account of this morning – was it really only this morning?

'Poor Jack,' she says. 'Still, it'll be good to have him here.'

We cross the cobbled market square, empty of people this drowsy summer afternoon, with shops closed and The Wheatsheaf's ancient wooden door fast shut till evening opening.

'Do you remember when we used to play at being sailors?' I say.

'With the bunk bed as our boat – or were we pirates?'

'Both.'

We go on recalling moments from that time when we three children, closest in age to each other, created a world of favourite characters and their adventures. I feel my spirits lift.

'We'll make him well again,' says Phyllis, and I hear, in her optimistic tone, her own enjoyment of our recollections. We take the shady path up through the churchyard and, under a black wrought-iron lantern arch, out onto St. Saviour's Lane. At its start the vicarage, a pretty double-fronted building of the Regency period, stands in the middle of its own small plot, surrounded by modest lawns, but with a deep herbaceous border running on either side of the narrow path straight up to the panelled front door with its fanlight. Phyllis tugs at the iron bell-pull, and we hear a dull note sounding in the space of the hall. We wait a moment in the fragrance of the butter-coloured rose which frames the door. I tilt a bloom, full yet still fresh, and take in a draught of its intoxicating honey.

The door opens to reveal Dee, whose expression changes in a flash from downcast to glad. 'Oh! Auntie Rose and Auntie Phyllis – lovely!'

I'm touched not only for myself but for Dee's recognition of that extra something which Phyllis, who would never admit to being attractive, always brings with her presence.

Dee ushers us in saying, as we stamp our shoes on the mat, 'I expect you've come to see Mother.'

'Well, yes...'

'She's in the garden.'

'But seeing you first is a nice surprise.'

'A bonus,' Phyllis adds, as we follow Dee down the dim but pleasant hall with its bees-waxed floorboards and ancient rugs, whose harmonious colours retain a glossy sheen. As we pass the hall stand, a white bone-china bowl with fluted edges yields the scent of lavender.

Dee leads us into the family sitting room, whose French windows stand open onto a garden, the second such room, I reflect, which I have seen today. This room, in contrast to the first, is slightly shabby, with well-worn chair covers, and a fireside rug bearing the odd tell-tale black spot where, over the years, sparks have jumped out and singed it. But the antimacassars are spotless and, on the upright piano, a vase of sweet peas gladdens the atmosphere. Next to an armchair, an occasional table bears a bookmarked novel, entitled: In the Prime of Love, with Hilda's spectacle case beside it. We pass the sofa, where Dee's school books lie open. Her fountain pen, discarded when the doorbell summoned her, rests on top of a page of writing in an exercise book. I glimpse the underlined heading: 'The Divine Right of Kings: The Root of Charles the First's Downfall.' Discuss.

We find Hilda with a pair of secateurs, dead-heading. 'Goodness me,' she says, as surprised as Dee was to see us, 'to what do we owe this double pleasure?'

'I've been to see Jack. I'm afraid he's not well,' I begin.

Hilda recomposes herself almost immediately from the anxiety which these words have obviously provoked in her. 'Come and tell me all about it.'

She moves as if to take us indoors, but Phyllis says, 'Can't we sit out here on your swing seat?'

'I was going to offer you a barley water or – '

'We don't need anything,' I say, 'let's sit on the seat.'

'Very well,' says Hilda, slightly disgruntled at our spurning her hospitality. Then, to Dee, still caught in thoughts of sympathy for Uncle Jack, 'You can join us when you've finished your homework.'

As Hilda turns and walks ahead of us, Dee pulls the slightest of downturned faces, but goes back to her books.

'I don't know,' says Hilda, arranging herself at one end of the opulent, if ageing, swing seat with its fringed canopy, 'we'll be like the three wise monkeys.'

'Not exactly,' I begin.

'The one in the middle'll have her head screwed off with all the to-and-fro-ing.'

'I've already heard what Rose has to say, so she doesn't have to look at me. I'll sit like this,' Phyllis does so, facing Hilda and making a lap of her legs.

'Perfect,' I say, climbing on board. I lean back against Phyllis's chest, feeling her arms gently lying on either side of me and smelling the faint aroma of fresh wood-shavings from the linen smock she wears for work, a smell which takes me back to our childhood, when Father would bring that breath of his carpenter's workshop in through the door at home.

'How did you find out about Jack?' Hilda brings me back to the present.

I only get as far as describing the ambulance trip when Dee comes out, dragging a basket chair. In her other hand is her exercise book, which she shows Hilda. 'Done.'

Hilda nods, not wanting to interrupt the flow of my narrative. It looks like exactly the same page I saw earlier but Hilda, with or without her spectacles, is in no position to make an evaluation, even had she wanted to do so.

From time to time, during my account, Phyllis rocks the swing with her grounded foot. It's very pleasant and relaxing in the mellow garden with bees buzzing from rose to rose to sweetly fragrant stocks, but there's no danger of falling asleep because Hilda says, 'Not too much, you'll make me seasick.'

I come to the point where I saw Jack extricating himself from the motor car. Hilda claps a hand to her mouth, her blue eyes filling. Dee looks down, fiddles with a loose piece of wicker. 'Is it a war wound?' Hilda asks in a hushed voice, but neither of us knows. I repeat his searing question to me, and how it became abundantly clear that mine had already been elected as his convalescent home.

There is a moment's silence in which compassion is uppermost amongst the emotions vying for control of Hilda's face. Her brows knit, then calm into her usual unflappable expression. 'Yes, of course, Rose, you are the one with two spare rooms.'

'One spare room,' says Phyllis.

'Oh, I know about Leonard's study,' says Hilda, waving an arm which dismisses both the study and the interruption, 'but it's such a pity we can't have Jack. I'm here all the time, I could look after him.'

I can feel what Phyllis is thinking.

'If only we hadn't had to relinquish our fourth bedroom to make a bathroom,' Hilda is saying, 'and that's another thing – no bathroom – and you haven't even got gas! I wonder... Do you think Ambrose would mind, Dee, while he's away, if we lent his room? He's not coming home at the end of term, so –'

'Hilda,' I say, 'it's very kind of you, but let's just see how Jack gets on with us.'

'That makes sense, doesn't it?' says Phyllis. 'It's what Jack's expecting.'

Hilda sighs. 'Well, all right. But we can keep it under review, can't we? And we'll give you all the help and support we can, won't we, Dee?'

'Of course,' says Dee. 'I like Uncle Jack.'

'Even if we didn't like Uncle Jack, it would still be our Christian duty.'

From inside the sitting room, an antique clock drops its pure notes into the air like liquid gold. It is a quarter to five.

'I must go,' says Phyllis.

'So, must I.'

We both get up, then Phyllis steadies the seat for Hilda to rise. As we cross the lawn, Hilda says, with the slightest exasperation, 'I suppose neither of you saw Gerald on your travels? He was supposed to be discussing the Sunday School Outing with me.'

'Actually, we didn't see anyone much on our travels, did we, Phyl?' I say.

'No, very quiet in town,' says Phyllis.

Both our faces are studies of mild ingenuousness, which we maintain until we are out of sight.

Miss Briggs, Louisa, has been suffering from toothache, which came on during Saturday. She is such a conscientious dear that she tried to carry on working, sucking cloves to keep the pain at bay. Leonard insisted that she should not come in on Monday, usually a quiet day, but should go to the dentist straightaway. In his concern for her he overlooked the fact that, of all days, he was expecting a substantial consignment of new books which would be better entered up that day rather than being left until Louisa was recovered and back to help him. Not that this would in any way have changed his mind towards her absence.

It being my day off from Quinn-Harper's, I immediately offered to help him, and so, after leaving Lizzie Munns to peg the washing out, I'm on my way to Pritchard's Bookshop, my first love along with its owner, which will always hold a corner of my heart. I cross the High Street and make for Bridge Foot, where the old boys like to lean over the parapet gazing at the river and setting the world to rights. At the brow of the bridge, there, down Holywell End, lies the row of shops containing dear Pritchard's, as homely to me as my own cottage in Blessings Yard. I pause on the other side of the street. I can see, beyond the displays in the shop's two modest windows, my husband holding a book and talking animatedly to two young women, no doubt from the training college, who stand gazing up at him, spellbound. It is remarkable how, even when they are supposed to be at lessons, there are nearly always one or two hovering around. I cross the road and cast a professional eye over the display in the nearer window. A new book of poems by John Masefield, whom we both like, takes pride of place, together with another poetry book compiled by Lady Gregory, apparently translated from the Irish.

I glance at the other window as I move to enter, and spot The German Treaty Text. So, it's permanent, then, this peace...

Now, Leonard has seen me and bounded to open the door. 'The light of my life,' he exclaims to his audience.

I have to laugh as I go straight through to the comfortable sitting room, where I leave my hat and gloves. By the time I'm back, he is alone in the shop.

We work well together. While Leonard carries out the documentation, I find space for some, at least, of the new books. The rest will have to stay packed, and Leonard will carry them through to the back of the shop. Shelving and tidying is a job I enjoy, moving the existing books around, slipping the newcomers into the appropriate slot. Most satisfying of all is pulling forward, with the gentlest of touches, each book on a shelf by the top and bottom of its spine, and then nudging them with the back of my hand to create a neat, straight line. I love that soft 'clunk, clunk' of moving books and the smell of new paper, print and bindings. This has been evident at Quinn-Harper's since we transferred all the new fiction there from Pritchard's shortly after I took over the shop in 1910. There it is diluted by the palpable presence of all my antique stock, a scent I also love, leather and mildew, reminding me a little of church.

At lunchtime, Leonard strikes off for his usual walk along the river. I cross the road to say hello to greengrocer Kate and buy some watercress for our light meal tonight. It is almost too hot to be outside, so I retire gratefully to the cool sitting room, leaving the back door open for what breeze there is. My spirits have been dampened by the number of war memoirs from every conceivable angle which, this morning, have passed through my hands. Leonard says they still make up a large part of his stock. It's inevitable, I suppose. To counterbalance them, I start to read a book about the importance of bees and other pollinating insects – or rather what ought to be their importance – to farmers or anyone involved with crop production. I don't get very far before Leonard is back, we eat our cheese sandwiches, and it's time to open up again.

Leonard props the shop door open with the wooden owl roosting on a block which Phyllis carved for the purpose. We finish our task. No one comes to see us.

'You could go home, really,' says Leonard.

Perhaps I will a little later, but this has the dreamy quality of a Monday afternoon when I first worked for Leonard, Mr. Pritchard, as a sixteen-year-old. Before the training college opened and we became busy, we would spend this time after the lunch-hour on a Monday, always our quiet day then, reading to each other, usually poetry. I have noticed a new edition of one of my favourite collections, Peacock Pie by Walter de la Mare. I take it from the shelf, sit down on the stool behind the counter and open it. Leonard takes the other stool next to me, his familiar presence both reassuring and arousing. I find the page I want and, at an encouraging nod, clear my throat and start to read.

Leonard refrains from pointing out what he might think are the poem's deficiencies, and enters into a wholehearted enjoyment of all the images, particularly the one I picture most vividly, the horse with big, gentle mouth pulling at the sweet-smelling hay. I pass the book over to Leonard, and he reads The Little Green Orchard, with its mysterious but friendly other presence, or presences, besides the writer. Again, the natural detail is evocative. I pick out 'the horned snail' in the moonlight. I read about Nicholas Nye, the old donkey drowsing in his meadow 'while the birds went twittering by', and Leonard reads A Widow's Weeds, a play on words about the 'poor old widow' who isn't diminished at all by her situation, but sows 'weeds', then 'peeps at her garden with bright brown eyes' because she celebrates, as the poem does, the beauty of wild flowers in a garden 'drowsy from dawn till dusk with bees.'

Perhaps classes have dismissed early, but here are a group of young women pausing at the window. Soon, the first workers from the city will be stepping off the train and passing by, or lingering at the window and coming in.

'Honestly, I can manage,' Leonard says.

So, I decide that I will go on ahead and remove the now-redundant note to Dee and Alex from under the knocker, apologising for the cancellation of our usual Monday meeting and, before they arrive, bring in the washing from the line.

I cross the bridge and, as always, look at the classic view of the river winding west. The sun, still high though the solstice is now passed, almost dazzles me. I shield my eyes before I cross the High Street. Walking beneath the arch to Blessings Yard, I feel its sustaining peace.

I open the front door. On the mat is a letter, which must have come by second post after I left. It is addressed to me. The hand looks rushed and erratic. It takes me a moment to recognise that it is Dot's:

Sawdons, 27th June 1920

Dear Rose,

Well, I never thought I'd live to see the day when I'd be ashamed to have once been an Alleyn! Thank goodness I've been a Landers for twenty years, and Upstairs have forgotten my maiden name. It's earned itself enough black marks here and no mistake!

Hilda leaving – well, that was justifiable

I should think it was, given that the young master of the house would have ravished her if she had stayed a moment longer. I can feel the slow pulse of anger at the thought of all that business. When I came with news of Mother's death, Hilda begged me to let her take my place at home looking after Father. I would replace her at Sawdons, the threat to me being far less because I wasn't beautiful. I agreed but, in the meantime, I met Leonard, a point not lost on Dot.

But then there was you letting them down, Ralph going off to a grander garden and never coming back and as for Phyllis –

Yes, Phyllis... I feel anguish even now for what happened to her, relieved never to have been noticed by Master Greville, on account of what she considers her lack of prettiness, only to find that she had become the focus of his attentions, as if she were a challenge.

There's half a line crossed out but my current mood lends me the ability to decipher it with no difficulty.

if only she'd called out, surely one of the men

'There was no one else anywhere near!' I shout at the sitting room.

No wonder, when Greville made his assault, she defended herself with the nearest thing to hand - grabbing the Royal Photograph and smashing it into his face. This action earned her instant dismissal, which was how she came to Widdock, just in time to nurse me through the serious illness which has left me with a heart which skips to its own beat.

The least said about that episode the better.

Dear, brave Phyllis. I try to overcome my dismay at Dot's mental alignment with Upstairs. It's understandable. All the same...

And now Jack has disgraced himself - over something so trivial, too. He can tell you in his own words, I'm too upset. He's here under sufferance this week, while they find a replacement chauffeur, but Father will bring him over to you on Sunday, that is, 7th July.

I'm sorry Rose, I didn't mean to sound off like this, but it was all so unnecessary. I will be thinking of you all on Sunday.

Your loving sister,
Dot x

Chapter Four

I tell Dee and Alex, after they've chatted and written something and read it out, that Uncle Jack will be arriving this Sunday. I mention nothing of the cloud which seems to overhang his departure from Sawdons.

'So we should see him, then, next Monday,' says Alex.

'Ye...es,' I say.

Dee reads my hesitation. 'Provided he's well enough.'

'If he is, I'm sure he'd like to see you, so come anyway. By all means tell your parents he's going to be living here for a while. Hilda and Hubert ought to know about their brother, but do emphasize to your mothers that I can cope.'

While Leonard was away during the War, I took his place at meetings of the Chamber of Trade. He has yet to resume his role there, though he says he will after next month's summer break. It being the third Monday of the month, I am pulling on my gloves ready to go. There is a knock at the door.

'I'll let him in,' says Leonard, assuming it must be Gerald. 'Oh!'

It's my dear friend, Lettie, carrying a covered basket. She greets us both.

'Come in, come in,' says Leonard.

'What a shame I'm just going out,' I say.

'I know you are,' says Lettie, crossing the threshold, 'I'm representing Gifford's this evening, so I'll come with you. Now then,' she marches to the table, plants her basket down and throws the cover back, 'you'll need plenty of sheets and pillowcases, and these are absolutely beautiful.' She holds up a swathe of fine, snowy cloth. 'Gifford's best Egyptian cotton. Look at the finish.'

'How lovely,' I begin.

'We haven't got to buy them, have we?' Leonard asks.

'No, of course not, they're mine but I haven't used them yet. You are very welcome.'

There is another knock. 'Ah, this'll be Gerald,' says Leonard, with relief. He flings open the door. 'My dear cha –'

'I'm sorry to disappoint you, Leonard,' says Hilda, stepping past him, 'he's had to obey the call of duty. You won't see him this evening.'

'Hello Hilda,' I say. She, too, is carrying a covered basket.

'Hello Rose... Lettie.' Her eyes are on the luxurious fabric. 'Well, what a coincidence! I've brought you some bed linen, too.' She advances to the table, uncovers her basket and firmly holds up with both hands a pillowcase and the border of a sheet, both with a wild rose and honeysuckle motif worked in silk thread. 'So, really Lettie, it's terribly kind of you, but you could keep your sheets for your own family, and Rose can use this set, which is spare. I embroidered them myself.'

'They're sweetly pretty,' says Lettie, 'but the thread count on these is superb' – I catch Leonard's bemused look – 'and for someone who's an invalid, they'll give maximum comfort.'

Suddenly, the thought of the Chamber of Trade meeting becomes tremendously appealing. 'I've got to go,' I say. 'May we keep both?' And that seems to settle it.

The three of us are walking the same way until Lettie and I enter The George in whose upstairs room proceedings are about to begin. In that space of time, cordial relations have been more or less restored, chiefly because Hilda likes to hear town gossip and Lettie always has plenty, this time centring on the fact that a distinguished stranger came into the shop, looked around in a discerning way, then asked if he could make an appointment for his wife to be fitted for a complete new wardrobe.

I meant it when I said I could cope with Jack's arrival this weekend earlier than anticipated but, all the same, it couldn't have come at a worse time. Today, Saturday, is Widdock Day, a celebration of the town by its inhabitants intended to bring in custom from the surrounding villages and beyond. Before the

War, so great had been its success that the event had expanded to become Widdock Weekend. But, during those years of loss and hardship, and despite a faction who seemed oblivious to what was happening abroad, no one, fundamentally, had the heart for it. Last year, we were all still coming to terms with who had returned and who had not. It would have felt like indecent haste to resurrect it then. Now, though, it is twenty years exactly since the very first Widdock Day, which I attended as a sixteen-year-old, so a cautious attempt to reinstate the institution is taking place. Much of Monday evening's meeting of the Chamber of Trade was concerned with last minute details about the co-ordination of events as varied as a holiday fashion show at Gifford's or a veterans' rowing race on the Blaken in support of Toc H, followed by a talk from one of the boat builders ready to take orders, afterwards, for barges, lighters and dinghies or even pleasure craft.

Over the last few weeks, Louisa Briggs has been crossing town to help me, particularly on Saturdays. This is the time of year, with summer term drawing to a close, when Pritchard's Bookshop is least busy. Here, at Quinn-Harper's, the approaching holiday season brings an influx of customers looking for a novel or collection of short stories to entertain them.

I always enjoy Louisa's company, intelligent but gentle in manner. We had got to know and like her as a student at the training college, and missed her bright presence when she left for her first posting. In 1910, after I inherited Quinn-Harper's, we took on dear Ned as our assistant, but he went to the Front and was killed in that very first year. Although we could hardly think to write, we put an advertisement in The Widdock Courier and, in the midst of our sorrow, Louisa's reappearance seemed like a miracle. She'd had her own serious troubles, having been sent to a rough school where she could not cope. That much we know. She turned her back on teaching, and we welcomed her with open arms.

We walk over to our right hand window to unveil the book in pride of place whose display we set up yesterday behind a screen, then covered with a velvet cloth before we took the screen away.

Louisa nods towards our left hand window. 'I'm rather glad that she will now have to share star billing.' She is referring to the authoress Rose Macauley. Her new novel has been described as 'coruscating'.

'I thought you were enjoying Potterism,' I say. It has held prime position for a fortnight with steady sales to Widdock's intellectuals and literati.

'I know it's a witty satire and you're actually supposed to despise practically all the characters, but I'm not sure that I like to find myself sniggering.'

I stop, my hand about to pull back the velvet cloth from the other book. 'No, that's what I thought, really,' I say. 'It just shows how unsophisticated we are.' We laugh. 'Are you ready? One, two, three!'

We carefully peel back the covering to reveal Daisy Ashford: her Book. This compendium features, of course, her much-loved novel, The Young Visiters. It was written in 1890, when she was nine years old, then it was put away, rediscovered, and eventually published last year, with all her childish spellings. Also included, amongst other tales, is a story by her sister, Angela, and Daisy's first novel. At the age of eight, she dictated this to her father who, according to her foreword, lovingly wrote down every word. I suffer a renewed pang thinking about that, and how my father can do little more than write his own name, and that not always correctly, the 'b' in Robert sometimes back to front.

'Has Mr. Pritchard read The Young Visiters?' asks Louisa, as she places a small pile of the compendium at the end of the counter, in the hope of sales.

'Oh yes, he liked her mixture of precocious talent and naivety. The book came out at just the right time.'

Louisa looks grave. 'What he must have gone through.'

I'd rather not be reminded of what he went through, so I tell her, 'He laughed out loud at the opening sentence: 'Mr. Salteena was an elderly man of forty-two.' That was exactly my husband's age last year.' We're both giggling now.

The morning passes without incident, there being a steady flow of customers, but not a multitude. Like so many days this month, it's cool with a hint of rain. This may be putting people off. Others are at market. We still sell three copies of Daisy Ashford's book, and two of Rose Macauley's. The afternoon is a different matter. The sun has broken through and, suddenly, the shop seems filled with people, here for the various Widdock Day events.

I have just sold, packaged and passed across another copy of Daisy Ashford: Her Book, when who should appear outside, wheeling a bicycle each and looking at the window display featuring Potterism, but Fred and Gladys Rawlins. My heart sinks at the sight of them. They are both wearing knickerbockers, rucksacks and working men's caps. They move over to the other window, glance in, exchange a look and lean their bicycles against the bay.

'Are you enjoying Widdock Day?' I say, after we've greeted each other. I hear how inane my voice sounds.

'I'm here to cover it for The Gazette,' Fred Rawlins answers. Of course.

'And I thought, while I'm at it, I'll pay a visit to the illustrious Quinn-Harper's and, given the appropriateness of the subject matter, buy myself a copy of Potterism.'

The eponymous Mr. Potter, of the novel, runs a newspaper and has no scruples about printing sensational and sentimental stories because he knows that these will sell. He has done very well for himself, and both his children go to Oxford. They deplore their father's lack of publishing morals and set up the anti-Potter league but, as they are loathsome prigs, the reader cannot sympathise with them.

As I put Potterism in a brown paper bag and fold the sides neatly to fit it, Fred Rawlins says, 'There's a character isn't there – Gideon? – who upholds truth and integrity, but since the masses feed on what Potter peddles, he ultimately fails...' His eyes hold mine.

For a bizarre moment, it's almost as if he isn't talking about the book. 'I'm not going to comment on the plot,' I say, refusing to be daunted by any implied parallel with what he considers to be our divergent business ethic. 'That'll be seven and six, please, Mr. Rawlins.' I give him a steely smile.

He counts out the coins.

Gladys, in the meantime, has picked up and is reading the Daisy Ashford Compendium. 'Charming,' she says, and replaces the book on the pile, slightly askew.

'And very popular, no doubt,' says her husband, picking up his purchase and making me feel, once again, like some kind of Potter figure, entirely motivated by financial self-interest.

'I shouldn't think the price is,' says his wife, 'seventeen bob.'

'Both novels are popular,' I say. 'Will you excuse me, please?' I turn to the next customer. They take the hint and leave our now busy shop.

Later in the afternoon, I am serving one of my regular customers. Out of the corner of my eye, I am aware of a tall, fine-featured gentlemen with white hair, wearing a beautifully-cut light linen suit. He is absorbed in some of my antiquarian stock, so I will leave him alone for a while to browse in peace before I ask if I can help him. The next time I have the chance to look for him, he has just left the shop and is walking away, a lady on his arm. Even from her back view, it is clear that she is his distinguished match. On the gentleman's other arm are two large cardboard bags bearing the name Gifford.

'Do apologise to Leonard for me, won't you, Rose?' says Gerald, as I follow out of church the dozen or so parishioners at the conclusion of early, unsung communion. 'My services were urgently required elsewhere on Monday evening.'

I can tell, from his compassionate face, the exact nature of the call upon him. 'There is never a need to apologise.'

I hurry home, relieved not to have encountered Hilda with any last-minute instructions or exhortation to join the family for Sunday lunch. She will, no doubt, attend the later service.

As I enter the kitchen, Leonard rises from the remains of his scrambled eggs on toast, newspaper propped against the milk jug, to make me a cup of tea. I barely have time to drink it, whilst slipping a shoulder of lamb into the oven, before we hear the clop of hooves and the trundling of a cart's wheels. I have never known my father to be late, and this occasion is no exception. We exchange a supportive look and go through to open the front door, welcoming smiles on our faces. I have forcibly to hold mine in place, and see Leonard doing the same, at sight of Jack.

Although there is no sun, it is not a cold day, but Jack is wrapped in the old woollen rug which, usually in more inclement weather, accompanies passengers on the cart's bench-like seat. He seems huddled into it, either with cold or discomfort – or both, for that hard wooden surface would have no respect for the condition of his back. But oh, his sweet, dear face is drawn with fatigue and pain. My blue-eyed, flaxen-haired brother is a shadow of himself. I could howl. I do nothing of the sort of course, but step forward, greeting Father and reaching up to Jack to assist him. He takes my hand and gives it the faintest squeeze, 'Rose,' with the flicker of a smile, but the men have to help him climb slowly down the steps to the ground and, as slowly, make his way into the cottage. We guide him to my armchair, which will be in the sun should it choose to come out and which, thank goodness, I have already had the foresight to prepare with the patchwork quilt. Jack sinks into it, and I tuck the quilt around him. 'Thank you,' he says, his voice a wraith.

Father is standing by, turning his old summer hat in his hands.

'Will you stay for tea – or lemonade?' I ask, but I know what his answer will be.

'No, thank you all the same, Rose. It looks to me as if that dirty weather is coming up sooner than they think. I'd like to get the mare back and into Sturgess's stable. He's got a big funeral tomorrow, and he won't want her covered in mud.'

For as long as I can remember, my father has worried about a mare, the first Sable and now this one loaned to him, when not in use by the undertaker, in recompense for her summer quarters in our field.

By the time Leonard and I have come back inside from giving Sable a drink, and then seeing Father off, with our love to Cousin Grace and best wishes for George's better health, Jack is sound asleep.

We tidy up the kitchen, conferring in whispers. I assure Leonard that I don't need him to fetch potatoes and greens from his potager for at least an hour. I know he would like to go on reading the paper which, normally, I would share, sitting in my armchair opposite him, feet resting on my little footstool which Phyllis made years ago, and Jenny embroidered with a striped Gallica rose. I try sitting on our sofa but after a while feel restive, so I take a bowl into the garden to pick blackcurrants and raspberries for our desert. I wish I'd thought last night to make a summer pudding. Ah, well...

Out here, big, piled-up white clouds now thin to show skeins of blue against which swooping swallows are dark silhouettes uttering their sharp, clipped notes. I part leaves to reveal black jewels, taking one to test for ripeness, and savouring its distinctive taste, tart yet sweet. As I work on, gathering a bowl full of fruits, firm shiny black and delicate bobbled pink, I find the restorative rhythm the garden gives me. I look up with a start on hearing Leonard, coming out for the vegetables. I take my bounty back into the kitchen, together with the scent of mint which I have picked for the sauce.

Jack wakes up naturally, in time to be escorted across the room to where I have laid the table in the alcove under the stairs. The niceties of carving and serving occupy us, and then Jack tucks into his roast lamb and mint sauce with a relish I am glad to see. It is clear that he has no wish for conversation, and this is not the time to ask him about his health and certainly not about whatever it was which led to his dismissal. As usual on a Sunday, Leonard enquires what Gerald had to say.

'Today's the festival of St. Thomas the Apostle,' I tell him.

'Ah! Thomas Didymus, the twin,' says Leonard. 'I think I can guess the thrust of the sermon.'

'Well, yes, not being a Doubting Thomas, but believing in the Lord without needing proof, but Gerald managed to bring in the generally more open attitude both of Mary at the tomb, in the passage before, and of the other disciples when they saw Him.'

'The difference being, though, that both parties saw Him – or thought they did,' he adds, dryly.

'That was what some people in church were saying afterwards, of course.'

'Good old Gerry, though, he gets'em thinking.'

After a brief period of silent eating, I make the observation that today is American Independence Day, and wonder what our two eldest brothers, Bob and Ted, who have lived and worked in New York City for nearly thirty years, are doing to celebrate it. Leonard recalls a place called Coney Island, which he says has a fun-fair. I say I'm sure there will be fireworks. These whimsies last us until well into the summer berries and cream.

'They're about due for another visit, aren't they?' Leonard says.

This is true. They have come at ten-year intervals, first in 1900, then 1910. Having worked their way into senior positions in the furnishing and fabric section of a departmental store, they pooled their resources with another man in electrical lighting to become Alleyn & Malkin, thus becoming part owners of an exclusive store in what they tell us is a prime location.

'They haven't written, as far as I know,' I say. 'They may be too busy.'

'Perhaps they want to make certain there isn't going to be another war,' Jack says.

I get up to clear the dishes.

Leonard helps Jack to my chair, which he has said he found very comfortable as, indeed, I know it to be. I return to the table, noticing his wry look now that Leonard is also helping to take out dirty crocks. He offers Jack the paper and, as I've made a start on washing-up, he joins me. We make short work of the chore.

In our living room, Jack is labouring through the leading article, finger underlining words, mouth framing them. Of course... though not illiterate like poor Father, Jack was never really one for reading.

'You don't have to sit with me,' he says. 'I can make my way out the back, if I need to, you just do whatever you usually do.'

On a normal Sunday, we might take our bicycles off somewhere all day or, at this time of year, spend a long afternoon working then sitting in the garden. Sometimes, we simply go for a walk along the river. This seems an attractive option.

I pull the front door shut behind us and slip my arm through Leonard's, as we start off through the yard. His presence, connected physically to mine in this familiar way, is both a tonic and an affirmation of unity. I glance his way and catch his smiling gaze. He squeezes my arm. 'It'll all work out,' he says, and it is as if my heart expands and feels lighter for it.

We do the full circuit, up to the old mill, which is the pharmaceutical factory where the scientist sisters, Winnie and Meg, go to work, then back through the park and the High Street. But this morning's brief patch of blue has disappeared. The day has dulled, and I can smell rain in the offing. After little more than an hour, we are heading home to find Jack sitting gazing into space. He perks up at the mention of tea. In the kitchen, under cover of the water boiling, Leonard mouthes the offer of his armchair. In the same manner, I decline it.

Once Leonard and I are seated, Jack clears his throat. 'It's very good of the two of you to have me here' – the slightest chink of china as Leonard and I both lower our tea cups for what is clearly going to be a speech – 'firstly, at all, and secondly... earlier than you thought I was coming. I'm truly sorry for that.'

'You don't have to apologise,' says Leonard.

'Or say anything more,' I add.

'No, no, I must tell you what happened,' Jack says, 'it's not a secret. In fact...' There could be a number of interpretations for the look which crosses his face, 'anyway, what it is - when I came back to Sawdons after the War, the first person I met from Upstairs was the Squire on his own, which was good because I'd worked out what I was going to say to him, on the quiet, you know.'

'You'll tell us,' Leonard says, with perfect gentleness.

'Yes, well. Of course, I said - and I would have said this anyway never mind anything else - how very, very sorry I was about their loss. The Squire thanked me, and I could tell he was touched. Then I said: 'If Master Greville came walking back through that door, I'd fall to my knees on the ground in honour and thanks to God.' The Squire looked a bit taken aback. Didn't expect that kind of thing from me. But he agreed, naturally. Then I said: 'But I want to say something about the War, Sir, and I hope you'll understand.' 'I'm listening,' he says, so I told him: 'After what I went through for this country, my country, I'm now of the opinion that I'm worth the same as any other man, no matter what his rank.' 'Quite so, Alleyn,' says the Squire, sort of evenly. Then, I said, 'The point is I can't, in all conscience, bring myself to touch my cap to anyone anymore, no matter who they are. It doesn't seem right.' He stood there a bit stony-faced for a moment, then he says, 'You're a good man, Alleyn, I respect your conviction, but I am -' how did he put it? - 'fundamentally opposed to all it implies', that's it!'

'Of course he is,' says Leonard, quietly, but Jack goes on.

' 'I may be prepared to overlook your unconventional behaviour' - he says, 'but I can't speak for my wife.' He used a fancy form of words, but the meaning was clear: she wouldn't reckon I'd done enough in the War to get on my high horse. In case I hadn't got the message, he says, 'She's of the opinion that Salonika was a bit of a sideshow.' 'I'd be glad to give her some of the details of my experience there,' I said, pleasant, like. 'That won't be necessary, Alleyn,' he says. 'I'll convey your intention,' and he stomps off. '

'Oh...' I say, 'so Madam didn't like the fact that you dared to have principles, and that's why – '

Jack cuts across me. 'No, she didn't like it,' he gives a mirthless laugh, 'but she had to live with it. I was pretty indispensable – first class chauffeur and mechanic and the best groom they had. I wasn't rude to them, I did my job. Then, I started to get ill, which worried the Squire and displeased her. So, she found the perfect excuse to sack me. In fact, I handed it to her on a plate. They'd kept their entertaining down to a minimum since I was back, what with Master Hector being so poorly and having the convalescent home at Sawdons, but for the first time since before the War, they had Lord and Lady Pressinghurst to stay. They all wanted to be driven on a picnic. I was waiting at the bottom of the steps with the Armstrong Siddeley. Lord and Lady P. arrived at the car just in front of Madam and the Squire. The guests got in without noticing me. Madam glides up. 'I'll speak to you later, Alleyn,' she hisses. I knew what was coming. I'd shamed her by not showing deference to the aristocracy, so there was no place for me at Sawdons.'

'Bravo, Jack!' Leonard says, as we both applaud him. 'Your place is here.'

I make a smoked mackerel salad with lettuce, cucumber and tomato, all of which Leonard picks from the garden, and I butter some bread to go with it. This is followed by the Madeira cake I made last night in Jack's honour, it being his favourite. I'd forgotten, though, how he likes to dunk it swiftly in his tea. After we've cleared up, and Jack is in the armchair, I explain that we normally spend Sunday evening quietly reading.

'I suppose you would,' he says, 'with all those books.'

He declines further reading matter, so I offer him a tray and a pack of cards. He used to love patience, but that was when we were children. I settle on the sofa and open my Bible, to read again this morning's passage from the Gospel of St. John, but I have to admit that the sound of the cards being played is a distraction. I steel a glance at Leonard, whom I know is reading a book, Little Essays, by the South American poet and philosopher George Santayana, someone he has admired and, indeed, met when once he ventured to these shores. The very studiousness of Leonard's expression suggests to me that he is having difficulty in maintaining his concentration. I try again to find my own, but it is as if Jack is attuned to our discomfort. He gathers up the cards, places both tray and cards beside his chair and pulls himself to stand.

'I'm going to get myself ready and then go up – no, I can look after myself. You carry on reading.'

He slowly makes his way into the kitchen. We've told Jack that his room will be the one above it so, strictly speaking, he doesn't need our help. We both return to our books, trying not to hear the back door twice and the sound of the kitchen plumbing. After he has made his painful progress up the stairs, I wait a decent interval, then go up and knock.

'It's me. Do you have everything you want?'

'Come in, Rose, come in.'

It is strange to have our back bedroom occupied again, especially by my dearest brother, propped up in bed, clothes folded neatly on the chair. Competing with the whisper of lavender from Hilda's bedlinen (I thought Jack would be more at home with this than with Lettie's arguably finer product) there is an indefinably masculine scent.

'I have more than everything I want,' says Jack. 'Thank you both.'

His head is nodding even as he gives me a blissful smile. As I used to help my patients at the hospital, I ease him down into bed without waking him. In sleep, he looks an innocent boy again. I kiss my fingers and touch his soft hair. I move out of the room, soundlessly closing the door, down the stairs and back into the living room where, I'm glad to see, Leonard now looks truly absorbed. He does not notice as I hesitate, then assume my own armchair.

I re-read St. John: Chapter 20, the story of St. Thomas and, in verse 27, the Lord's inviting him to touch him, if that was what he needed to believe in the Resurrection. Then, I go on reading Chapter 21, where the disciples are out fishing on the Sea of Tiberias, catching nothing until Jesus, standing on the shore, tells them to put out again and cast their nets to the right of the ship, whereupon their net becomes so full 'they were not able to draw it for the multitude of fishes', at which point John, 'the disciple whom Jesus loved' was the one to recognise their Lord. And here, at verse 9, I can see so vividly, as they saw it, the shoreline and 'a fire of coals there', sea-coal, glinting like jet, gathered from the beach 'and fish laid thereon and bread' all of which, no doubt Jesus had prepared for them, as He tells them to 'bring of the fish which ye have now caught', so they draw their net, heavy with 'great fishes, an hundred and fifty and three' and Jesus says, 'Come and dine', and I hear the lightness of His tone, and see them all there, enjoying that meal outside with Him. And yes, I know it's symbolic of the task ahead for those disciples. And yes, I know that later, He goes on to allude, so gracefully, to the way in which St. Peter will meet his end, but for me, now, what has caught my imagination is a meal between friends as if, I dare to say, they were equals, even though all those men will never forget, on another level, that they are in the presence of the Divine.

I look up from the Book, and see the glimmer of the late sky through the window, the pools of light next to each of us, though I hadn't been aware of Leonard moving to the lamps and, in everything in this room, wooden table, hearthside rug, bookshelves, a heightened but consoling brightness. And the half-formed affirmation runs through me, Ah... Sunday...

Leonard meets my gaze as if he, too, even in his atheistic mind, has had some kind of spiritual experience. He closes his book.

'Shall we go up?'

I have little to do to ready myself for bed. I tread quietly, but the room on the other side of the landing is still. I put on my nightdress, brush my hair and say my prayers.

Leonard is swift and neat in his preparations. I have noticed this orderliness, no doubt instilled during his time away. He enters the room and softly closes the door as I slip between the sheets. I lie back, watching him undress and fold his clothes as Jack had done, placing them on the chair beside the bed. Outside, the world is Sunday quiet. Here is my world, caught in a candle's gentle light. Leonard snuffs the wick and slides in beside me.

Our arms find each other, our lips meet. We move closer still. Leonard's hand reaches under my nightdress. I pull the weight of him onto me, into me.

A cough. The slightest trace of sound, but clearly audible from the room across the way.

I cannot help my tense reaction but - oh - how I wish I could have concealed it.

'Drat,' says Leonard, quietly.

'I'm sorry,' I say, trying to relax.

'Never mind, never mind,' Leonard murmurs. Then, after a while, 'let's just hold each other.'

'But - '

'That's more than enough. Believe me.'

Chapter Five

Tapping... ...odd tapping... ...night... ...who...?

'Rose... Rose...'

...pushing... ...pushing me...

'Wake up, my love, it's morning.'

Morning...? ...dark... ...ohh... Now I have placed the sound which was beginning to wake me. All else becomes clear... clearer. Rain sputtering in the gutter...

'Here's your tea.'

His lips brush my forehead. I catch the fresh morning scent of him, that hint of lemon which enticed me right from the start.

And in the moment when saucer touches bedside table, accommodating the cup and spoon with the slightest clink, it all rushes back to me. I start to lever myself into a sitting position.

'It's all right,' says Leonard. 'Not a peep out of him.'

I smile and thank him for the tea, which I do enjoy whilst listening to my husband downstairs, quietly moving about the kitchen. The gentlest scrape of a chair tells me that he is sitting down to his porridge and this morning's paper, which he has just been out to fetch, propped against a bottle of fresh milk. But there is everything to do.

I pause by Jack's door before I slip downstairs, but my straining ears detect nothing to suggest that he stirs. I wash quickly at the sink aware, though my back is to Leonard, of his appreciative gaze on my half naked body. I turn and, as I towel myself dry, we exchange a complicit smile. I am relieved that he appears to bear no trace of disappointment about last night's curtailed lovemaking. I place the towel over the back of a chair and re-address the sink, reaching for my special flannel on its discreet hook at the back of the cupboard underneath. Moistening it in the bowl of warm water I've been using, and soaping it, I lift my skirt with the other hand and lower my drawers enough for that practised swipe, rinse and quick buff with the towel. I am alert to hear any movement from the room above but there is, mercifully, none. And in any case, how could Jack, in his current state move so quickly as to be downstairs before I was decent? Restoring all to order, and placing towel and flannel in the dirty linen basket, I flick the curtains open again to the sight and sound of rain drumming on the area between the kitchen and outhouses. A wet wash day. What a curse!

Behind me, Leonard is collecting his breakfast things which he will leave in soak with mine. As I turn, he breaks off. 'I know it would mean more work,' he says, with concern, 'but if you're going to be anxious about washing down here, you might want to re-instate the old regime.'

This is the expression of a thought which has been forming in my own mind, together with an image – a candle in the darkness of a winter's morning, its light catching the pretty details of a bowl and ewer placed on a fine linen mat on top of our chest of drawers. And yes, I know that fetching warm water is, of course, an extra chore, but there is something almost hallowed about performing the act of cleansing in such an intimate space, and so my nod of agreement is un-tempered by reluctance.

We both put on our waterproofs, Leonard to go and fill the hod, me to take the first pan of water out to the copper and light it. He has the worse journey, as the coal-shed is the further port of call, the wash house being a matter of steps from the back door. In this sort of weather, though, and with the necessary repetitions, mine is no pleasure either.

Lizzie Munns arrives, fluting greetings, shaking out her umbrella, stamping the doormat and apologising for any extra wet she might be bringing in. We call reassurances, and she comes through to where I am washing up and Leonard is stoking the range.

'How far have you got?' She asks.

'Half full,' I tell her.

'Right.' She grasps the pot-holder and takes the biggest saucepan through to the wash house, leaving me the easier job of carrying the kettle, which can be done one-handed. About to follow her example, I hear the creak of floorboards. My eyes meet Leonard's.

'You go, I'll do that,' he says, reaching for his waterproofs again.

Upstairs, I knock on the door. 'It's me, Jack. Everything all right?'

'Oh... I can't tell you, dear Rose...' Emotion chokes him on my name. My hand is on the latch, but then he says, in his normal voice, 'Yes, now I'm here, I'm more than all right.'

I feel the release of tension like a weight, dropping through my body. 'Would you like some breakfast?'

'I can come down,' he says.

I imagine him negotiating the busy kitchen – and Lizzie and I having to skirt round him. 'No, that's all right,' I say, quickly, 'I'll bring it up. It's only porridge and tea.'

'That'll be grand, thank you, Rose,' he says.

Downstairs, I discover that Leonard and Lizzie have practically filled the copper, which gives me a pang of conscience. Ridiculous, I tell myself.

'I must go,' says Leonard. 'If you need me – '

'I'll be fine,' I say.

'Yes, you will.'

Alone for a moment, Lizzie already in the wash house, we hug. Then, he kisses me on the lips, and leaves. I stand for a moment after the front door has closed, as the kitchen returns to orderly normality.

I lose track of time, as Lizzie and I work, paddling the washing, draining the copper and re-filling it with fresh water for the rinse to which, for the sheets, we add the little blue bag of starch. Her strong arms are much better than mine for wringing, but we work as a team, well-oiled by practice, when it comes to folding sheets to go through the mangle. Lizzie turns the handle, grasping the flattened sheet with her other hand, while I hold the wet end.

In this pose, I notice Jack making slow progress past the window. He is dressed in an old suit and cap. In one hand, he holds the spare umbrella, which I'm glad he found by the back door. The other hand carries the chipped jug which, apparently, Dot gave him twenty six years ago when he started work as a groom's lad at Sawdons. This he told us yesterday in the faintest of voices, as Leonard and Father helped him from cart to armchair. Carrying his small portmanteau, I walked ahead, which evidently gave him licence to begin to extol its superiority for the male physique – until Father told him to save his breath for what was clearly a taxing exercise.

The thump of the privy door is followed by the lesser knock of the seat and lid in contact with the wall. The following sounds are more muffled, but are still just audible as being those of Jack emptying the jug and lowering the seat. Lizzie goes on mangling unperturbed but, in this cold room, my cheeks are on fire. The thought enters my mind, another unforeseen aspect of Jack's arrival. Before I can stop its development, the thought concludes its process, with a flourish of ironic self-criticism and a nasty sting in the tail, by commenting on its own arrival like an unwelcome guest.

I seize an inspiration, and suggest we spare a thought for poor Will Sturgess and his important funeral drenched in rain. Dear Lizzie understands and, mangling all the harder offers, in a loud voice, the question whether it is worse for the mourners to see off their loved one on a day whose gloom matches their own or on one whose sunlight only underlines their loss in contrast. My mind flashes to the day of Mother's funeral, twenty years ago, one of such sparkling winter sunshine, it would have filled her heart with joy.

'Gone, but not forgotten,' says Lizzie.

We exchange smiles of sympathy, both having lost our mothers before time, hers dying in childbirth, mine at a late stage in a troubled pregnancy.

Lizzie carries through the basket of clean laundry, and I lower the pulley in front of the range. Jack is sitting in the armchair from where he calls through, in answer to my question, that he is perfectly content. I notice, as we start to drape the pulley, his washed and dried breakfast things which he has placed, neatly, on the table. My washing up brush, back in its vertical position in the front of the plate rack, is slightly the worse for wear. He must have tackled his porridge bowl straight away without letting it soak. Never mind. I don't have time to clean it now, so I put it in a small basin of lukewarm water to which I add a squeeze of lemon from the one I keep for such purposes by the sink. I give Lizzie her weekly money. She will be in again tomorrow to do the ironing, and on Friday for the cleaning. She thanks me as always, as if I am doing her an enormous favour rather than the other way round. Then, she leaves.

It is mid-day, and I am hungry. I offer Jack bread and cheese. He says he will come through and eat at the kitchen table. I am just about to call him, when – a knock, and the latch opening on a 'Yoo-hoo.'

'Phyllis!'

I hear the joy in Jack's voice, and hasten through to see the wide smile on my sister's face, which makes a good job of trying to deny the concern in her eyes. 'Hello there, Little Brother,' she says, 'up to mischief again?'

This makes Jack giggle, just as if we were the three desperadoes of our childhood games, making each other laugh with ever more preposterous ideas for how the story we were enacting should develop.

'I've just made cheese sandwiches,' I say, 'you will stay and have some, won't you?'

'Yes, please,' says Phyllis, placing her umbrella in the stand.

Jack gets to his feet, the rug falling away from him, and Phyllis darts forward to support him. In the time it takes them to arrive and be seated, I have made another round of sandwiches and put the tea to brew. Phyllis and I take the ends, Jack sitting between us. He looks, perhaps, the happiest I've seen him yet. He recounts, once more, the sequence of events which led to his dismissal.

'Good for you!' says Phyllis, with heat. 'You're better off out of that place – take it from me. All we've got to do is get you well.' She rises. 'And for that you need rest, which is why I'm going home now.'

I remind her, as I see her off, that I won't be able to call at Apple Tree House on Thursday because it is the long-awaited day of Leonard's reading at the boys' school.

'No, that's why I thought I'd come today.'

'How are things?'

'Much the same. They're both still fed up that nothing seems likely to happen about the War Memorial till next month, after the Bank Holiday.'

Neither of us needs say it, but we both are no doubt wondering how much the preoccupation over this undoubtedly important scheme is costing Mrs. Fuller and Beatrice in terms of fortitude to cope with their own grief.

'That was lovely,' says Jack, but his eyes are closing even as he sits at the table.

I offer to move him to the armchair, but he says he thinks he'll rest on his bed, assuring me that he can make his way upstairs unaided. I run the washing-up brush under the tap, glad to see that it comes clean easily. Then, I apply it quickly to our dirty crocks.

I'm just picking over the lamb joint to make a shepherd's pie - tap at the door, rattling latch, thump-thump on the doormat - 'Hello? Anyone home?' Hilda.

I call her through.

'Where's Jack?' She demands, as if I have done away with him.

'He's just gone upstairs to rest.'

She makes a slight tutting noise, but says she'll go up.

'He might be asleep,' I warn her. 'I'm sorry, I can't come.' I lift my greasy hands.

She dismisses me. 'I'll be quiet,' and makes for the stairs.

I hear her definite tread pause at Jack's door, where she knocks and, at his voice, enters. They spend a few moments in conversation. Then, she comes down again, looking pleased.

'After the rough life he's led, especially over the last few years, he said how much he appreciated the little feminine touch.' It takes me a moment to comprehend. 'Oh, Rose! My embroidered sheets.'

Thank goodness I chose them over Lettie's.

Hilda leaves. I just have time to finish our dinner before I hear Jack coming down again. He says he's had a nice little nap. I tell him to go and sit in the armchair. I'll make tea when the girls arrive. His face lifts at the prospect. I'm glad he is rested and looking forward to their visit. They both like him, and I would have been sorry if I'd had to turn them away. I hear the sound of the latch, then Leonard asking after Jack's health. My heart leaps. 'Not so bad,' Jack says, 'thanks to Rose.'

He comes through, and we kiss. 'All well?' He mouths. I nod, vigorously. He says he thought he'd call by after banking his takings, but as he can see I'm busy getting ready for Alex and Dee, he'll leave me to it. We hug. 'At least, it's stopped raining,' he says, going through and saying good-bye to Jack. I hadn't even noticed.

As usual, Dee arrives first.

'Quite the young lady,' says Jack, which is broadly what he says to Alex who arrives minutes later. Both, in turn, are bashful but pleased.

I leave them asking about Jack's illness. 'No, I don't know what it is,' he says. 'All I know is that my back hurts.' Their sweet faces crumple into moues of sympathy. I make the tea. At some point I shall need to impress on Jack, with the lightest touch, how important it is that neither Hilda nor Lettie should get to know about their daughters' regular visits here on a Monday afternoon.

But I needn't have worried. As I carry the tray through, Alex says, 'We've told Uncle Jack that if our mothers knew we came here to enjoy ourselves, they'd find tasks for us.'

'Or parish duties,' Dee adds, darkly.

'So, you mustn't tell them,' says Alex, 'on pain of death.'

'My lips are sealed,' says Jack, looking delighted. 'I must say, I'm very impressed – all this schooling. When I was your age, I was already out at work. Oh, I've said something wrong. Don't you want to go to work?'

Of course, it isn't as simple as that. Neither of my nieces has articulated her misgivings about the role perceived for her in adult life, and now is not the moment for either one to feel obliged to do so, as it were, on the hoof. I intervene. 'We just put all thoughts of the future aside for an hour on a Monday afternoon. Dee and Alex write their diaries and then read out an extract.'

'Oh, well,' says Jack, 'you'd better get on with it, then.'

I join the girls at the table. 'Would you like to read us anything you've written during the week?' Unsurprisingly, I sense their shyness. 'If not, I wonder whether you can recall any incident from Widdock Day which could be written up.'

Even as I am speaking, a wry smile flickers across Alex's face. She turns to some notes she's already made. Dee, too, has the draft of something she can refine. When they've finished writing, it is Alex who reads first.

'After The Fashion Show,' she begins, this being her title. 'During it, they'd been catching each other's eye, a man and woman in old breeches and cycling clips. Now, they were drifting about fingering the goods. What a cheek! Sometimes, people like that can be light fingered. Mother had spotted them, but she was serving a nice foreign lady, collecting a big order. So, I went up to them. I'd had an idea. 'Perhaps you'd like to see our dual-purpose cycling cape,' I said. 'Sun protection combined with a lightweight mackintosh, which rolls up inside the collar. Perfect for a July downpour.' Then I had another inspiration. 'It's called St. Swithuns.' I held my breath, but my gamble paid off. Though they looked amused, they thanked me and left.'

Dee has written a poem.

After she has read, I ask to look over both pieces of writing. Alex's talent for language and the comic is clear even in this short piece. She has a quicksilver mind. I see that Dee's poem scans throughout in iambic pentameters. She's worked hard on this already, I think, quickly re-reading it.

At the Fete

I was on the Bring and Buy with Mother.
In a lull, she granted me the chance to look
Around the other stalls. I had a go
At throwing hoops, and won a small rag doll
With merry, painted face and scarlet dress.
I put it in my bag. Back at our stall,
Mother was bending down beside a lady,
Someone she knew from church, whose little girl
Was inconsolable because, amongst
The crowd crossing the footbridge, she was pushed,
Which made her drop her dolly in the river.
Cautiously, I offered her my jolly toy.
Tears stopped, a smile flickered like pastel sunlight.

I am proud of them both.

After they've gone, I have to leave Jack nursing his second cup of tea. I re-arrange the laundry on the pulley and re-hoist it. Then, I venture out into the steaming garden to pick some beans and whatever summer fruit may be available. Would a crumble be too much after cottage pie? Something tells me not. I just have time to make one and get both into the oven before Leonard arrives home. He's had a quiet day, now that term is nearly over. He and Jack empty their dinner and dessert plates, enthusing over both courses. Jack returns to his chair whilst Leonard and I quickly clear the dishes, after which Leonard joins him. I make tomorrow's porridge, then go through to the living room, ready to open the door to Gerald who, unless his pastoral services are required a second time, should arrive any minute now.

As he crosses the threshold he says, 'No, don't try to stand, Jack. How are you feeling?'

Jack embraces the room and the two of us in his gesture. 'A lot better for being here, thank you.'

'Well, that's good,' says Gerald, sitting next to me, on the end of the sofa nearest Leonard.

'Before you get started, I must say what a lovely young –' Jack claps a hand over his mouth.

'It's all right,' says Gerald, with a tired smile, 'I've made my peace with the clandestine nature of the arrangement between my daughter, my niece and their aunt, given that it clearly benefits all three.'

'That's a relief,' says Jack.

I'm tempted to remind Gerald of last Thursday afternoon when he should have been discussing the Sunday School Outing with Hilda.

'On the topic of peace, it being my turn to open proceedings,' Leonard says, and Gerald nods, 'publication of the German Treaty Text might stimulate some thoughts from us all on the philosophical cast of mind required to sustain peace.'

Thoughts from us all...? I glance at Jack. He's looking at Leonard with admiration.

'What this means in pragmatic terms and whether we believe the participants in this instance to be in accord with it.'

'Certainly,' says Gerald. He turns to Jack and me.

'Well,' I say slowly, 'if part of the appropriate cast of mind for peace is acceptance of everyone's right to work for it, then excluding certain... members of society from the table at the very start doesn't seem particularly peaceful, does it?'

'Spot on,' says Leonard. 'And all credit to the women for staging their own peace conference.'

'And getting proposals included in the main draft,' says Gerald.

'But they shouldn't have had to go it alone, should they?' I say.

'So, can we say that inclusion is fundamental to promoting peace?' says Leonard.

'As exclusion is the opposite.' Gerald stretches his legs in front of him so that they are nearer the fire which Leonard lit at dinner time and which now is settling into a rosy glow. 'I've naturally been reflecting over the League of Nations and the exclusion of Germany. I know, Leonard, you're not keen on every aspect of Lord Robert Cecil, but I'm sure we both recall with dismay the dusty answer he got in Paris...'

Cecil... Surely, that name must be the same as the Cecil who was advisor to Queen Elisabeth...? I come to with a start. Leonard and Gerald are looking at Jack. I find I'm holding my breath.

'Sometimes,' Jack says, 'I feel I don't know what I think anymore –' murmurs of agreement – 'but it seems to me that if you're wanting people to be less war-like, the last thing you do is say to them, 'No you can't join,' when it's something which is supposed to be about maintaining peace.'

'Precisely so,' says Leonard.

I relax.

'Even leaving aside consideration of the moral aspect,' Gerald begins, 'the short-sightedness...'

'...Rose...?'

'She's dropped off.'

Jack's voice... why...? Of course! Oh, my goodness. I struggle to wake up.

'She's been running round after me all day,' Jack says.

'If you'd like to go on up, we can help Jack if he needs it,' Leonard says, full of concern, Gerald seconding him, and Jack saying he can cope.

I say goodnight, do the necessary bedtime things and go upstairs. I pull the curtains against a sky still subtly blue. After I've put on my nightdress and said my prayers, I lie in bed listening to a blackbird and the chirps of other birds still going about their business. That lovely poem from A Child's Garden of Verses by Robert Louis Stevenson comes to mind:

In winter I get up at night... And dress by yellow candlelight... In summer... ...quite the other way... I have to... ...go to bed... by day... ....I have to go... ...to bed and see... ...The bird... still... hopping... on the... ....

I drift in and out of sleep with the light, not waking properly till Leonard brings my tea at seven o'clock. He pulls the curtains on a dry, if pale morning. He has been up an hour already, writing in his attic study and making his final selection of poems for Thursday's reading.

I go through my routines, listening out for Jack, but there is no sound.

I am just at the point of wondering whether I dare slip out for a few things at the shops.

'Rose!'

I am faster than an arrow up the stairs. I barely knock before opening the door.

'Oh, Jack!' Barely raised on his pillows, my brother looks grey with pain, his face shrunken in on itself.

'It's all right. Don't worry. I have days like this - especially after days like yesterday. I just wondered - could I have my porridge up here?'

I take up a breakfast tray, which brings a smile of gratitude. He will probably stay in bed most of the day.

'At least I can do that here. I'm not required to drive a bloody motor car - sorry, Rose.'

I tell him that he will hear Lizzie later. 'So, if you need anything...'

'I won't.'

After we've said good-bye, I gallop to the shops, come back and unload everything, and then make my way to Quinn-Harper's Bookshop. Even though this is my busy period, it feels quite restful after being at home, and having the bright company of Louisa Briggs to help me is a delight.

'Old Hubert's been round here,' says Jack. 'I got up to - er - relieve myself, glanced out the window and there he was, sitting on the bench in your garden.'

'He does that sometimes.'

'I thought he must have come to see me, so I made myself get up. It took me a lot longer than I'd hoped, so I was convinced

75

I would have missed him, but when I got down to the kitchen and looked out, there he was still, looking as if he was communing with nature. When I called out from the back door, he started up like a pheasant at the gun. He came down to the house then and asked after me, but it almost felt as if he'd forgotten I was here and would have preferred not to have been interrupted.'

'He would have wanted to see you,' I say, carefully, 'but he does come and sit in our garden when we're not here. He finds it more restful than his own because there's always things to do in his, he says. We're nearer the station than the park, and nobody's going to buttonhole him and ask him what happened to the 9.15 last Tuesday.'

'Ah...' says Jack. 'I remembered not to mention what a lovely young lady Lettie is.'

Jack applauds. 'You've got a wonderful reading voice, Leonard. I could listen to you forever,' he says. 'Even if I don't always know exactly what you're going on about.'

He is looking much better now, with a large helping of bubble and squeak inside him and two strawberry jam tarts.

'That's very kind of you, Jack,' says Leonard. 'I hope the boys will understand what I'm going on about.'

'Oh, well, they're all intelligent lads, aren't they, or they wouldn't be at that school.'

Leonard looks as if he feels he should say something emollient. He has put so much into planning, and now rehearsing, this reading. I have to admit that Jack, for all his sterling qualities and notwithstanding the fact that he is my beloved brother, isn't exactly the ideal audience.

'You might like to know that you took exactly twenty minutes, so that's perfect.' I have been using Leonard's stopwatch to time him. Prior to the war, requests for him to read in public were not as frequent as I would have liked and as he deserves, given that he is a published poet, so I am relieved that he has this modest opportunity, and proud that he has lost none of his unassuming confidence.

'If you can bear it, we'll do it again tomorrow night,' Leonard says.

'It'll be music to my ears,' says Jack.

Train journeys are rare events in my life. Consequently, I might have felt some sense of anticipation about making this short trip to the next stop on the line and back, but Widdock's other, newer station is irrevocably bound up in my mind with a pain whose source is still too close to have settled into a dull ache. Leonard knows this and, under the guise of what was most practical, he did raise for discussion, with Jack chipping in, the merits or otherwise of having Olly Bates, senior or junior, take us to Cotteringbury School, it being just too risky to cycle there and back, quite apart from punctures, given the unpredictability of the weather so far this July. But I insisted on the train for reasons both of economy and common sense. Besides, we could not be sure what time we would be returning. 'Who knows, they might want to chat afterwards,' I said. Although Leonard dismissed this, I could tell that the thought had crossed his mind.

And now, here we are drawing out of Widdock North towards countryside which flattens into field after field of prime arable land. I am surprised and glad to see the wheat still standing high after Monday's downpour. Transportation of crops was one of the justifications for this railway line, but it is also the main line north. The thought of that unknown terrain brings another wave of sorrow and adds a different shade of regret. If I were to board one of the great express trains which thunders on to that far destination, I could probably visit my brother, Ralph, on the grand estate where he has been Head Gardener for more than a decade. But he would have no time to see me, I suspect. It is his wife, Delphine, who signs their Christmas card.

At Cottering's small station, we are the only passengers to alight, which is probably as well, there being only one cab in evidence. We take it and move off, the driver turning his horse away from the High Street, which looks pretty and interesting, reminding me a little, with a pang, of my old home town, Markly, out to the east of Widdock.

After a short stretch on a road passing between tall hedgerows and overhung by trees in their summer glory, we turn onto a wooded drive. At our cabby's enquiry, we work out when we'd like him to return, and he offers a very reasonable price for the round trip, saying he will get us back at the right time for a specific train.

Woodland gives way to a certain formality, specimen trees and clumps of rhododendrons. Then, there is a lightening of the sky as the drive opens to reveal a lawn and a sweep of gravel before a large, institutional building of yellow Widdock brick with doors and windows in the mock-Tudor style of the last century. On one side of the school are a block of newer classrooms, beyond which can be glimpsed some tennis courts. On the other side is the chapel and a path leading round to what presumably is a garden and parkland. No one else seems to be about, though there are several bicycles in a rack by the central staircase. We say a temporary good-bye and mount the stairs.

Through the porch, we enter a hall, a dim cavern of oak-panelled walls. The armorial bearings of the school's founder, a grim helmet and halberd above a black shield, surmount a noticeboard covered in pinned-on papers. There is a faint smell of boiled cabbage. We stand, somewhat at a loss, Leonard, smart in his light summer jacket, holding a large envelope containing three copies of his poetry book. 'Hello... hello... anyone there?' he calls, his voice echoing up to the rafters. A grandfather clock ticks away the minutes. Somewhere, a pigeon coos. Could it be nesting indoors? In the still quiet, we hear the scrunch of two slim tyres on gravel and a bicycle being placed in the rack. Moments later Mr. Vance, Eustace, joins us.

'Oh,' he says, 'where is everyone?'

'Exactly,' says Leonard. He produces, from his inside pocket, the Headmaster's letter of confirmation. 'This is the right day and time.'

'I'll go and see if I can find someone,' I say. I start towards a series of closed doors. Somewhere down the passage, one opens.

A flustered young woman comes towards us, clutching a sheaf of papers. She looks bewildered at our presence, then, 'Oh God,' she says, her free hand flying to her mouth, 'the poetry!'

Leonard is trying hard not to look disgruntled. Eustace Vance does nothing to hide his displeasure. 'Are we to take it that there has been a failure of communication to the school at large concerning our engagement?'

'I'm terribly sorry,' she says, gesturing towards the noticeboard, 'it got covered over. The Headmaster's indisposed, and I'm not here every day or else I'd... I'll see if I can round some of them up - only they have Thursday afternoon free, so I don't know - '

'Please,' says Leonard, 'I don't want anyone here under duress. If the event has been forgotten - '

'I have not forgotten it,' says a cultured female voice, with a foreign lilt.

The three of us turn, as one, to face the person heard entering and quietly standing behind us during the foregoing exchange.

'I made a note of it,' she says, 'and I can assure you I am very much looking forward to hearing your poetry.'

Chapter Six

She cuts a trim figure in her beautifully-tailored costume of wine-red silk. Dark eyes look out from under the brim of a stylish summer hat, which also reveals a glimpse of strawberry-blonde hair. She could be in her fifties, she could be ten years younger.

'Haven't we met...?' The young secretary, if that is what she is, asks. It is a question half-forming in my own mind.

'Yes, last month. I am to teach some classes here next year. Linda Watson.' She extends her hand, which the young woman clasps, murmuring her own name, Susan Sewell, or something like it. Mrs. Watson, for that I see is what she is, turns to the three of us with a charming smile. She shakes my hand first and I tell her my name. 'Bella,' she says, before moving on to Leonard.

'Where are we to go?' I ask Miss Sewell.

This seems to galvanise her. 'Let's see who's in the Sixth Form Common Room,' she says.

We follow her up the wide staircase and through to the back of the house and what turns out to be a rather charming, wood-panelled room. In the bay window, overlooking the garden, is a large table with some chairs, two of which are occupied by what my sister Hilda would call bookish-looking boys. In the distance, beyond their heads, I can see a cricket field, figures in white moving upon it. Faint cries drift through the open window. So, that's where everyone is. Bookish or not, these two pupils don't seem best pleased to be interrupted by the prospect of a poetry reading, but they dutifully stand up to be introduced, Leonard starting to chat to them about what they are reading and if they like the books. I see the crabbing tension ease out of their tall bodies and a loose, gangly sort of confidence take its place. Meanwhile, Eustace Vance is getting in the way as Mrs. Watson and I, wordlessly, start arranging a row of chairs, and he insists on trying every one of them. 'My back,' he says. 'If I sit down in one of those,' he nods towards two armchairs on either side of the fireplace, 'you'll never get me out of it.'

Miss Sewell returns with four more glum boys and a pair of colleagues who teach, respectively, Science and Religious Instruction. I glance across at Leonard, searching his face for signs of disappointment, but he and all six boys are chatting and he's making them laugh. From what I gather, one of the latest comers has met him in the bookshop, where he helped the lad. This seems to raise his stock with all. Mr. Vance has found a chair he likes by the window, so that the light will fall upon the printed page. Leonard takes one on the other side, and both put their books on the table. The teachers suggest the boys should occupy the front row. We are about to slot in behind them, but Miss Sewell insists that Linda Watson and I should sit on a two-seater sofa against a wall. I have my misgivings, as we won't be head on to the speakers, but as Mrs. Watson is already moving towards it, I step quickly to make sure I am the further away, so that she gets the better view. As she walks in front of where I've placed myself, I now recognise her back view. She is the elegant lady whom I saw outside Quinn-Harper's. Her husband, the distinguished-looking elderly man who had been browsing, joined her and carried her Gifford bags.

The door bursts open and a scarlet-faced man enters, clutching a tennis racket. 'Sorry,' he says to the room and then, advancing and transferring the racket to his left hand, introduces himself to Mr. Vance and Leonard, who have risen. 'Frobisher, English,' he says.

I am relieved for Leonard that the one teacher who might have a professional interest in his work has joined us.

Eustace Vance stands up and introduces Leonard briefly but, it has to be said, well, speaking of him as 'a distinctive and original voice.'

He sits and Leonard stands. He begins with a short poem which helps to settle his audience into an attentive mood. It seems like a straightforward nature poem, perhaps taking its inspiration from the Water Meadows at Widdock, but the listener realises that there is more to it. The bird call described could be the honking of a goose but the flight, like the build, is more graceful – and the bird is pink. We realise, with a frisson of unease, we're in a desert. This is Egypt. Now, he has his audience completely absorbed. He introduces the next poem, which has won a small prize, by telling us that, despite the way in which it opens, it isn't going to be a love letter. There is a slight chuckle of relief from the boys. I know, however, that the first stanza contains a secret message to me. Leonard reads:

What I Replied and What I Didn't

Dearest One, I'm so sorry for the delay
In thanking you for the notebooks, pencils,
Card and your letter, full of heart. It filled mine,

Bringing you to me like the sweetest attar,
Your unflagging spirit. You don't say how
Things are at home, but I see through your blithe mask.
This is my first chance to write, to relax.
They gave us a belated dinner, of sorts.
Did their best. As I write, I'm eating segments
Of Jaffa orange and some dates, which I hope
I won't regret. Glad you liked the poem.

It's all I could give – but wait, how could I
Forget? You had the perfect present early,
From my comrades and me. One which our esteemed
P. M. divined was just the ticket to boost
British morale for Christmas: Jerusalem.
No doubt you've already written to thank him
For tipping the wink in no uncertain way
To the General in November, giving
Us time to sort out Gaza first, after
His predecessor's two pig's ears, both of which,
I mustn't add, involved me, less and more

> In turn. Decent chap, Edmund Allenby.
> A ruse with a haversack and false papers
> To deceive the enemy is one thing.
> It's quite another to drop from our planes,
> Along with propaganda, cigarettes
> Laced with opium to drug the Turk's soldiers.
> He drew the line there, but was over-ruled.
> All this I found out later. Perhaps you did.
>
> The rest you know, but not the half of it.
> Our progress up the coast. Each place ticked off.
> Each tick cost the lives of soldiers, friends of mine,
> But it was worth it for Jerusalem.
> To show respect for the three great religions
> Of the city, Allenby walked in. Good man,
> As I said. I'm told the bells rang out at home.
> Alleluia! I hope you're still enjoying
> Your Christmas present. Me? I can't complain.
> After all, it's only what I signed up for,
> Isn't it? This Egypt-Palestine Campaign.

Leonard allows a moment before he speaks again, so that we can all return from our thoughts. Then, he says that, at the end, he'll gladly answer questions about how he wrote these first two or any other poems. He says he'll read two more. Both are upbeat sketches of camp life, one about the informal adaptions made to uniform to suit desert conditions, the other about the Horse and Hound Show. He closes his book pleased to hear, but braced for the sound of, genuine applause.

The Religious Instruction teacher's hand is first up. He introduces himself smoothly as Deacon Hicks. 'Being one of those back home who drew great comfort from the Allied victory at Jerusalem, I detect a certain... note of irony in your most arresting epistle. I wonder whether you'd like to expand on your argument.'

'It's my opinion, rather than my argument – based on first-hand experience,' says Leonard. 'I think the poem speaks for itself. But I'll talk about the practice of writing poems, if you would like me to.'

One or two of the boys glance at each other with a look which suggests that their master has been put in his place, for he gives no answer but the slightest huff. The moment of potential conflict passes with Mrs. Watson's question: does Leonard draw inspiration from the great poets of the past or does he confine himself to those of today?

'Absolutely not. I seize inspiration from wherever I can find it – Dante to de la Mare.'

'Dante in the original?' she asks.

'Sometimes,' says Leonard, and Mrs Watson gives a little sigh of what sounds like pleasure.

The English teacher asks about his daily routine. 'I write first thing while my mind is fresh,' Leonard answers, and there is a question from one of the boys about how to start writing poetry. 'Read a poet you enjoy, then see if a word or phrase sparks something in you which makes you want to write. Always include the senses. Think, how does it taste, smell, feel, sound? – not just, how does it look.' After more applause, Leonard introduces Eustace Vance as 'a significant force in the world of poetry', which is one way of describing him.

Mr. Vance stands and opens what he has himself described as his hoary tome, a large volume published over twenty years ago. He starts to read the rather leaden verse – and doesn't stop, poem after poem, as if he has lost all track of time. Leonard's polite face is a study of willpower over emotion. I try to hide my utter dejection, for I'm not convinced that this little audience will remember Leonard's jewel-like poems in the face of such an onslaught. I become aware of Mrs. Watson's perfume. Something which I had thought delicate and fragrant about it now seems to have a cloying undertow. I feel slightly sick. Eventually, the monotonous sound ceases. The English master jerks awake to the brief, forced applause with which Leonard copes by dint of its feebleness. There being no questions, the master thanks both poets, and people start to move. Hoping Mrs. Watson won't think me peremptory, I make my way to the front, taking drafts of as much fresh air coming in from the open windows as I can without drawing undue attention. Leonard is looking at his watch. 'We must go.'

We walk downstairs with Mrs. Watson. When we get to the hall, she says discreetly to Leonard. 'That was superb. I only wish my husband could have heard you.'

Leonard thanks her graciously, but he has his eye on our cabby, waiting at the door.

'I will write to you at Pritchard's Bookshop,' she says, as we prepare to leave. 'You must both come over to Ash Manor, and perhaps you will give dear Jeremy a private reading.'

'I should be delighted,' Leonard says.

We say good-bye, she boarding a little trap which has come for her, and we the station fly.

Glancing warily at Leonard's face, I feel like blowing Mrs. Watson a departing kiss. She has restored the look of pleasure which his performance and its enjoyment by his audience gave him, and she's added something beyond price: validation of his achievement and, thus, a real incentive to go on writing.

'Try to relax,' says Leonard, close to my ear.

'I am.'

The evening has had a rather celebratory feeling, with Leonard's justifiable satisfaction over the way this afternoon turned out, and Jack having had a better day than the last two, so what follows, though unusual during a working week, is not unprecedented. But I'm dismayed by my own inability, however hard I try, to enter wholeheartedly into the act of love. Although I am not consciously withholding my participation, far from it, it is as if I were listening for that cough – which is ridiculous. I am not.

'Well,' says Leonard after a while, 'it's been lovely, but it's getting late.'

We hug and kiss goodnight. I hear him fall asleep.

I must have drifted off. Suddenly, I am lurched awake by that terrible keening, which turns my blood to ice. Who knows what devastating images his mind is showing him? I sit bolt upright in the darkness, but do not attempt to touch the darker shaking form beside me. Sometimes his anguish turns to a sobbing frenzy and he lashes out, batting away the flies which - dear God - covered everything in the desert. I light the candle on the chest next to me. By an act of will, I regulate my rapid breathing. Keeping my voice low and calm, I say, 'It's all right, it's all right, you're safe, Leonard. Look, you're at home with me, Rose,' I repeat these lines, as I have so many times before. Eventually, they make some impression.

'I'm sorry, my love...'

We hold each other tight. He is bathed in sweat. 'Let me make you comfortable,' I say, gently.

He does not demur, so I remove his sodden clothes, quickly sponge him down and dry him, glad that I have gone back to the bowl and ewer on the chest. He is dropping asleep, exhausted, even before I've finished so, it not being cold, I roll him naked into bed and cover him, cuddling up and resting my arm across his rising, falling chest. He sighs, I think with comfort. I pray there won't be another episode tonight. I'm trying not to be despondent. How long has it been since the last one...three months, four? Neither of us has dared mention it, but I think we both had begun to hope he might be cured.

'Yes, I did hear him,' says Jack, 'but it didn't frighten me. I knew what it was. Poor old Leonard. I think he copped it worse than me.'

We're both utterly exhausted long before bedtime. Jack says he'll help Leonard do the washing up while I make porridge, set all to rights for the morning. I have to be grateful.

No, no, please God no, this cannot be. This time, I'm alert before the shaking starts. I take a chance and hold him, caress him, crooning in his ear till he quietens, falls into natural sleep.

We both wake up subdued – and, again, exhausted. Saturday. Quinn-Harper's is likely to be busy, but...

'Yes, you go,' says dear, game Louisa. 'If it's clear he's not coping, he won't be able to fob you off.'
But as I walk down Holywell End, keeping to the other side of the road so I can spy, I see my husband laughing and chatting with that trio of old friends, Messrs Davison, Nash and, yes, even irascible Mr. Vance, no doubt holding forth about his superlative performance last Thursday. The shop isn't crowded, so I turn round and head back to bridge-foot noticing, as I hurry along the tow-path, the quickest route to Quinn-Harper's, that the river is picturesque with boating parties.

'Where's Jack?' Hilda asks, as we stand outside after Church, 'Leonard hasn't got at him, has he?'
'No, he hasn't,' I say, with rather more asperity than I would usually allow, but I'm still so, so tired after the two broken nights and a busy Saturday at Quinn-Harper's. Leonard, too, is still recovering. After helping Jack through bath night, while I changed our sheets, he was asleep within minutes as soon as we got to bed. And Jack...
'Jack has good days and less good days,' I tell my sister. 'He certainly wouldn't have been up to coming to Church.'
'H'm,' says Hilda. 'When he was at that place, I don't suppose he ever saw a doctor.'
'I haven't asked him,' I admit.

The only time that I ever visited the doctor was after my bad illness, twenty years ago, when he told me not to worry about my irregular heart-beat. That was nice Dr. Brownlow, with his twinkly eyes and manner like a kind uncle. His practice was located in a little shop further down Holywell End from Pritchard's. The waiting room was at the front, with voile curtains across the bay window, screening his patients who sat in the old sofas and assorted chairs around the walls. His surgery was the equivalent of our sitting room at the back. But Dr. Brownlow has been dead for many years, and that building has reverted to its commercial use.

If we were to need a doctor now, the nearest is the one who operates from a smart villa on the other side of town, not much further on than Quinn-Harper's. Having tentatively broached Hilda's question, after Sunday lunch, and gained the answer she'd expected, I got Jack's willing agreement to a diagnosis, so I went first thing and luck was with me. The doctor will call here after morning surgery, at half past eleven. This couldn't have been better as, it being a fine day, Lizzie and I have finished the washing early and hung it out. Lizzie slips away.

I am just checking on Jack when there is a smart knock. I hurry downstairs. As I open the door, the doctor is looking at his wristwatch. He's almost across the threshold before I greet him, and is right behind me as I go to open the door at the foot of the stairs. 'My brother's room's to the rear,' I call to his mounting back. 'I've put a towel by the bowl and ewer – ' but he's knocking, entering, 'Dr. Warnish,' and closing the door behind him.

I can't stand it in the kitchen, hearing the muffled voices, the floorboards overhead. It sounds as if Jack's out of bed which is, of course, perfectly reasonable. I go through to the front room and sit in Leonard's chair, which still retains a sliver of sunlight before the sun moves round towards the back. Please, please, dear Lord…

Suddenly, Jack's door shuts and the doctor is on the stairs. Ten minutes must have passed. He bursts through into the living room, the stair door banging shut behind him.

He places his bag on our dining table, where I am now standing. 'There is nothing wrong with your brother.'

My first shock is that he should see fit to share his patient's private business.

He misinterprets my stunned silence. 'Oh, I saw plenty of this during the War, believe me. Stomach cramps, back ache - you name it. All under the heading of 'shell shock'.'

Something inside me snaps. I look at his pebble eyes in features set like a sneer. My voice, coming from somewhere deep and true grinds out like a whetted knife. 'If my brother says he is ill, he is ill.'

The doctor gives a high, jeering little laugh. 'Oh, well, if that's what you want to believe, my dear, you'd better find the nearest quack.' He opens his bag, produces pad and pen. 'Who shall my wife invoice, Mr. Alleyn or Mr. Pritchard?'

'Tell her to send it to me,' I all but snarl, 'Rose Alleyn-Pritchard.'

I'm reeling. Whatever made me call myself that? I look up to see the front door gently moving in the breeze.

'He had it in for me right from the start.'

Jack's face has more colour in it than I've seen all week, flushed with anger. I sit on the bed and take his hand. 'But why?'

'When he came in, announcing himself, I didn't like the way he looked at me. I reckon he thought I should have got myself to the surgery rather than take up his precious time. Still, I bid him a civil 'Good Morning', and while he was sitting down next to me and getting out his stethoscope, I said, thinking I was saving time, 'Apart from my bad back, which I don't understand, I seem so tired. If I have a good day - by which I mean a few hours awake on and off, I pay for it the next and often the one after. I could stay here and sleep the clock round.' 'Well, you'll have to get out of bed after this,' he says, putting on his stethoscope, 'if I'm to examine your back.' He listens to my chest and takes my pulse. Then he tells me to stand up. I managed it quite well, not keeping him waiting, and I thought he might be pleased, but he said nothing while I was moving into position in front of him. Still trying to be helpful, I said, 'I was in the War, of course, and I wondered whether what happened to me had any effect -' 'I make the diagnosis here,' he says, and starts feeling my back, and generally prodding around. 'All right, you can get back into bed, if that is your wish,' he says, washing his hands and drying them, 'but I must tell you, Mr. Alleyn, I can find nothing wrong with you which a regime of good food, fresh air and daily exercise couldn't put right. Your sister will no doubt provide the former,' he's at the door by this time, 'and the other two are your responsibility. Good day.' And he's gone.'

Not mentioning the bill, I tell him what I said when the doctor spoke to me.

'Thank you, Rose. At least I've got someone on my side.'

'We both are. Try and calm down now. And if you want to sleep, then sleep.'

As it turns out, we have lunch first, me sitting beside the bed with my plate and sandwich while Jack eats his. After a little tussle about the bill, which he's now remembered and insists on paying, though he's touched and amused by my retort to the doctor, he says he thinks he will be able to rest, so that he's downstairs in time to see his nieces. It is Alex's thirteenth birthday and, although I'm sure Lettie will have ordered something elaborate from Askey's to follow the evening meal when she gets home from work, I dart across the road to see what's in their window. I manage to secure four Swiss buns and as many of what the Askeys used to call Coburg cakes but which, at the outbreak of the War, they swiftly changed to Windsor.

Jack is awake and downstairs, looking refreshed, by the time his nieces arrive. Despite the Alleyns generally not sending cards and presents because there are too many of us to cope with it, I give Alex what I always give each girl on her birthday and at Christmas, a small notebook with a marbled cover. This one has a swirl of sea blue shaped like a breaking wave, fusing with tones of emerald and purple. She clutches it to her chest as she thanks me. All eyes light up at the sight of the cake stand. All hands dive for the Swiss buns just as, 'It's Auntie Phyllis!' both girls chorus with delight. She's brought, as usual, a pencil inscribed by herself 'Alex Alleyn' in a rather angular, modern-looking script, which Alex likes. Phyllis has the same taste as Leonard for the spicey, gingery Windsors, so I take the last Swiss bun. As expected, there is no writing today. It's a joyful occasion, completely cancelling out what happened earlier, which neither Jack nor I bring up, though I would have loved to talk it over with dear Phyl. She leaves first and, at the door, I say I will come up and see her on Thursday afternoon. Our eyes meet. 'Do,' she says.

Shepherd's pie again – that was such a lovely piece of hogget we had last week, I plumped for repetition while lamb's in season – and here I am again, behind with my tasks and racing to get the dish in the oven. Like last week, I failed to make a summer pudding to follow yesterday's roast, so it's just as well we have the cakes. I'll pick some raspberries, too, when I go out for the greens. All this activity has one good result. It's helped to keep at bay my growing sense of annoyance with myself. How I wish I hadn't rushed to act so quickly on Hilda's suggestion about the doctor! If only we had waited a little longer to see how Jack would fare. One thing's for certain, given that she doesn't even know the doctor's been, I'm in no hurry to inform her of developments.

I will just have time to pick some broccoli and make a fleeting re-acquaintance with my roses, dead-heading and collecting petals from those which are full-blown, so I can dry them. This I used to do by laying them out on muslin on the chest in Jack's room. Now, the only places where they will not be disturbed are the two window ledges downstairs, front and back, but I have to make sure to do this when the sun is not directly on them, or it will turn them to flakes. It occurs to me that Jack, currently in the living room might, if I bring some cushions, like to sit on the bench under the apple tree.

He gives me a slightly wry smile. 'Making sure I get some fresh air?'

'That wasn't what I was thinking.' I can't help smarting at the misconstruction of my honest invitation, but I say nothing more and, as we make our slow progress outside, he apologises. This illness of Jack's is such an unfamiliar landscape.

Once amongst my namesake flowers, I calm down. On one side of my basket, I collect spent flower heads in order to dry the petals, reserving the other side for blooms with which to replenish the rose bowl on the dinner table. Feeling restored, I choose three stems from my delicate pink moss rose whose heavenly fragrance wafts me back indoors just as Leonard walks in.

'Ah, glorious!' He says.

Our lips close above the scent.

'You look in good spirits.' I say, as I place the roses just so, without disturbing the others in the bowl.

'Ah, well, I've had a letter.' He taps his top pocket. 'Good news. I'll show you. But first, what about you?'

I can't bring myself to puncture his good mood. 'Not too bad,' I say, 'let's see this letter.'

It turns out not to be what I had thought. It's an invitation, yes, but not from Mr. and Mrs. Watson rather from the school, prefaced by a handsome apology from the Headmaster. Would Leonard be prepared, next academic year, to give a talk and reading to the new sixth formers, at a time to suit him and for which he would be paid?

'Look,' he says, tapping the figure given. 'I can hardly refuse at that price, can I?'

Jack is as delighted as we two are. 'Credit where credit's due.' He must also feel like me about the episode with the doctor, for he says nothing about it either.

We toast the occasion with the three remaining Coburg-Windsors.

Later, Gerald arrives wanting to debate the motion: Modern inventions will destroy the contemplative mood. When he leaves, we all go up to bed. Perhaps because I am so tired, I manage to find the words to tell Leonard matter-of-factly, without emotion, about the doctor's visit.

'Don't worry, let's just see what happens over time,' he says. 'I'm proud of you.' He kisses me.

We hold each other. I am soon asleep.

As Jack had told Dr. Warnish, a good day is often followed by several steps backward. I come home on Tuesday to find Jack resting on his bed. Perhaps all the varied excitements of Monday took their toll. This is how Leonard reassures me. Wednesday is no better. I feel as if I'm being gnawed from the inside.

'Try to relax,' Leonard says. 'You're doing your very best.'
'But what if he's really getting worse,' I whisper.
'Then we'll discuss it tomorrow.'

Thank goodness today, Thursday, seems to be a better day. Jack's up and smiling, ready for a sandwich when I come home a little after one o'clock.

'Yes, you go, I'll be all right,' he says. 'Besides, Leonard said he'd be home about two.'

In the past, on a fine early-closing afternoon, Leonard might have gone for a walk or taken his bicycle out, but I expect he feels concern for me. If he's satisfied that Jack can be left, perhaps he will follow his fancy. I hope so.

All in all, though, I am relieved that it looks as if I will be able to visit Phyllis. There's something on which I'd like to seek her views.

In the front garden of the house which bears its name, I pause to gaze up at the lovely tree, abundant with green apples. Passing the blank side wall, I cross the terrace and take the path down through the ornamental garden, ablaze with the colours of high summer. Noble hollyhocks, shading from darkest crimson through pink to lemon and purest white, vie for supremacy in height with the gentle gold of mullein. In the understorey, flame bursts of gallardia, the blanket-flower, offset the scent and subtlety of lavender, which never fails to delight both bees and me. The vegetable garden and The Byre are screened by trees of cherry, plum and damson, ripe with fruit, and the gorgeous roses which climb into them. My eyes are almost closed as I drink in the perfume of the deep-pink Bourbon rose nearest the path.

'Goodness me!' They're wide open now.

Phyllis comes out of The Byre, bearing a tray with two glasses of lemonade. 'It's all right, isn't it?' She is wearing her breeches, a collarless blouse and jerkin, hair pulled back into a covered band.

'You haven't bought it, have you?'

'No, no, it's hired. But if I like it, I can buy it and get the hire money discounted.'

'I say, Phyl – how exciting!'

What we are both admiring is a two-seater motorcycle in smart black livery with a chrome trim.

'I picked it up this morning,' says Phyllis, moving towards the south-facing bench against the wall opposite The Byre. 'Let's sit and look at it.'

'But what about – ?' I jerk my head towards the house.

'They've both gone to Cornwall.'

I clap my hand to my mouth. 'Good Lord!' I move as if numb, find the seat, and gratefully take a sip of home-made lemonade.

'Yes, it was all very last minute. Beatrice has some artist friends down there. She was going anyway, and she managed to persuade her mother to join her. They left yesterday. I can tell you, it's been... interesting getting them both ready. They had to have all their equipment with them – travelling easels, boards, paints and palettes. You should have seen Olly Bates's face when he came to pick us up.'

'You went to the station with them?'

'I went to Paddington with them! I wanted to make absolutely sure they got on board that train to – St. Erth, that's it. Whoever was supposed to be meeting them could help them off it.'

'Oh Phyl, you must be exhausted.'

'I'm all right,' says Phyllis. 'But what about you?'

I tell her everything - well almost everything - from Hilda's suggestion of calling the doctor to Jack's slight improvement today.

She sits, taking it all in. 'And it can't be easy for you and Leonard?'

'It's... changed things,' I say, feeling the colour come to my cheeks.

'Perhaps I should have Jack up here,' she says, almost to herself.

'Good gracious, no. You need a break as much as anyone. You have two people to look after - besides each other, I mean. Not that Jenny needs looking after.'

'No,' Phyllis gives an inward smile, 'she's what keeps me going when it's... difficult up at the house. But Jack... I think I'm inclined to agree with Leonard, do nothing for now. In fact,' she looks slightly uncomfortable, 'do nothing for two weeks - Factory Holiday Fortnight. The thing is...'

'Oh! Are you going away? That's wonderful!'

'Well, it did seem like an offer we couldn't refuse, especially as we never get the chance normally.'

It turns out that, by way of celebration and to give the Temperance Club support, Phyllis and Jenny called in yesterday evening. Whom should they see but our old friends, Meg and Winnie? So, they joined them and, over blackcurrant juices, learned that the scientific sisters were planning to spend the factory summer holiday touring the Norfolk coast.

'You know they've got a motorcycle and sidecar combination?'

'Er... yes,' now I come to think of it.

'They store the tent and their belongings in the sidecar. Anyway, they suddenly said, what about us coming, too? If I could get hold of a motorcycle, we could put our tent in with theirs. And if it rains a lot - well, we'll just find a couple of rooms where we can put up for the night.'

'That sounds marvellous.' I have a vision of the four of them, laughing at assembling their tents, frying sausages on a camp fire, pointing to the white shape of an owl hovering over reed beds, the distant whisper of the sea.

'I've got to pick the tent up from that place on Swan Mead. Then I'll collect Jenny from work.' Though I hadn't heard of the tent manufacturer, there are a lot of factories and workshops down by the river, off the London Road. 'I'll give you a lift home. You'll be my first passenger.' My face must be a picture. 'It's all right, Rose, I won't go fast. I don't want to be accused of raising a dust storm.'

Phyllis wheels the motorcycle up the path, round the side of the house and into the drive under the apple tree. I clamber onto the pillion seat, which is situated over the back wheel. I'm showing a good deal of leg, which reminds me of the time when I was sixteen, had just written to Leonard, asking for a job at Pritchard's Bookshop, and Father, having been to speak to Leonard who was working out his notice at Sawdons, came to collect me from my aunt's, where I had gone with the news of Mother's death. Father was riding Old Sable. What a fuss Aunt Mary made about my sitting behind him astride! What would she think of me today?

Riding Sable was an intimidating experience, but no more so than this beast of a different stripe. In the same way as I clutched Father's ample waist, I throw my arms round Phyllis's slim one. She spurs the motorcycle into monstrous life.

Just as with a horse, I'm trying not to let my nerves communicate themselves - either to Phyllis or the machine. Before she moves it off its stand, I speak into her ear. 'Leonard will be home, so - '

'It's all right,' she calls back. 'I'll switch it off before we reach the yard.'

To say that I move down New Road in a dream doesn't convey the noise and vibration nor the level of sheer terror I am feeling, as the familiar landmarks of that long road slip by. I clutch even harder, as I sense - I dare not take my eyes from Phyllis's back - her turn the front wheel to the right, and now - Glory be! - we're in East Street, empty this afternoon, thank goodness. The engine cuts away as the wheel turns right again, and we pass through the archway under our own momentum, coming to a stop outside our cottage. I am shaking as Phyllis helps me to get off.

'That was exciting,' I say in a weak voice.

Phyllis rests the motorcycle on its stand and takes my hands. 'Perhaps I shouldn't have done that with you. Are you going to be all right?'

'Yes, yes,' I say, as my breathing returns to normal. 'It was fun,' I manage. It almost was. 'You'd better get on,' I say, to show that I've recovered.

'I shall be thinking of you while I'm away,' says Phyllis.

'And I shall be thinking of you. Do be careful.'

'I will. And I'll really give Jack and his illness some serious thought.'

'Don't spoil your holiday,' I say. 'Any ideas what you'll be doing?'

'Eating Cromer crabs, isn't that what you're supposed to do?'

'So it is. When do you actually go?'

'First thing, Saturday morning.'

Of course. So, I don't ask her opinion on what I'd had in mind to do. It wouldn't be appropriate or fair.

It is as well that Quinn-Harper's is busy on both Friday and Saturday. It helps to keep my mind from returning to Jack, who is not so well and, on Saturday, imagining my sister and three friends on the road to Norfolk, wishing I could be with them. There is also the absence of any communication from the Watsons, which I'm sure has struck Leonard also. Perhaps it is too early to be concerned.

On her way home from market, Hilda calls in at the shop.

'Has Jack seen a doctor yet?' She says in a stage whisper.

At Louisa's nod, I take Hilda through to the sitting room. I have spent the days since Monday rehearsing a range of answers which aren't direct lies. 'I can't talk for long,' I say, not offering her a seat, 'but yes, he has, and we're doing everything beneficial for him.'

'Did the doctor say what's wrong with him?'

'He mentioned shell shock.'

'Oh,' says Hilda. 'That's what he thinks it is, does he?'

'The important thing is that it could take quite a while to see an improvement.'

'H'm,' says Hilda. She peers at me. 'You're looking peaky, Rose, like you did during the War. I hope you're taking care of yourself.'

'I'm sorry, Hilda...' I walk towards the door.

'We must talk about it on Sunday,' she says, as she leaves.

I say nothing, having other plans.

Chapter Seven

Thank goodness it's sunny. I'm on my bicycle, with a cake tin secured in the handlebar basket, making my way over to the Station Master's House, a substantial brick cottage which Lettie considers old-fashioned, but I think rather pretty with its decorative bargeboards and crest tiles, just like those of the station. In fact, it overlooks Widdock East from a slightly elevated position just across the tracks on the town's 'favoured' south side, which climbs to a ridge with commanding views of Widdock Moor to its own south and, to the north, the town of Widdock laid out below, beyond the railway line and the glint of the river Blaken. This being Sunday morning, the crossing gates stand open. I have a good chance of finding both my brother and nephew at home. As I dismount and start to feel the strain of pushing up their garden path, which is only a fraction of the way up the steep hill, I can't help thinking not for the first time, that although it must be wonderful to freewheel from the highest street of imposing residences, the wind flying through one's hair, down to the bottom, it must be quite a different story to have to trudge, heavy-laden with shopping, right to the very top. I suppose, up there, they all have servants or arrange for their goods to be delivered.

I leave the bicycle propped behind a juniper bush, gently freeing my precious cargo. As thanks for Lettie's kindness in lending me the sheets, I have made her some shortbread, which I know she likes and never makes. She has a cook-cum-cleaner, one of the redoubtable Munns family who helps her during the week, and baking is something she rarely does herself.

Alex lets me in with a glad cry, 'She's here!' then shows me through to where the family is sitting in the back garden with glasses of soda.

Lettie jumps up. 'Come and sit here.' She indicates an empty deckchair beside her. 'Ooh, what's that?'

I present the cake tin. 'Jack really appreciates those lovely sheets,' I say, which is true.

'You naughty girl,' says Lettie, gazing at the shortbread with delight, 'you know you didn't need to – but I'm going to have one. Alex, you can pass them round.'

'It's for you,' I say, declining a piece.

'Make yourself comfortable and I'll bring you some pop,' says Hubert, who stood up when I came in, and now moves to un-stopper the bottle and pour me a glass.

'Thank you.' We exchange a fond smile.

'How are you at tongue-twisters, Auntie Rose?' asks Tom.

'Not good enough to try one,' I say.

He is holding a book entitled, Quips and Tips for Shining Slip-Shod Wits.

'He got that from the station bookstall, of course,' says Lettie.

'Well, he wouldn't have bought it at Pritchards!' Alex says.

Hubert brings my drink over to me, next to Lettie, 'I don't know what's worse,' he says, 'him reading them out, or him sniggering to himself.' The love in his look belies his words.

It takes me back to that morning early in 1918, which none of us will ever forget. I was at Pritchard's. The shop being empty, I was absorbed in paperwork. Something made me look up out of the window. A few feet away stood the Recruiting Officer talking intently to Tom. Although I couldn't clearly see his face, everything about Tom's stance looked frightened and helpless. They both started walking towards the Drill Hall which had been built further up Holywell End, and where the Recruiting Officer had his room. By this stage, I'd locked the shop, hands shaking, heart pounding. I ran to catch up and, just before they reached the door, almost without thinking, I stepped across their path. 'You're not trying to conscript my nephew, are you?' I said, my voice loud but uneven with an anger I could barely control. 'You know he's under age.' The sergeant, gazing at a point above my head, said, 'Yes, it's a very fine day for the time of year. Now, if you'll excuse us, Madam.' He made to move towards me, as if I would have to give way or he might, perhaps, walk right through me. I stood my ground, or rather my body stayed grounded, while my mind - or was it my soul? - was so afraid it had taken flight, for a moment, looking down on the scene. I tried to find words. 'Tom, have you told him you're only seventeen?' 'He took no notice,' Tom said in a small voice then, uncertainly, 'He says I've got a duty to my King and Country.' 'Not until you're eighteen,' I said. Then, I folded my arms, and with that action, brought myself back together. 'I'm just going to stand here, in front of this door, till I see you turn the corner for the station, Tom. Tell your father, the Station Master, what's just happened.' At this point, the Recruiting Officer stood aside. So, I took Tom's arm and we walked off together, wordless and shaking but entirely dignified, back to Hubert, who was beginning to worry what was keeping his son on a simple errand to purchase stamps. After that, Tom was not left unattended in public. This episode explains the great affection in which I'm held by all the family.

Lettie finishes her shortbread and goes on shelling peas for Sunday lunch. She bats away my help, but wants to know all my news. I give her an undramatic version of events, finishing with Hilda's verdict on my own state of health, which I treat light-heartedly.

'Well,' says Lettie, pausing, an unshelled peapod in her hand, 'We all know Hilda can be a bossy-boots' - and I know what Hilda would say: takes one to know one - 'but this isn't just her wanting to interfere. She does care about you. After all,' Lettie returns to her task, 'let's face it, you are looking after two sick men.'

'I hadn't thought of it like that.' Suddenly, I feel rather hot. I try to adjust my deckchair so that I'm more thoroughly under its little canopy with the tasselled fringe but, even in cool muslin, my legs, stretched out on the chair's extension, are exposed to the sun. 'I'll have to move,' I drag the chair into the shade of a large hydrangea, opulent with pink, mop-head blooms. This is a garden full of shrubs, which more or less look after themselves, since neither Lettie nor Hubert has time to lavish attention on it.

'Do think about it like that,' Lettie is saying, 'Leonard's not out of the woods yet and Jack - ' She shrugs.

It occurs to me that this is how we all have to think about Jack, like an unfinished sentence because - 'It's difficult to know what to do for the best.' At least I finish my present thinking about him.

'Best for who? It's never for you, Rose, is it? If you're going to help those two men in your life, you do need to look after yourself.'

She's quite right. Lettie always helps me to be practical. 'But what about you? What's your news?' I ask, at which she gives me chapter and verse of Widdock's gossip.

As she is seeing me to the door, she says, 'I'm looking forward to tomorrow. Remember that very stylish woman who came in and ordered an entire wardrobe?'

My interest quickens. 'Mrs. Watson?'

'Very good, you do remember.' I haven't the time to go into why. 'Well, she's coming in to have a mourning costume fitted. So, they must be going to a big funeral, I should think. Her blonde hair would look lovely against black marocain. Very elegant...'.

So, that's why we've heard nothing from the Watsons. It would be entirely understandable for such a funeral to have taken all their attention especially if, for instance, it's in a distant place.

Leonard, trying not to look relieved at the explanation, agrees.

Today has been a better day for Jack. The fact that I'm at home on Mondays probably helps. Consequently, we are feeling rather cheerful over dinner, though I am slightly distracted by the fact that, because Jack and I are deemed to be part of the discussion group on Monday evenings, tonight's topic will be broached by me. Since, during our Sunday quiet reading last night, I happened upon the well-known poem 'Dream-Pedlary' by Thomas Lovell Beddoes, with its image of 'A cottage lone and still, with bowers nigh', I thought we could start by thinking about the individuality or universality of a daydream or ideal. I'm not very confident. Perhaps this is why I'm off my guard. At the expected knock I, being nearest, open the door. 'Come in, come – oh...'

'I shan't take up a moment of your time,' says Hilda, stepping across the threshold. 'If you hadn't gone to early Communion, Rose, I could have told you all about it after Church yesterday, but we've got a proposition for you, haven't we, Gerald?'

I offer them the sofa, turning a dining chair, for myself, to face them.

'Go on, dearest,' says Hilda.

'Rose, you'll have heard me talk about The Chantry, yes...?' This is a name I know, but more than that I don't have to acknowledge, as Gerald goes on, 'It's a house shared by the diocese at Hocton. I think the fact that we didn't see you yesterday may have been for the best, because what we now have is a firm proposal for you.'

'The point is,' Hilda says, 'because of the disappointing weather this summer, they've got a vacancy over the Bank Holiday Weekend and I, we, thought what a wonderful opportunity it would be for you, Rose, and you, Leonard, to have a little holiday. We, of course, would be more than pleased to look after Jack for two or three nights. Oh, and you don't have to pay. You just make a donation for upkeep. They're glad for the room to be filled.'

I can't help wondering whether, in this last sentence, Hilda is echoing her own understandable ache. When term ended Ambrose, with a party of Cambridge friends, went directly on a tour to Durham and Holy Island, after which he will go into retreat. We shan't see him till the end of summer.

I glance at Leonard, then across at Jack both, like me, recovering from the shock of Hilda's suggestion.

'Well, I think that's a very good idea, if you'd like to do it,' Jack says, looking at Leonard and then at me. He doesn't convince me entirely, but he's nodding at me to say yes.

'I'm sorry if I appear ungracious in the face of such a generous offer,' Leonard says, 'but I wouldn't be expected to participate in any services or what not, would I?'

'Absolutely not,' says Gerald. 'Chantry House is a place for restoration and reflection, not evangelism.'

'Well, what do you think, Rose?' He looks almost enthusiastic.

I glance at Jack willing me, for my own sake, to say yes. Really, there's no reason not to. Both shops will be closed. And I've never seen the sea.

We settle into what I suspect will be the pattern of our life – at least for the next couple of weeks before we go away – Jack having a good day and then, as if the malign spirit of his illness, whatever it is, has to make up for its negligence in allowing him some ease, a day or even two when pain and fatigue keep him to his bed. I ask myself whether he is getting worse, and what I should do.

'Nothing for now', says Leonard. 'He's only been here just over a fortnight.' Can it be true? It feels much longer. 'That's no time at all. He isn't suddenly going to deteriorate. Wait till we've been back in our normal routine for a couple of weeks. Then, we can have a reassessment.'

This is sound advice which, forgive me, I'm glad to follow. Apart from Christmas, these weeks up to the August Bank Holiday are my busiest time. Daisy Ashford's book, although quite pricey, is doing well, as are all the summer novels. Even Mr. Conrad's new one, the final part of his seafaring Lingard Trilogy though set before the other two, is making a surprising showing. It is not, however, the holiday reading matter which some of my customers may have expected from its title, The Rescue, A Romance of the Shallows, and has sometimes found itself firmly put back on the shelf. I'm glad to say that Mr. Hardy's novels are still enjoying the revival in popularity stimulated by his eightieth birthday, which took place in June.

Wednesday morning, and I'm in the kitchen, getting ready for work. I hear the letterbox flap. On the mat is a post-card featuring a view of the seafront at Cromer, with wide sands and an impressive pier. It is addressed to the three of us, and bears the message:

> *Crab salads consumed with relish. Wish you all were here. Really.*
> *With much love from the four of us xxxx*
> *Phyllis*

I can't deny a momentary pang.

I leave the card propped up against the cruet for Jack, not yet stirring, to see when he comes down. I step out into the sunlit yard, thinking about the sea and what I shall make of it.

Jack tells me he's feeling better, and I've had another day of good sales. It's Friday evening, and I'm in the kitchen garden with a bowl full of raspberries, picking mint to go with our home-grown new potatoes, which will accompany a lovely piece of salmon. I was lucky enough to catch the fish man on his rounds before I left for work.

I hear someone stepping outside the cottage. It's Leonard, carrying a folded copy of today's Courier. Although he greets me cheerfully, asking after my day, there is something about him which gives me a flutter of anxiety. 'And how about you?' I ask.

'I've got something to show you,' he says.

I follow him inside. He opens the paper towards its end, finds what he wants – I notice the page heading – folds it and hands it to me, pointing out a small announcement. I read:

> The funeral of Mr. Jeremy Watson, late of Ash Manor, Cottering, will take place at 3p.m. on Monday 26th July at St. Michael and All Angels, Cottering, after which mourners will be received at Ash Manor by his widow, Mrs. Linda Watson.

'Oh, goodness! No wonder we didn't hear from Mrs. Watson, poor thing,' I say.

'Indeed,' says Leonard. 'It must have happened shortly after we met.'

Of course, neither of us mentions the door now closed on the invitation to give a reading, and what that might have led to.

'Should we send our condolences?' I ask, 'or will it seem... too forward of us?'

'It's a bit tricky, isn't it...' says Leonard.

'It might seem rather callous not to,' I suggest. 'I mean, we do know her, if only as an acquaintance.'

In the end, we both agree on a short, formal note conveying our sympathy.

It made such sense, tomorrow being Early Closing, for us to gain a whole extra day away, especially as Louisa is more than capable of opening the two shops for the consecutive morning hours best suited to them - early for Pritchard's, late for Quinn-Harper's. All the same, I lock my door and turn away with a slight tinge of regret.

Visible through a window, and audible through the open door of Hocton Station, a bus waits, engine running. We are helpless, caught in the press to leave the building, and see it filling up with the many people already alighted from the train, which picked up holidaymakers at every stop along its route. The bus pulls away as we come out onto a street noisy with assorted vehicles, motorised and horse-drawn, some clearly private and others, just as clearly, for hire. We stare after it, temporarily at a loss.

'I wonder when the next one is,' I say.

'We could walk,' says Leonard, 'Gerald said it's only twenty minutes or so.'

'Where you going, Sir?' asks a cabby with a horse and trap.

'The Ness,' says Leonard.

'Well, that wasn't your bus. Where exactly in the Ness?'

'It's a place called The Chantry,' I say.

'We're going to The Chantry,' says a pleasant voice behind us. We turn to see a couple of about our age, with the same amount of luggage. They look friendly.

'Shall we share?' Leonard asks.

Now we're all smiling.

'I can get you to The Chantry quicker than any bus,' the cabby says over his shoulder, as his horse starts to trot in response to a tap of the reins and a giddy-up. 'They have to go along the front. What with the trippers, it'll be stop start stop start all the way. And you'd still have a walk.'

We've taken a course which I assume, because the railway track is intermittently visible, will bring us slightly inland. Am I never to see the sea? Veering right, running parallel with the coast, I think, we pass under the railway bridge and into a wide avenue. Set back from the road are substantial villas with names such as Sea Breeze or Bella Vista, some of which offer Bed and Breakfast accommodation. In the well-tended gardens tamarisk trees, with their thin, whippy branches, attest to a maritime location and, in one or two very well-sheltered places, I spot a dracaena palm. It gives me joy to recognise these specimens from drawings of them in the books owned by my Grandpa Clarke, a part-time nurseryman and gardener at heart. I hope dear Grandpa would be pleased. The general air of quiet prosperity in these streets bears witness to what Hilda was at pains to impress on me, namely, that this is Hocton's favoured side which, unlike Widdock, is its north. We turn again coast-wards, I think for, unless I am mistaken, the tang in my nostrils must be salt. I feel quite excited. We are in a quiet lane with houses hidden behind their greenery. They are randomly spaced, some of the gaps between them large enough to suggest grounds rather than gardens. I notice that, underfoot, dirt is mixed with sand. We turn into what must be the driveway of one of them.

'My word!' I say.

'It's an enormous cottage orné,' says Leonard in a tone of some awe.

The building before us looks like a traditional cottage made of wattle and daub, but one which has been stretched to at least six times the normal width. At each end is a half-timbered jetty or overhang. Crowning the structure in its entirety is an impressive thatched roof, dipping down to cover each first floor window bay, a theme repeated by the porch.

'You're right about it being Regency,' says Sam Baker – for we've introduced ourselves already – 'but it really does have a mediaeval core, the chapel.'

'Or Chantry,' says Alice, his wife. 'We know all this because we've got the pamphlet at St. Barnabas.' We've learnt that Sam is a vicar in the East End of London.

We disembark, pay the cabby and step under the porch. The thatch is likely to be reed-straw, judging by what we saw in the flatlands approaching Hocton, but its sweetness reminds me of hay, horses and my old life as a child in the country. The bell-pull's toll is answered promptly by a grey-haired lady with a kind face who turns out to be the Manageress. Although the building's outside took me aback, I have seen enough of its ilk not to be surprised by this entrance hall. The word 'baronial' falls neatly into my mind, though the days of any barons who may or may not have lived here are past, if the well-worn easy chairs and coffee tables grouped loosely around the fireplace are anything to go by. I find myself relaxing. We are handed our keys and given directions. With many assurances of our comfort and well-being, the Manageress leaves the Bakers to take the staircase to the left, 'the west wing', Leonard and I mounting its duplicate to the right, or east, up under the big drop of the latticed window which was a feature of the two mediaeval-looking jetties outside. We find our room at the end of the corridor.

'H'm,' says Leonard, as we close the door behind us.

It is clear, from the way the ceiling moulding cuts off abruptly on both sides, that our room has been made out of one which was originally much larger. We have already noted that we are next door to the bathroom - 'A mixed blessing,' says Leonard - and it doesn't take a genius to work out that part of our room has been relinquished for that purpose, whilst the remaining third has gone to make what's probably a similar room next door - 'Supposing there's someone in there!' I cry, under my breath, as Leonard taps the partition wall.

'H'm,' says Leonard, again, 'not much chance of cwtching here!' This is a Welsh word which Leonard learnt when once we took a week away from work, our honeymoon really, not close to our winter wedding but in the summer lull. We spent it with his cousin in a small town in South Wales, from whence the Pritchards - originally ap-Richard, son of Richard - hail. The word 'cwtch' means 'to cuddle up' but we have adopted it for a more intimate form of cuddle. Free from the inhibition of Jack's presence, is that what he's been thinking about? 'Of course, we could...' he begins, not needing to finish the sentence.

I look at him with dismay. Whilst still on the train, we had worked out a plan to take advantage of any available bathroom now before all the guests return and claim it for their pre-dinner ablutions. I cannot wait to shed my clothes, soiled by travelling generally and filthy from all those engines with their descending plumes of steam, and the smoke and smuts trapped under the glass vault of Liverpool Street Station.

'It's all right, Rose,' he says, seeing my expression, 'I'm as anxious as you to have a bath. Next door looked free. You use it. I'll see if I can find another bathroom. If we take our valuables with us, we don't need to lock the door - not that I'm expecting thieves here - then whoever gets back first won't have to hang around outside.'

I simply take the towels provided and my portmanteau straight into the bathroom, lock the door and run the bath - what bliss! It reminds me of being back at Apple Tree House. I love our little cottage, but the convenience of turning on a tap and having hot water flowing out of it was a boon in that year I lived there. I would never own this to Hilda, who is always on at us to have a room converted and gas put in, as if money grew on trees. In any case, we would hate the disruption. I'm thinking about all this as I allow myself to drift in the healing water. But I pull myself together. Leonard, if he's found a vacant bathroom, will be back already - he's so quick - and besides, someone else might need to use these facilities. I quickly dress and gather up my travelling clothes, shocked anew at the dense black grime round collar and cuffs.

Leonard is back first, of course, neatly unrolling his few clothes and hanging his clean shirt in the wardrobe. 'I'm ravenous. Where are we going to eat our sandwiches?'

I pause from drying my hair with the hand towel. 'If this place really does have its own beach, I'd like to find it. I'd like to see the sea.'

Our bedroom faces north but, I'm pleased to say, the window overlooks a lovely garden surrounded by an old wall made of flint. Beyond this is an open stretch of heath. Against the sky, a line of scrubby bushes and trees blasted westward by the prevailing wind suggest the proximity of the sea.

Armed with our sandwiches and books, in my case one of the better holiday novels which have proved so popular at Quinn-Harper's, in Leonard's a small collection by one of the new poets, we go back downstairs. Following Hilda's instructions, we push a door, slightly ajar, marked 'Lounge', and pass through the large but faded, homely room towards French windows, which stand open like an invitation, out onto a terrace, then down three steps to a lawn. By the house, to the west, is a kitchen garden extended, no doubt during the War, into the adjacent flower bed but, as we walk slowly down the lawn, we are accompanied on either side by borders in their late summer glory, swathes of bright, metallic sea holly underpinned by bright red montbretia. Tough Rosa Rugosa, with its crinkled leaves, rambles up and along the weathered wall in blooms of pink and white. I think of Grandpa Clarke again but also of Mother, who grew up with her father's love of gardens and all things green and living. August is, was, her birthday month, the garden risen to its apogee, as if to offer praise and thanks to her for all her care throughout the year. I feel her pleasure fusing with my own.

We turn an iron roundel on an old wooden door festooned with ivy, as if it were auditioning for The Secret Garden. Now we are out on the heath, springy grass under our feet, salt in the air, together with wheeling birds, gulls and another bird I don't recognise, white with a black cap and shrill, twittering cry. We walk towards the trees and bushes, and now I catch glimpses of a grey-blue which is not that of the sky, but is defined against it by a darker line – the horizon. We come out on the other side of the scrub – and there it is, stretching before us calm and infinite, what was once German, but renamed The North Sea. I stand for a long time, breathing in its unique odour, feeling as if it must be scouring my lungs, freshening my thoughts, doing me good. Eventually, I become aware of Leonard, who has also been silently communing, but is now smiling at me.

'Oh, goodness, we must eat,' I say.

'Look, there's some steps,' he says, and we make our way down onto a sandy, shingly beach where the waves, far enough out not to be a threat, suck and break with mesmeric endlessness.

We find a sheltered spot – though against all odds, there is no real breeze – between sandy clumps of what I recognise to be marram grass. There may be others on this beach – occasionally I hear a sound which might be human voices – but we are not interrupted. Most of the holidaymakers must be in Hocton. We eat our sandwiches, and Leonard lies back against a grassy outcrop, finds his spectacles and starts to read. I try to do the same, but my eyes are always drawn to the sea where, now, sunlight looks like stitches on every wave. A flotilla of white-sailed boats comes into view, tiny in the distance.

I think at some point both of us fall asleep, and come to ready for a cup of tea. We stand up, brushing sand which seems to stick to everything. 'You should try the desert,' says Leonard. 'At least this doesn't burn your feet.'

At the same moment, another couple appear from behind a little dune further down the beach. It's our friends Alice and Sam Baker, apparently with the same idea about refreshment.

We go back to the Chantry where, yes, we can purchase tea and Madeira cake. I think of Jack and hope with all my heart that he is happy. We take our trays to wicker chairs and tables on the terrace.

'After this, we're thinking of walking to the end of the Ness,' says Sam, 'would you care to join us?'

Of course, we'd be delighted.

We go back through the lovely garden. 'You know a lot about plants,' says Alice, so I tell her all about Grandpa Clarke and Mother. Then, I ask her about herself. The men are walking in front of us absorbed in conversation about low wages and the need for cohesion as well as militancy in the major unions.

'I'm working with Sylvia Pankhurst,' Alice says. 'We must do more for women's rights.'

'You make me feel like the country cousin,' I say.

'I'm sure you're not. Tell me what you do.'

So I give a brief account of how I met Leonard, became his assistant at Pritchards and then, how I felt sorry for his rival, Auberon Quinn-Harper, who really had no inkling of how to run a successful bookshop. 'He dealt in antiquarian books – buying up libraries from houses, like his own, which had fallen on hard times.' I do not mention how he had gambled his inheritance away. 'The trouble was that he could never reconcile himself with the fact that he was in trade. I was passing, one day, and couldn't bear the inept, ugly notice he'd attached to a board outside – the letters wrongly formed and all falling off the page because he hadn't allowed enough space to fit them in. I'm no artist, but my mother taught me calligraphy. I went inside and asked him if he'd like me to re-write his poster. He wanted to pay me, but I refused. I didn't want to end up feeling beholden and doing his cleaning to make up for it. The back room was an absolute tip. I wanted the freedom to help him under my own terms. From then on, I just made a habit of calling in from time to time and sorting him out. But imagine the shock that morning after his death – I still can't quite believe it – when a letter came from his solicitor, asking me to call – Leonard came with me – and we found out he had left his bookshop to me.'

'He must have felt he could trust you, Rose. That's a wonderful story.'

All the while, we have been taking in the view, the sea at low tide revealing an endless stretch of smooth beach punctuated only by occasional breakwaters. Inland is scrubby vegetation. Here, tufts of marram grass sculpt our path, and low-growing sea holly scrambles across it, tough plants adapted to their maritime location. I glance down and recognise, from drawings, the needle-like leaves and cup-shaped flowers of thrift, a soft pink.

Now we are reaching the end of the headland, The Ness. Ahead is a broad estuary of rippled sand whose rivulets of glinting water run away to the sea. Almost indecipherable in their dun-coloured plumage, small wading birds dip their long beaks into the wet, compacted grains, their fluting cry barely audible against the slightest of breezes carrying the muted roar of distant surf, the occasional flurry of raucous gulls. There is a strong, bracing odour which must exude from clumps of gleaming seaweed stranded on the shoreline.

The four of us stand under the wide blue sky. If we were to follow this track further, it would lead us round a bay and on northwards up the coast. We turn south towards The Chantry.

On the way back, Alice confides that her husband is worked to the bone caring for the impoverished people in his parish who live in utter destitution. Added to this now, there are all the men returned from the War unable to find work, many of whom have families dependent on them. It was the Bishop who suggested Sam should have a holiday. My heart goes out to both of them.

We go up to change our clothes for dinner. 'You won't be wearing a gown will you, Rose?' Alice asks me, and we burst into giggles.

'No fear!' I say. I shall wear a serviceable dress in apple-green lawn.

Six large circular tables dominate the dining room. These are taken by groups who all seem to know each other. At the far side of the room is an oblong table. This is occupied by war veterans. Between the windows is a table seating only four. Our friends are already there, and wave us to come over.

Grace is said, Leonard standing head bowed, lips unmoving, but then we settle down to casseroled beef, potatoes and fresh vegetables from the garden. The conversation is more general, what we plan to do tomorrow – walk into Hocton – and how we find the meal – excellent – by the end of which the four of us are clearly ready for bed.

Once in, Leonard and I reach for each other. We move soundlessly, as if in a dream, then fall asleep to the susurration of the sea.

Chapter Eight

We come down to breakfast feeling rested and equal to whatever the day has to offer. It is intermittently sunny, again not windy, so a morning walk along the front into Hocton seems a good idea before it gets too crowded.

'No sign of the Bakers,' says Leonard, with a hint of disappointment. 'Perhaps they're early birds.'

'I don't think so,' I say, as we seat ourselves. 'Look, this table hasn't been used.'

We indulge in a hearty breakfast, after which the proposed walk is all the more appealing. We're just coming down our stairs, ready to set off, when we see Alice and Sam about to cross the hall to go in to breakfast. Leonard calls out good morning, and they pause, looking up and waving. We join them.

'I'm afraid we slept in,' Alice says.

'My fault,' says Sam.

I notice how tired his dark eyes look and how pallid his skin. 'Well, don't let us stop you getting served in time,' I say.

'Perhaps we can catch up at dinner,' says Leonard, to which they agree wholeheartedly.

We walk up the drive and reach the lane, looking left along it. 'That looks like a cul-de-sac,' I say. 'There's no way through on either side of the house at the end.'

'I fear you're right,' says Leonard, his short-sightedness not helping him. 'We'll have to go up to the main road and then see if the next one down seems more promising.'

It takes us longer than we thought it would. We stop exclaiming every time we see a palm tree.

On the main road with the discreet B&Bs, we retrace yesterday's route but dither at the next easterly turning, which has a similar appearance to our own road. 'Pity we can't actually see the end of it,' Leonard says. 'I suppose we could walk down until we can.'

'And then have to come all the way back. It just doesn't look like a definite through road.'

'You'd have thought,' says Leonard scanning the main road both ways, 'there'd be hordes, all with one purpose.'

This is true, but there's not a soul in sight.

'Let's go to the next one. There must be a way to and from the front, surely, or there wouldn't be a bus along it – for all the houses in between, I mean...' I tail off, not at all sure if I'm making sense.

'You may be right,' says Leonard, slowly. 'Let's try it.'

Luckily, I am. The next road presents itself as a much clearer thoroughfare. At the far end of it, we can see the blue-grey wall of the sea, and ahead of us are groups of people all walking towards it. A slight breeze, salt-laden, freshens my face, disturbs loose tendrils of hair. We pass more gracious properties, some with verandas and terraces, most with nautical names. Sea View has a curious windowed turret built out on a corner and looking like the prow of a ship. Gradually, the villas become less grand, more closely spaced, their ornamentation no longer so individual. As we carry on down, I realise that they have coalesced to become terraces, most still named, however, and offering accommodation. As we approach one, the front door opens and four young children tumble out onto the path of black and white tiles. They are arguing over who should carry the bucket and spade which, presumably, they must share between them. 'What did I say?' warns a stern male voice, reminding me of London. The children fall silent, watching as both parents now appear and close the door behind them. The little party makes its way just ahead of us. They are a pleasure to observe, the children trying so hard to control their natural exuberance, the parents, clearly immensely proud of them and loving. As we walk on, though, I find that there is something about these meaner properties which I dislike for no good reason. I shiver.

'Are you all right?' asks Leonard, 'you've stopped pointing things out.'

'I'll be glad to get onto the front,' I say.

'Yes, this is a bit dreary, isn't it?' says Leonard, nodding towards the yard, outbuildings and rear of a large building on the corner we're approaching. From its many windows and ugly fire escapes, we suppose it's a hotel.

We are now near enough to catch random shouts, laughter, low traffic noise, keening gulls, the distant notes of a hurdy-gurdy. The promenade is busy with holidaymakers of all ages. The sea comes to us on the breeze.

We pass the hotel's side wall and turn determinedly south along the front, towards the centre of Hocton. On our side, the wide road is composed almost entirely of hotels built during the last century, many with glassed-in verandas. On the other is the expanse of sea, with a promenade which leads the eye towards a focal point. Although it must be half a mile away the long pier, with two flag-topped, turreted domes at its entrance, is a striking feature. I gaze at it.

'What's the matter?' Leonard asks.

I have stopped walking. 'I... it's just...'

'Rose, I think we'd better get you to a seat.'

In a daze, I let him thread us between others crossing the road, and find a bench whose sole occupant leaves as we sit down.

'Are you ill, my love?'

'I... don't think so...' I'm taking in drafts of sea air. It's calming, but slightly dizzying. 'The thing is, I feel as if I've been here before.'

'And that's why you went quiet on the way here,' Leonard says, almost to himself.

'I didn't realise then, I just felt... odd. But when we turned the corner and I saw the view...'

'Perhaps you came here as a child.'

'How? How could I - from Markly?!' I make an effort to curb the snappish tone brought on by my puzzlement. 'It would have been far too complicated - the travel - all of us. And besides...'

'I know,' says Leonard, well aware of my parents' modest means. 'I was just trying to help you find an explanation.'

'Of course you were, dearest love.' I slip my hand into his and look into his eyes, an even deeper blue with concern. 'And I'm sorry to be so surly and ungrateful. I think there is no explanation – except the fact that I've read about the seaside so many times, I must have made my own mental version of it, and this is it.'

'Well, I suppose that's possible,' says Leonard.

'I shan't think about it anymore,' I say. 'Let's walk on.'

And I do try not to think about it.

We follow the example of many others and take a stroll to the end of the pier, where the little breeze is pleasantly bracing. We stand leaning against the rail staring at the blue horizon and working out where, if we were aboard ship and sailing in a straight line, we should strike land. 'Somewhere in Belgium,' says Leonard. Our moment of mutual silence grows wings which take it with our heartfelt good wishes to the Janssens.

'Oh, look!' Crossing my line of vision are three elegant, tall-masted craft with many umber-coloured sails.

'Thames barges bringing coal,' Leonard says.

Their appearance and number have the quality of a fairy tale to me.

We walk back down the pier and out, past its twin towers, onto the promenade, now much busier in the last hour. A steady stream of people makes its way down the road which must lead from the station. The beach on either side is packed. Men and women walk with dogs straining on leads, children are being led on donkeys or playing in the sand, others dodging, with shrieks, the gentle wavelets which tease the shore. Mothers dish out sandwiches, towels, admonitions, whilst fathers direct the construction of castles, try to read the paper or feign sleep under handkerchiefs or hats. There is hardly a square inch unoccupied. In a booth on the sand, surrounded by a ring of wide-eyed children, a puppet I recognise from story books waddles across the stage to beat his wife, an idea which I never found amusing and which is even less so in the flesh. A little further along the prom, queues wait patiently to pay for a turn to paddle a canoe, dodging others, on a little boating pond. All along the prom are booths and trestles selling cockles, whelks and mussels. These, too, are surrounded by throngs eager to part with their pennies.

Leonard's wordless gaze is eloquent, summing up exactly the reason why, on the very few occasions we have ever had the odd day or two's holiday, we have never considered coming here, but have either gone to London or to Cambridge.

'I expect it's better out of season,' I say.

Leonard looks about him. 'If you want to have a go on one of those swing boats...' he says.

He seems as if he might like it himself, so we walk the way we came towards a little funfair on the front, the hurdy-gurdy thumping through our heads, but that's not the cause of all the noise. There is a firing range. I can feel, through Leonard's arm linking mine, his whole body tensing each time a shot hits its target.

'Come on, let's go back to the Ness,' I say. 'We can walk on the other side, away from all this.'

'If you're sure.' I hear the relief in his voice.

'Quite sure.' I tighten my hold on his arm, propel us across the road from the prom and face north.

Although Leonard made the bed the army way – the same as hospital corners – and I tidied all our belongings, I can tell, as soon as we walk in, that our room has undergone the subtlest of re-orderings. I see it, for example, in how the towels hang on the stand. We leave those of the hotel where they are. Leonard rolls the ones we brought from home, my tiny guest towel – in case I paddle – inside his modest bath sheet and packs these in the rucksack, together with our books. I have released my stockings and peel them off, my feet immediately relishing the polished wooden boards. Each of us has noticed the outside tap at the back of the building, so now we are uninhibited in walking barefoot downstairs over the cool tiles of the hall, through the lounge and out into the garden, the lushness of whose lawn tickles bare arches. Then comes the scrubby transition, our passing feet catching the occasional prickle of a sand-shrouded wayside plant, this being enjoyable in its way, a sort of purging before we step down into the blissful yellow, like warm flour.

Today, we are not alone, but the beach is nowhere near as crowded as the one we gladly left after we'd eaten fish and chips outdoors at a little café, and used their tap to wash the grease from our hands - what a tactile business being at the seaside is, and how Leonard laughed at my fastidiousness - then took the last two seats on a charabanc going our way back to the Ness and on to the bay beyond.

We walk on up the beach a little further than we did yesterday. Soon, we come to a less populated stretch, and find a sheltered hollow. Here, without constraint, Leonard strips off his shirt and trousers, which he rolls and puts in the bag. He is wearing a stylish navy swimming costume bought, with a great deal of advice from Lettie, at Giffords. We leave the bag and make for the sea. The tide is further out than yesterday, but not so far that he can't swim without first walking for miles. I keep an eye on him as he bobs and slaps water onto his arms and legs, then suddenly plunges. Now, all I see is his dark head, his moving hands and feet, as he lies on his back, propelling himself lazily across the water. I watch him for a while, but he is in his own world, and looks a master of it, so I walk gingerly to the tide line and let the next frilly little wave - oh! so cold, but oh! so exhilarating - claim me. I do this till I'm used to the sensation, then dance along the breaking foam, sometimes dodging, sometimes jumping into it. I come back to where Leonard is swimming seriously on his front. Holding my skirt as high as I dare, I walk in up to my knees, feel the pull of current, breathe in the good sea air. I am in a daze in which I come to recognise a strong sense of wellbeing. This is understandable but it highlights, by contrast, my earlier mood today of quite unreasonable disquiet. I break off this contemplation, realising that Leonard has been joined by another swimmer, hair darkened by wetness. It is Sam Baker. I look back quickly to the beach.

Alice waves. She is sitting by our bag. I hurry, as best I can through sand, to join her.

'If I'd known you were here, I'd have come away sooner,' I say.

'That's why I didn't interrupt you,' she says. 'I could see you were at one with the sea.'

It turns out that she isn't bathing because salt water might exacerbate the eczema which lurks between her fingers and her toes. I tell her I can't do more than paddle. After the bad illness when I was seventeen, which gave me my irregular heartbeat, the doctor advised against swimming, not something I would have thought of anyway, having never been taught. We both agree it's doing our husbands good, the bathing and the camaraderie.

'Sam doesn't get much time just to enjoy himself,' Alice says.

'Nor do you, judging by all the admirable things you're involved with,' I say.

For a moment, she doesn't answer, and there is just the distant sea, with the cries of birds and random shouts of holidaymakers. Then, she says, 'I threw myself into work - I had to.' And somehow I know what's coming. 'Our little boy died. It was four years ago, but it could have been yesterday.'

As she is speaking, the image of my dear ones, my sister Annie and behind her my brother Jim, stand, forever not yet five years old. 'I'm so sorry,' I say.

She is not crying, but just staring out to sea.

I take a risk, and ask gently, 'What was his name?'

'Robin.' And now, she tells me so many details of that sweet, young life until both of us are crying, but with tears of a sort of joy in sharing.

'He's a part of you. That's how he lives on,' I say, thinking of Jim and Annie and of Mother, who seems strongly with me in this place.

'I knew you'd understand,' she says. 'You're carrying a burden too, I think.'

I know she doesn't mean my worrying about Leonard's recovery, of which she has already guessed when we were talking about the War last night over dinner. And suddenly I am telling her all about Jack.

She waits for me to finish. 'He will get better,' she says, looking me straight in the eyes, so that I take in hers, nut brown, clear and intense.

We arrive for dinner at the same time and, like a charm, our table by the windows is waiting for us. Over fresh cod in parsley sauce with peas and new potatoes, our easy conversation flows on.

'I respect what you did during the War with Sylvia Pankhurst – the clinics, the cheap canteens – everything,' says Leonard, 'but what I find most admirable is that you stepped forward, Alice, and joined the Quakers to work on quelling anti-alien prejudice. That's putting yourself in the firing line.'

'I take that as a profound compliment from you, who were in the real firing line,' says Alice, with her sincere, burning look. She is just the kind of person in whom Leonard, who is so little susceptible to physical appearance, finds the inherent richness.

Leonard bows his head, at a loss for once, I think, so I say, 'You all three have made your remarkable contributions.'

'Let's not forget hospital visiting, running two bookshops and giving hospitality to refugees,' says Sam, gallantly.

'Well...' I begin.

'No, don't dismiss all that,' says Alice. 'You must have run it as tightly as a military campaign whilst not short-changing anyone, if I've understood anything about you.'

'She did,' says Leonard, and I bathe in the warm dark sea of his gaze.

After dinner, we walk through the garden whose blooms and leaves are tinged with fire by the westering sun. In a spirit of curiosity, we turn south towards Hocton. On the right of a rough track runs The Chantry garden wall, joined to that of the next property and the one beyond. It's impossible to discern whether the track goes on or peters out. On the left is a small stretch of tussocky grass, the edge of the cliff, then the murmuring sea.

'I'm for turning back before it gets too dark,' says Alice, voicing my thought, one which we both conclude with our concern about rabbit holes and twisted ankles – and stumbling into the sea.

Leonard, who is leading us with Sam, stops at the end of a wall, which turns out to be a corner. 'Voila!'

The ground drops steeply giving us a view, about a mile away, of Hocton, the silhouette of its pier, the glimmering flares of its fairground darkening the sky to night.

I hear the others discussing how they wished it had been made more obvious, by a discreet notice, for example, that this was a way to the front, but that probably residents of the Ness, anxious for their properties' security, were resistant to public access. I nod in agreement when Sam says, 'I take it we're all of one mind?' and we retrace our steps. What I can't get out of my own mind is the conviction that I've been here before.

Breakfast is a distracted business, laced with regret. Our friends must leave this morning, as Sam cannot be spared any longer from his duties, and must be back in place to take Communion on Sunday.

We have each said what we can about keeping in touch, and we all mean it, but no one underestimates the ability of life's demands to push aside the best of intentions. We wave them off in the trap which brought us and has just brought more guests.

So as not to be reminded of the Bakers' absence, we strike out on the fresh plan we made last night before bed to follow the Ness right round into the next bay. Here, a handful of white weatherboarded cottages with dark window frames run down to a shingly beach and slipway where boats rest at an angle, the tide being out, or lie overturned for protection, showing the graceful ellipses of their panelled hulls. On the quayside in front of The Admiral Nelson public house are trestle tables and benches, some already occupied by a party of cyclists, their machines propped, one upon another, against a row of mooring posts for boats, whatever they are called in nautical terms. From an open window in the bar, a woman does a brisk trade in sea food, at the same time telling us all about today's catch. I cannot face the thought of oysters, but I do my best with the pin provided to enjoy our salty, vinegary bag of cockles, before resorting to the slice of toast and marmalade, packed on itself, which I slipped from the breakfast table. Leonard samples the local beer and, after I've finished a homemade lemonade, I comb the shore for pretty shells, iridescent in sunlight, and screw them into the clean handkerchief which held the toast.

But when we get back to The Chantry, common sense tells me to scatter them in the garden, for they will never survive the journey. They look entirely at home on the rockery amongst the flowering pinks. I am filled with gladness.

At dinner, a whole new set of people has arrived. We find, to our dismay, that our customary table by the window is occupied, the only two places available being on a large circular one in the middle of the room. It becomes clear, as soon as we are seated after grace, and introductions have been made, that everyone else knows each other. They all seem to have been involved in an administrative capacity with the forthcoming Lambeth Conference.

'Fascinating,' says my neighbour to the left, a man of about fifty called Giles Neville. 'All encompassing,' he adds, including Leonard in the conversation.

I say, 'Are we allowed to know what's on the bishops' agenda?'

'I see no harm, Mrs. Pritchard. The main topic will, of course, be International Relations and the Reunion of Christendom. But the position of women is also to be discussed.' He gives me a smile like a pat on the head.

'Oh,' says Leonard, 'Extending the priesthood to women? About time!'

There is a half-beat before Mr. Neville gives an embarrassed little chuckle. 'Steady on, old chap.' What he says next, I could parrot with him, I've heard it so many times when it comes to women's rights. 'One step at a time. But I think I can confidently say that their Lordships will agree to the right of women to be heard in the Councils and Ministrations.'

'That'll be decent of them,' says Leonard with a straight face.

'May I ask,' says Mr. Neville with a genial smile and in a reasonable tone, 'Are you a believer?'

'No,' says Leonard, just as an elderly jewelled hand touches his sleeve on the other side. 'We've been very lucky with the weather today, haven't we, Mr. Pritchard?'

Leonard allows himself to be diverted.

'I go to St. Saviour's, Widdock,' I say, trying to rescue the situation.

Mr. Neville takes up my olive branch, beaming, 'Gerald Armstrong's parish. Fine man. Inspiring, wouldn't you say?'

I agree, and light upon the example of how, after Gerald's sermon, I went on reading about Jesus waiting for the disciples by the Sea of Tiberius.

'It's actually a large freshwater lake,' says my companion. So much for my vision of Jesus collecting sea coal! 'I was in the Holy Land in 1910.'

He pauses, either for breath or for effect. I say, 'My husband was there – from 1917 to early 1919.'

'Indeed, so.' Mr. Neville dips his head a moment. 'I must have a chat with him about his impressions of Jerusalem.'

Please don't. Although Leonard has told me nothing of all the great battles he underwent, he has vouchsafed how shocked he was at the tawdry commercialisation of that sacred city – especially compared with the simple dignity accorded it by its Muslim population. But I needn't worry, Leonard is otherwise occupied. Having wolfed his smoked mackerel and watercress salad, he has turned his chair slightly, enabling him to chat with some Indian and Gurkha veterans on the table behind ours, not that he or they are talking about the Egypt and Palestine Campaign, beyond acknowledging that they all were there. Undaunted, Mr. Neville carries on with his reminiscences, but I'm barely listening. I'm coming to a slow realisation. Not only do I feel certain that I have been to this seaside place before, but what I'm almost sure of is who was with me: Jack.

I put on my dirty travelling clothes, for what's the point of soiling fresh ones? Leonard takes an early swim, I go to the chapel, the oldest part of the building containing its mediaeval heart. There are no set services, but those few of us here at this hour have no need of intercession on our behalf. I ask for guidance. Weak sunlight brings to life the red and blue of ancient glass. I lose myself, start when Leonard puts his head round the door, whispers, 'Coming to breakfast?' There is hardly anyone in the dining room. 'Good,' says Leonard. 'I'd rather avoid being this morning's entertainment, so they can practise their tolerance.' We claim our old table. Afterwards, we pack our bags ready to leave straight after Sunday lunch, having booked yesterday's cabby. A keen easterly drives us back indoors from walking on the Ness, but we enjoy the morning reading the papers which have been provided, 'even though they're not my choice,' says Leonard. Again, we are first in the dining room. Afterwards, we make a generous donation for all we have received here.

Leonard insists on carrying our two small portmanteaux, so I am the one who tries to turn the key and finds the front door unlocked. As I open it and step inside the cottage I hardly need to see, propped on the mantelpiece, the postcard sent last week by Phyllis – three donkeys on the beach at Hunstanton – which Jack took to keep him company whilst away, to know he's home before us. He had the opportunity to stay at Hilda's till tomorrow. I feel as if I'm suddenly compressed by heavy weights.

 He must be resting in his room, so Leonard wastes no time in getting the bath down for me. There's hot water in the kettle, so it can't be long since Jack went up. I set it to re-heat, with the saucepans, and tiptoe to our room to fetch clean clothes and towel.

 ...The perfect temperature. Though mindful of the need to hurry up, I allow myself a moment's luxury... ...I know that tap-

tap on the front door, the confident step across the threshold as Leonard opens it and greetings are exchanged. 'Rose is in the bath,' he says, as if that will make any difference. I hear the determined tread.

The kitchen door opens and my sister's head pokes round it. 'Honestly, Rose, I don't know how you can put up with this.'

'I was enjoying it, actually.'

It transpires that Jack slipped out of Church during Communion, 'of all times to leave,' Hilda says. 'Good job Dee told me he'd left the house or I'd have served him Sunday lunch! Seems to have managed to walk round here perfectly well. I don't know what got into him.'

'Perhaps he just needed to be alone.'

Hilda snorts, underlining my own awareness of simply coming out with a pat response, lips moving without reference to brain. This is because that observation, 'seems to have managed to walk' has seeped into me like poison. Of course she's nettled, but I hope we're still on the same side. I deflect her by telling her what a marvellous time we've had. Leonard can hear me and joins in. It does the trick.

'I knew it was just what you needed. It's such a lovely place.'

We thank her again. 'I'm sorry not to have brought anything back for you, but sea food would have gone off and we didn't think you'd want a stick of Hocton rock.'

'Your thanks and the fact that you look so well – what I can see of you – is a gift in itself. Anyway, I'll say good-bye now before you catch your death and undo all the good.'

I hear her telling Leonard about the food she has brought for us to tide us over the remainder of the Bank Holiday. 'There's plenty of cuts from the joint – he could have had it hot with all the trimmings – but never mind. Gerald may call round tomorrow evening for a short discussion, Leonard. He can bring the baskets back with him.'

'Right you are,' says Leonard. I imagine him saluting.

'You're very kind, Hilda,' I call.

'It's what family's for,' she calls back as she leaves.

I towel myself hard, trying to dispel my irritation. An hour or so sitting on a hard pew does no one's back any good. No wonder Jack had enough. All the same, I do wish he'd either been strong enough to refuse to go to Church altogether or, having left the service, gone back to the vicarage and stayed the course. I feel I've had to work hard to maintain Hilda's good will. And I wasn't mouthing platitudes when I praised our holiday and her kindness. She wants the best for us.

I'm right in my diagnosis of what drove Jack from Church.

'Agony,' he says, with feeling, tucking into a second helping of roast duck. 'Anyway, I'd had enough. She means well, Hilda, but I wanted to be back here where I belong. I do belong here, don't I? – Leonard? – Rose?'

He suddenly looks so vulnerable and anxious. I swallow all my unworthy emotions and join in with Leonard's unequivocal response: 'Of course you do, Jack.'

But maybe something of my earlier resentment lingers because, although I have resolved not to trouble Jack, clearly tired, with my all-consuming question, I find myself seizing a quiet moment, regardless of its effect. Leonard is in the garden watering. Jack is sitting vacantly. I am supposed to be reading the Bible, which I close. My brother turns his gaze to me.

'I had the strangest feeling, while we were in Hocton – particularly at the Ness – that I'd been there before – with you.'

I've been watching his face clouding while I've been speaking. 'You have,' he says. 'We have. I did wonder, when the whole idea came up, whether you'd remember, but you didn't seem to. You were only a little tot, so I wasn't surprised. I was relieved. If you don't remember the rest, that's probably just as well.'

Chapter Nine

Although it is a Bank Holiday, Lizzie Munns offered to come and help with the wash, and here she is, plying me with questions about our holiday. Leonard has gone to sort his new stock in peace. With the start of the academic year in view, Pritchard's Bookshop will be entering its busiest time of year. Jack is not in evidence yet. After his firm refusal to disclose any further information about the circumstances in which he and I, as children, found ourselves at Hocton, he took himself off to an early bed. I conclude that he must retain some memory which he thinks I wouldn't like, or which makes him uncomfortable. Could I, perhaps, have embarrassed our parents, and by extension Jack, with a loud outburst objecting to a punch-and-judy show? I was always a shy child, so the likelihood of that is a slim one. What I find most disturbing is that I have no recollection of any detail, but only those feelings which overtook me. I can't help wondering if Jack, wary that I might not let sleeping dogs lie, is waiting for me to go out, which he knows I am due to do, before he ventures downstairs. None of this do I recount to dear Lizzie. She would be agog to know more whilst, at the same time, telling me that my interpretation of Jack's non-appearance is just my imagination getting the better of me.

In fact, my imagination has been quite fanciful enough already this morning. It's come up with a picture of my mind as being like one of those Dutch flower paintings Leonard and I have seen in the National Gallery, in which the elements are symbolic. My painting would depict a vase of bright flowers standing for the note I read from Phyllis when we got home yesterday in response to mine which told her we were away, when we'd be back, and inviting her and Jenny here tonight for what Mrs. Fuller would call supper, an invitation gladly accepted. In the vase, though, is a thistle. This represents my conscience, for also on the doormat was a brief letter from Cousin Grace, on her own behalf but also that of Dot, enquiring after Jack. The tone is entirely free from reproach, but I can just imagine how Grace and my sister, let alone Father, might have puzzled not to have heard from me over what is now three weeks. Heavens above! How could I have forgotten to drop at least a line to them? The fact that those weeks seem to have flashed past is no excuse. Glad to have no time to follow the floral analogy further, in respect of Jack, I sit down as soon as Lizzie has left and dash off a note to Grace full of apologies, telling her... What? I pause, pen in hand. I can't say that Jack is physically better. Jack is very at home here and doing well. I voice my usual heartfelt wishes for George's health, and sign with love. As I address the envelope and find a stamp, I hear Jack moving around.

His arrival for breakfast coincides with Leonard's return for an early lunch, as he won't keep shop hours today.

'I'll eat both now,' says Jack of his porridge and a cheese sandwich, which latter is what we're having. He looks gaunt with tiredness. 'All that took it out of me,' he says. I hope he means the stay with Hilda and its abrupt curtailment rather than my broaching the topic of Hocton. 'I'll sort myself out and then have another rest. I want to be bright as a button for Phyllis and Jenny.' The ghost of an animated smile crosses his face. How can I feel anything but utter tenderness towards him?

I have good reason to indulge myself in the pleasure of cycling up Park Road and into these streets which, together, form almost a discrete model village of well-designed houses for the workers at Hallambury's Pharmaceutical Company. This may be the only opportunity, before everyone returns to work tomorrow, to have a chat about Jack with my two knowledgeable friends, Meg and Winnie. I'd had the idea that afternoon with Phyllis and the motorcycle, but thought better of it when I learned that they were just about to go on holiday. I hope that, today being dull, I might find them at home. I turn into Margaret Fell Avenue and feel a never-fading satisfaction that my two former housemates were able, when names were being sought for the new roads, to put forward that of the co-founder of the Society of Friends. Not only that, their request to live in the so-named street was granted.

I stop at Number Seven and wheel my bicycle up the path between buzzing, aromatic borders of lavender. Attached under the front door knocker is a note, 'Callers', with an arrow pointing round the side of the house. Phew! It is almost as if I am expected. I prop my bicycle against the neat, weather-proofed shed which runs beside the house. It is both a workshop and a repository for garden and other tools, and must also be the home of the motorbike and side car combination. I walk past a barometer and thermometer attached to the house wall and a water butt at the rear. A gleam of sunlight picks out the oblong of visible back garden which frames Winnie who is wearing a sacking apron and working with a hoe amongst the sisters' beds of herbs. She looks like a figure from an illuminated manuscript. Meg is sitting in a collapsible upright chair, stringing beans into a colander in her lap. Both look up with smiles, as my footsteps echo in the corridor between house and shed.

'I don't want to interrupt you,' I say, after we've said hello.

'Please do,' says Meg. 'We've been working for hours.'

Win strikes her hoe into the earth. 'I'll make lemon balm tea, shall I? You take that one, Rose,' indicating the chair's twin with back and seat of scarlet canvas, 'I'll bring one out.'

I sip the tea which is hot but not boiling, full of the flavour of lemon but with a kinder, less astringent quality. Bees are in constant motion around, into and out of the white trumpets of a stand of balm flowers, their humming a congenial drone to our conversation. In response to my question about the Norfolk holiday, I hear about the long stretches of sandy beach which that county can boast, together with its many fine old churches. The sisters ask about my holiday, and I give them a brief account, but do not mention my peculiar experience, which I feel would be an unhelpful distraction.

'You do look well,' says Meg, 'that's a relief.'

'You may be surprised, but we were concerned about you,' says Winnie. 'It's a lot you've had to take on.'

I'm glad that the subject has come round, naturally, to Jack. 'Actually, there's something I wanted to ask you.' The sisters sit, all intelligent attention. I tell them everything to date. 'Perhaps I'm worrying too soon, but I had hoped there might be more of a sense of steady improvement. I just wondered... I thought I read in The Courier that Hallambury's were developing some sort of machine with rays – '

Winnie groans. 'Rontgen rays.'

Meg giggles. 'The ill-fated skelegraph. I'm afraid it was a bit of a disaster.'

'Not our specialism, of course, but as far as we know there aren't any plans to revive it,' says Winnie.

'Oh.' I feel deflated.

'But there's nothing wrong with Jack physically, is there,' Winnie continues, more as statement than question. 'He's a horrible man, Doctor Warnish, but he knows his anatomy. He'd soon have detected anything amiss.'

'Of course,' says Meg, slowly, 'something did come up when we were talking with Phyllis. Your brother does have a history of mental illness.'

I think back twenty years to the time when, as a sixteen-year-old, I nearly relinquished my new job at Pritchard's Bookshop to take up a post cataloguing the library at Sawdons because Jack was suffering from melancholia, and I thought he needed me. Thank goodness he began to recover before I had to go any further in that dreadful direction. I wouldn't know if he's had relapses since. 'But he doesn't seem to be in low spirits,' I say. 'Or perhaps he is, and I just can't tell.' I suddenly feel quite down myself.

The sisters glance at each other. Meg nods, imperceptibly.

'Do you think we could meet Jack at some point?'

It's as if the clouds have parted and the sun has come out.

'What do they want to meet me for?'

I have made a terrible miscalculation. Having announced to Jack that I'd invited Meg and Winnie to join us for supper, to which his response was an ominous silence, I've now made matters worse by floundering, the truth sounding like a platitude and provoking this blunt reaction.

'Because you're part of the family - and they are like family to me.'

Jack snorts. 'They won't preach at me, will they? I've had religion up to here,' he gestures to his chin, 'this weekend.'

'Of course they won't. Quakers don't do that, and anyway, Meg and Winnie are really quite quiet and retiring. In fact, they didn't want to intrude on our evening. I had a job persuading them to come.'

'Pity you did. I was looking forward to seeing Phyllis - and I could cope with - what's her name? - Jenny? But two more of 'em...' he mutters to himself.

'They're bringing a Madeira cake,' I say, as I leave Jack sitting in my armchair and go out to the kitchen to get the meal ready.

A roar dulled to an echoing popping under the arch to Blessings Yard, then silence announces the early arrival - thank goodness - of Phyllis, with Jenny as pillion. Jack starts from his chair in wonder. I'm just laying the table, which Leonard and I have pulled out into the room. We go to the door, but let Jack through first, as Phyllis is dismounting. 'Hello tyke,' she says, which makes him laugh.

After Jenny has been introduced, Jack sits on the bench, so that he can study the motorcycle. Jenny sits next to him. I barely need to acknowledge Phyllis. She starts talking about the bike, Jack chipping in and asking questions.

Leonard and I go through to the back garden. He disappears amongst his beanpoles. I start to fold the washing. Another pair of hands joins mine, unpegging and deftly folding. I tell Jenny that Winnie and Meg are coming, and why.

'Oh,' she says, when I mention Jack's reaction.

'I'm glad we didn't motorcycle here,' says Winnie, on arrival, 'your neighbours would have thought we were having a rally.'

'I wish you had,' says Jack, 'I'd have liked to have seen that piece of kit.'

'Another time, then,' says Meg.

Phyllis has, unwittingly, done such a good job on turning his mood around that now he's smiling at the newcomers, who look so thoroughly wholesome in their neat, un-showy dresses, their light brown hair pinned into plaits around their heads, matching the colour of their eyes.

Hilda, in her generosity, has given us smoked salmon, eggs, bread, milk, butter and ten perfect Victoria plums, fragrant with ripeness. We shall have one each for our dessert, and I will keep the other three for Leonard, Jack and me tomorrow. Phyllis and Jenny have also brought eggs, so I make the elegant meal to which Mrs. Fuller introduced me that Bank Holiday weekend, twenty years ago, when we were alone together at Apple Tree House, and I needed cheering up because my father was too ill for me to go home to Markly and – as Mrs. Fuller realised, though I did not – I was missing my true love, Leonard, who had gone to visit a cousin over the long weekend when the shop was closed. I try to cut triangles of bread and butter as finely as Mother would have done, holding the loaf against me to butter it, then carefully cutting towards myself, so that the slices are as fine as lace. We have some lemons which are soft and ripe, so Jenny slices these to squeeze on the fish. 'I'll just have scrambled egg,' says Jack, eyeing the salmon with distaste. I make frothy yellow mountains of the stuff, so no one will go home undernourished.

Talk of our two holidays circulates again, Jack interested in routes taken, the state of the roads. Leonard and I join in when appropriate but, at other times, look across at each other, letting it all open like a flower. I serve cups of tea and slices of Madeira cake. Jack dunks and eats his, then he leans back and, in a lull, says, 'What I want to know is how you two young ladies found your way to being scientists.'

Meg gestures to Winnie. 'Our father ran a chemist's shop, so we grew up with the knowledge.'

'Ah,' says Jack, 'but you didn't stay to help him?'

'There came a point - how old were we, Win - ten and eleven?'

'Younger,' says Winnie.

'When we understood that it would be our brother's business,' says Meg.

'Ah,' says Jack again.

'I still remember that feeling of... disillusion,' says Winnie, Meg nodding, 'but we pulled ourselves together and, when we left school, sought a future elsewhere - which was Hallambury's.'

'Disillusion, that's a good word,' says Jack, 'but disappointment, that's what I'd call it. I know about that all right.'

'Go on,' says Meg, quietly.

'You don't want to hear - '

'We do.'

'Well,' says Jack, 'I'd been working at Sawdons since I left school - I got that job by chance. Rose knows, she was there behind me on Sable - '

'The undertaker's mare. Father had his permission to use her,' I interject.

'Anyway, she was being frightened by a dog running out of control, so I told this young milord to call it off, which he did, and we walked on.'

'Oh,' says Winnie, 'I think I know this story.'

Meg nods.

Jack carries on regardless. 'When I went to Sawdons next day, about the post of groom's boy, who should walk into the room but him from the day before, turns out to be the Squire's son, Master Greville. 'I want this lad,' he says, 'he knows how to handle horses.' Anyway, so there I was for the next seven years, working up to being their Head Groom, but I knew which way the wind was blowing. They reckoned they'd got no money, but they'd want a motor car - Master Greville especially. I knew that if I didn't take on the role of chauffeur I'd be out of a job. I was going to be sent to learn about the nuts and bolts of motor cars. I wasn't looking forward to it but, much to my surprise, I took to it, which was good because earlier in the year I'd had...' he pauses to choose his words. I feel myself reddening in anticipation, 'a disappointment which I won't go into.' This was when I didn't do what everyone thought I would and go to Sawdons as a tweeny. On the day of Mother's death, I went to tell my brothers and sisters the shocking news. Afterwards, walking homewards through the garden there, I met the tutor, Leonard, and found that as his young charge was off to public school, he was about to open a bookshop. I applied to be his assistant. 'I cheered up,' Jack is saying, 'especially as the chap I'd learnt from – up the road at Harkerswell – ' he waves in a generally north-western direction, 'and I were supposed to be opening a motor workshop together when we'd saved up enough. I don't know how long it took me to realise he was just stringing me along, it wasn't going to happen. I couldn't afford to do it on my own, so that was another slap in the face. I got over it because, in the meantime, Master Greville was getting very interested in the idea of developing a particular type of motor car. But then the War came. He went off before he needed to and got himself killed.' By now, Jack's face is flushed, as if angry with the dead man. ' I went when I had to, and the thanks I got was a lot of ignorant people thinking we had it easy out there. They forget we saw him off, the Bulgar. Took some doing, but we saw him off. It was a successful campaign. And I didn't catch malaria like some of the poor blighters, I only got sunstroke, so I was lucky, but easy it was not. Again, stupid me, I'd pinned my hopes – well, it doesn't matter.'

'I think it does,' says Leonard, quietly, 'tell us.'

'Another thing was, all the time I was out there, they never let us home on leave. But that was all right, I didn't mind... I didn't mind because...' Jack is speaking quietly now, as if he's seeing within himself, 'my job, of course, was to look after the horses. I had to go on regular patrols of these little villages in the Struma Valley, it was called, making sure the enemy hadn't got a foothold there – I liked doing all that. I had a special mare, Kitty, a chestnut hunter. It was a place I'd never want to return to but sometimes, when it was just me and Kitty, before the day got unbearably hot, as it did – well, I imagined bringing her home, safe and sound, and presenting her to her owners, or even keeping her. But that wasn't to be. And when the War was over, that's when my back started playing up, so they were only too glad to get rid of me at Sawdons.'

'We heard about your brave stance,' says Meg.

'Admirable,' says Winnie, and we all agree.

Jack smiles, ruefully. 'Well, you could say, 'Look where it's got him,' but I'd reply, 'Yes, it's got me where I'm made welcome in the home of my dear sister and her heroic husband.''

Leonard and I are, of course, abashed, but everyone's saying hear, hear, and someone might, perhaps, have started clapping but there is a knock on the door.

'Is that the time?' Jenny says.

Leonard opens the door to Gerald, who apologises for interrupting our evening. 'Don't all get up and leave!' he says, only half-joking, but we make assurances that it's nothing to do with him and everything to do with work tomorrow. Despite my remonstrations, our four guests are clearing the table between them, so I encourage Leonard to sit down as usual with Gerald. I try to get Jack to stay with them, but he follows me through to the kitchen, where Phyllis is at the sink, deftly rubbing spent lemon quarters on plates and forks to dislodge recalcitrant scrambled egg. She is very quick, and will have rinsed them and be ready for hot water to do a swift proper wash by the time Jenny brings the kettle over. 'You can dry the cutlery,' she says to Jack, who has seated himself at the table, not quite out of the way. He accepts the cloth I hand him. I tell Meg and Winnie that no further help is required.

' It's been a very enjoyable and interesting evening.' Winnie gives the slightest glance towards Jack, who is engaged in his task. She lowers her voice. 'I think we can... do something.'

My spirits lift like a bird in flight.

'That's good,' says Jenny, now a quiet presence beside me, 'but', she, too, lowers her voice almost to a whisper, 'don't let him take over.'

We four know that she's looking back to the time when we were housemates and another resident made Jenny's life a misery – until she suddenly left, and Jenny blossomed. 'Bless you,' I say, 'but it's going to be all right.'

'This is just for you.' Meg takes from her bag a glass jar, which she presses into my hands.

I read the label: 'Lemon balm honey,' and think of the two white hives at the end of their garden and the constant, roving bees amongst those bell-like blossoms.

All four women propose to walk out through the garden and round by the side passage, so as not to disturb Leonard and Gerald's discussion.

'No, it'll be a lovely thing to do,' says Meg, setting out ahead with Winnie.

I go, too, with Phyllis and Jenny. Jack says he'll sit in the kitchen and listen to the blackbird on our apple tree. We take in the scent of roses and, as our skirts brush past it, lavender.

We all say good-bye, the sisters walk off, under the arch. Phyllis helps Jenny onto the motorcycle, then lifts it off its stand and, when we've said good-bye, starts to wheel it out of Blessings Yard. I retrace my steps through the dreaming garden.

'I've thought about it hard,' says Jack as I re-enter the kitchen, 'and it's only fair I shouldn't torment you about what happened at Hocton.'

My heart jolts.

'I could tell you now while they're having their talk.'

Instead of preparing porridge, I leave the back door open and sit down opposite Jack. It's that time of the evening when sunlight is kind again and white flowers begin to take on a magical glimmer. 'I'm ready.'

'I think I was six, so you'd have been five. And you were poorly. I remember that.'

'I remember that - starting school, and then being at home again.'

'Mother and Father were worried about you, I understood that much, and that made me worried, too. It was all to do with giving you a breath of sea air to try and make you well.'

'How could they afford it?'

'That I don't know. And I don't know why it was just Mother and Father and the two of us, but what I do remember is sitting in a train and feeling angry with you because you were the reason we were going away and leaving Gyp behind.'

'Oh, Jack...' Gyp was our little dog - Jack's little dog, a friendly terrier.

'It's all right, I got over it.'

And now I think, perhaps, I can remember feeling Jack's hostility radiating from the shoulder turned away from me.

'We must have been there two nights because we definitely had a whole day on the beach before what happened - happened.'

I'm feeling very cold now. 'Where did we stay? Can you remember?'

'Miserable place.'

'Was it in a street with other guest houses?'

'It might have been... yes. Anyway, on our second night - I think it must have been about our bedtime - Mother started feeling ill.'

And now, I'm suddenly back in that dark room with a view of the brick wall next door.

'She desperately needed to use the bathroom, rushed out of our bedroom - '

'But the door was locked.' I see my mother slump as she tries the door knob, a groan escaping the thread of her lips. I see her lurch back into the room, a spasm buckling her.

'Father tried to block our view, but he couldn't just stand there, he had to help her.'

I see the bedside cupboard open, my mother squatting, racked with pain but trying, trying to be careful. 'Afraid of spoiling that horrible carpet.' I can see its hideous pattern of what looked like brown chrysanthemums.

'Father said to us, 'You must find the lady - whatever her name was - '

'Mrs. Brewster.' It comes in a flash.

'And beg her for more towels.'

And now we're clattering downstairs, and that formidable woman marches out from the kitchen, frowning. 'What on earth - '

'And you said - '

'Please, please, Mrs. Brewster, give us some towels. Our mother's dying of blood.'

'Oh, Lord! I've forgotten the porridge!'

We've just got into bed.

'I'm not surprised, you're in shock,' says Leonard, gently pulling my arm to stop me rising. 'Never mind the porridge, we can have toast. Come here, dearest.'

I let him pull me into his arms, resting against his chest.

'It's all very well Jack apologising, but I'm not sure he should have revived that particular memory. You'd blanked it out for good reason.'

After our joint recollection of that terrible evening, Jack went on to tell me about the blissful day our little family had spent on the beach in a less frequented part of Hocton, how a small dog had come from nowhere to join us and Jack had thrown him sticks, but his words reached me as if muted, sliding over me. I couldn't, still can't, get out of my mind the thought that I was responsible for the trip to the seaside, and therefore I was to blame for my mother's miscarriage - for that, clearly, is what it was. It would not be the last.

'It could as easily have happened back in Markly,' says Leonard. 'Try not to dwell on it. Let's say good-night and then, why don't you rest here in my arms?'

And so, instead of me comforting Leonard in this way, after one of his bad dreams, he holds me to help prevent my mind from fabricating nightmares. His familiar, loving embrace soothes me into instant sleep.

I wake early, full of joy, still in the presence of Mother, Father, Jack and the playful dog. I feel as if I've spent a long, idyllic day at the Ness.

I wash and dress quickly. Leonard is up already. I sense rather than hear him overhead in his study. I tiptoe downstairs with my writing book and pen, and sit in my writing seat at the table under the stairs, where I can glance up towards the sunlight coming in the window. It occurs to me, before I try to turn my dream to prose, that the Ness is more than likely to feature in Leonard's morning contemplation, but this he will distil into a poem.

It felt strange walking out of the shop on Wednesday evening, knowing that I would not be seeing it again till today. It feels just as strange entering it this morning. I have only been absent for five days, but it seems much longer.

I have some post, two publishers' lists of forthcoming books, a letter on fine notepaper, and a fat package, hand-delivered. I think I recognise the plain, clear handwriting. With fifteen minutes before opening time and no Louisa for company, now that she is back helping Leonard in his preparations for the new term, I can satisfy my curiosity without further ado. I stand in the empty space, surrounded by the comforting scent of books, old and new, and open the packet. Inside is a letter folded round a brown paper packet on which is written: St. John's Wort. I smooth out the letter:

Dear Rose,

We hope neither you nor Jack will mind, but we've had a discussion about his illness, and think we might be able to help. A cup of boiled but not boiling water poured onto a spoonful of these dried flowers of St. John's Wort, left a few minutes and then drunk once every day may help Jack's state of mind. This might be a start towards his recovery.

Of course, if the tea does not agree with him, he must stop the remedy straightaway. We both believe it will do him good.

Do let us know how Jack gets on. If you, or he, need further help, you know where we are.

You are in our prayers.
With love,
   Meg   *Winnie*

These flowers come from the sisters' own herb garden and pharmacopoeia. I am quite overcome. Given that they start work at the factory when I am only surfacing from sleep, they must have got up extra early in order to drop this precious package here, a short detour from their route to Hallambury's, so that I would be able to start Jack on the tea treatment, assuming he agrees, as soon as I get home today.

I feel so uplifted by this ray of hope that I almost forget the letter on quality notepaper. I open it hurriedly as the Town Hall clock strikes ten.

In certain respects, it holds what I expected. Much of my antiquarian business is, as inherited from Auberon Quinn-Harper, that of periodically visiting country houses whose owners are in financial difficulties. In most cases, I'm called upon after they have discovered, from one of the major auction houses, that they are not in possession of an outstanding library full of prestigious works which could be sold to boost their income. The path has, therefore, been prepared for me. Usually, the books which I'm prepared to take do end up in my shop. From time to time, I do effect a sale. Occasionally, I am thanked, rather than merely acknowledged, for the cheque I write the former owner.

This letter, written and posted on Saturday, thanks us both for our sympathy and then goes on to ask whether, given the nature of my bookshop, I would be the right one of the two of us to come to Ash Manor and give a valuation of her late husband's library. If so, am I available at any time this week? The letter is signed, Linda Watson.

Chapter Ten

As I come out of Cottering station there is, besides the cab and horse, head in his nose-bag, a smart horse and trap whose uniformed driver steps forward with a smile, touching his cap – I think of Jack – 'Mrs. Pritchard?'

Instead of taking the road to Cotteringbury School, we turn right and pass through Cottering High Street, old cottages with dipping roofs and timbered jetties. A handful of buildings display shop fronts from the last century. Here is the butcher, there the baker, the essentials. My heart warms to this little town, so like my childhood home, dear Markly, and yet, what is it about the place – an infinitesimal severity in its architectural lines or in the very atmosphere – which tells me that we are on the way to the North?

Once through the High Street, we soon take a turning which, from the parkland on either side, I understand to be a drive. At the end of it stands a double-fronted house from the Georgian era, ivy climbing its mellowed red brick walls. It is not grand, but it is impressive. There was a time when I would have felt as nervous as I did that day in June, returning to Sawdons ostensibly with our last patients, but really to visit Jack. Now, though, I have the measure of such places, and a professional job to do, so I am quite composed as I'm helped out of the trap and invited to ring the front door bell.

A middle-aged woman with a homely face opens the door. I just have time to introduce myself before a door opens further down the hall, and a dark-clad figure advances wearing a boat-necked, slim-skirted afternoon frock which I see, as she gets close, is of black marocain. We greet each other and I hear again that charming foreign lilt. Even as I offer further condolences, and she thanks me, I am thinking that I must remember to tell Lettie how fine the dress looks, as she rightly surmised, offsetting Mrs. Watson's honey-blonde hair, which is piled up on her head with jet combs. She introduces the housekeeper as Mrs. White,

Peggy. 'Now tell me, my dear,' she asks me, 'which would you prefer – to look at the library before or after tea?'

'I'd like to see the books first, please,' I say.

'Very good, then we can relax in the kitchen,' says my hostess. 'Thank you so much, Peggy. I will be with you in a moment.'

She shows me into a book-lined room of not too formidable proportions which until recently was, I'm sure, a welcoming retreat. Two leather armchairs flank a cosy fireplace, and a writing desk stands by the window through which I catch a glimpse of green. Now, as if missing its owner, the room has drawn in upon itself.

'Are you wishing to sell the entire library, Mrs. Watson?' I ask.

'Linda, please call me Linda,' she says.

I tell her she may call me Rose.

'Oh, so pretty,' she says. 'To be perfectly honest, Rose, it breaks my heart to sell any of it, but...'

Ah... I can hear tears dangerously close. 'I understand,' I say. 'Shall I look at a sample – gain an idea – ?'

She draws herself together. 'Yes, that's very good. I will leave you for now. Then you come and have tea with me.'

'They are called 'brutti ma buoni,' says Linda, 'ugly but good. I'm glad you like them. They used to be Jeremy's favourites, didn't they, Peggy?' The housekeeper, who has said she will get on with dinner, if we don't mind, and is now unconcernedly doing so, agrees that they were. 'I made them myself' says Linda.

These unprepossessing biscuits, dun-coloured lumps of cooked dough, certainly are delicious, with the taste of hazelnut.

'He used to like to dip them in Vin Santo.'

A misty look has come into her eyes. I feel I have to draw the meeting back to order. 'About the books...'

'Ah yes, the books...'

'You have some very fine editions of the classics which I feel sure I could sell for a good price. But there is such a quantity of books in Italian...'

'Jeremy loved Italian art and music and literature. That's how I met him. It was one evening at the British Embassy. He gave such an interesting talk on the cultural crosscurrents between our two countries in the early nineteenth century. Everyone was impressed by him. One or two men asked questions, which he answered with such assurance. Then, I dared – I dared to raise my hand and I think, in the moment when our eyes met – he could have been fifty years older than me instead of twenty – that was it! Afterwards, he asked if I would care to join him for a light collation and this time, when we looked into each other's eyes, instead of a mature intellectual gentleman, I saw the vulnerable boy he had once been – and that was who I fell in love with.'

'That's very moving.'

'He was such a perfect English gentleman, and years working in the British Embassy, travelling the length and breadth of Italy, meant that he was never overawed by any occasion, any audience however large or small, any dignitary however important or self-important. He was such a success as a diplomat because he met Italians in their own enthusiasms.'

'I wish I'd met him.'

'Oh, so do I, Rose, so do I. He would have loved you. Jeremy was always utterly charming, with an easy manner that put everyone else at ease. But, do you know, I learnt that he had a reputation for getting his own way! He would win favours and funds from important people who had been determined to resist him and were left bewildered about how they had surrendered to him without a shot being fired, as he used to put it. He had been in the army in his youth, you know, and he did see active service, and acquitted himself bravely, but he was a man of peace through and through by nature.'

'He sounds remarkable. The thing is,' I have to break this reverie, 'I'm just not sure how marketable those books are. I don't speak Italian, but Leonard does. He would be able to give you a much more authoritative opinion than mine. Would you be willing to let him come and see them?'

'This is such good fortune,' she reaches for my hands, 'someone who speaks Italian! How I wish that when dear Jeremy was alive and we stayed with his parents here, we had visited Widdock instead of always going to Cambridge or London for intellectual stimulation! We might have met you both so much sooner. Yes, please do ask Leonard if he will come and look at the books. But do not let us lose contact, dear Rose.'

'Of course, I'm curious about Jeremy Watson's collection,' says Leonard, over dinner, the first chance I've had to raise the topic of my afternoon's expedition, 'but next week's already busy - what with Fabians on Monday and the Council meeting on Wednesday. So Thursday -' He makes a gesture as of thistledown blown in the wind.

'Well, you could put it off,' I say. 'I'm thinking of asking Hilda if Dee can be spared next Thursday afternoon, as I shan't see her on her birthday because of work, so if you wanted to see her -'

'I wouldn't base my plans around whether Hilda felt magnanimous on the day.'

'Ahh... these sausages...' says Jack, spearing another one. 'No wonder he calls them his Specials.' Our butcher's Special Recipe for beef sausages is a closely-guarded secret. 'It sounds to me, Leonard, as if it'll be more trouble than it's worth.' says Jack. 'After all, who's going to buy a load of books in Italian?'

'People who speak Italian,' says Leonard, with a touch of asperity, 'such as, for example, Italians.'

'How many of them've you got living in Widdock?' Jack says, guessing the answer and helping himself to more mash.

'I think there's some in Greenfield,' I say, racking my brains. 'And there's people who aren't Italian themselves, but happen -'

'I'll go next Thursday - get it over with. Let's talk about something else,' says Leonard. And then, with perfect equanimity, 'How are you, Jack? What have you been doing today?'

'I could be worse,' says Jack. 'As a matter of fact, I've been thinking a lot about that trip to Hocton – when we were youngsters, Rose and me. Well, about afterwards, actually, when we got home. It's been coming back to me.'

'Oh...?' I begin, my interest immediately quickening.

'If you're about to tell us,' Leonard cuts across, 'it's not going to upset Rose, is it?'

'No, no,' says Jack. 'All it is, really, is a picture I've got in my mind of a moment – a lovely memory.'

'Go on,' I say.

'It's of Mother, sitting on the bench outside the cottage, with a shawl round her, Father leaning over her. He'd got Gyp's ball in one hand. He was going to throw it, but I can see Mother laughing up into his face and reaching her hands up for it. And the look between them. And so he gave her the ball and she tossed it to Gyp. And then Gyp brought it to me, of course, and I threw it. And you were there, Rose. Sometimes, you went to pick it up, and sometimes Ralph did. He was there, too. And it was late afternoon, with the sun shining. And it seemed... as though everything was all right again.'

Friday, the sixth of August, was the Feast of the Transfiguration of Our Lord so today, the eighth, Gerald's sermon is based on a quotation, which he has found about it, from a saint called Irenaeus: 'For the glory of God is the living man, and the life of man is the vision of God.' Reminding us that 'man' stands for us all and that we are made in the likeness of God, Gerald exalts us to try to live up to this highest distinction by responding to and acting from what is transcendent within us. Afterwards, in the churchyard, I catch the drift of opinions ranging from 'inspiring' to 'tall order.' After Jack's description of that incident with Mother and Father, the image has stayed in my mind, so that I now see our parents as if transfigured, bathed in light, which seems a bit odd, since Father's still alive, but perhaps that's what Gerald meant...

'You seem to be in a brown study, Rose.' Hilda.

'You were chatting to people, so I was waiting.'

'I suppose Gerald won't see Leonard tomorrow because of your meeting, if you're still going, that is.'

I tell her that we are. 'Why don't you both come? It's going to be about the idea of a family allowance, an alternative to the living wage as a way of relieving poverty. Your kind of thing, I'd have thought.'

'You can tell me about it afterwards,' says Hilda smoothly. 'And we won't see you on Tuesday for Dee's birthday because you'll be at work,' she adds, with genuine regret.

I ask her about Dee coming to us on Thursday afternoon and, hoping it will make her more amenable to releasing her from parish duties, I extend the invitation to Hilda.

'I will if I can,' she says. 'You could invite Alex. She won't be let out of the shop on Tuesday you can depend upon it.'

I'd already thought of this, of course, but I don't say so. No other parishioner has stepped forward to claim my sister's attention, so I seize the moment. 'Hilda, when you and Gerald suggested The Chantry, did you remember that Jack and I once went to Hocton when we were little?'

Hilda looks blank for a moment, then her face clears. 'Oh yes, so you did,' she says. 'It was supposed to build you up, I seem to think. You were always such a scrap of a thing.'

'Jack and I were wondering what happened to all of you while we were away.'

Hilda gives me an exasperated look. One of her henchwomen, a bastion of the flower-arranging and brass-polishing group, is moving inexorably towards her, diminutive husband in tow. 'We'll see you on Thursday afternoon at three o'clock, Rose.' She turns to the couple with a beaming smile.

We've been sitting out here, stoically making the most of a rather indifferent afternoon. Jack is on the bench, Phyllis and I, 'like your hand maidens,' she says, on deckchairs facing him.

'Beginning to spit,' says Jack, raising his hand to the elements. 'Still, we haven't had a bad innings, considering...'

He doesn't need to say: this disappointing summer.

Neither does Phyllis have to say more to me than, 'Weren't we lucky?' Following Jack's thread, we will both have been thinking about our seaside holidays.

Jack and I have just given Phyllis our account of the childhood trip to Hocton and the Ness, and Jack's memory of that scene afterwards, back at home, Mother and Father, Ralph and me, playing ball with Gyp.

'Why weren't you there, Phyl?' I say, as Jack goes through to the living room and we store our deckchairs in the wash house.

She doesn't answer immediately but when we follow Jack, now comfortable in my armchair, she says, 'I think I was there, but perhaps not on that evening you remember. And not all of the time.'

'I don't know what you're driving at,' says Jack.

Phyllis turns a chair outward from the table, so that she's sitting facing him. 'Well, I know I stayed with Gran and Grandpa Alleyn once when I was little, and I can picture Ralph with Gyp – not with you, which is why it must have stayed in my mind. So, perhaps that was when you two were away with Mother and Father.'

'That would make sense,' I say. I'm on a dining chair the other side of Phyllis, leaving Leonard's chair for Hilda and the sofa for the two girls, hoping both come.

Jack nods.

'What I really remember,' says Phyllis, 'is Granny letting me play with some wooden bowls she told me Grandpa had made. They looked and smelt so lovely and felt so smooth. They were my friends. I forgot about all of you while I held them and placed them – just so.' Her face is filled with the light of joyful memory.

'They had a lot to answer for then – those bowls,' says Jack.

Phyllis had wanted to be a carpenter, but that was out of the question for a girl.

'No more than the day Father let me slip inside the door of the workshop, and I just sat watching him working for hours, it seemed. I thought he'd forgotten I was there, but after a while, he gave me a little piece of wood, and guided my hands to show me how to whittle it. I was in heaven, the scent of the fresh wood shavings and the feeling of the little chisel. It turned out to be part of Grandpa's miniature set, when he was learning, do you remember?'

'I remember you coming across to Gran and Grandpa Clarke's with a little boat you'd made,' I say.

'That was a good deal later, when I'd finished it. I'm talking about the day when I first started. Mother came with a flask. Father slapped his forehead. He must have forgotten it. Mother and Father kissed. There was no one else in the workshop, and they thought I wasn't looking. We all sat on the bench together outside by the door. And when he'd finished his drink, he stroked my hair and went back in, but we could still see him. He was making a wheel. I leaned against Mother, and she put her arm round me, and it seemed as if the sun was shining on us, not in a hard way, to make us hot and uncomfortable, but gently, and she began to hum a little tune. And that's all I remember, but it's a perfect memory to me.'

'Oh... that's lovely,' I begin, but we hear footsteps, voices and a knock on the door.

I've provided my usual treat – Askey's Swiss buns which, though good, are in no danger of competing with the birthday cake made by Hilda. Phyllis, who called by on the day, tells me it was a feather-light sponge, with apricots and clotted cream. Also, to please Jack, I've made a Madeira cake. I can see, from the corner of my eye, Dee and Alex wanting to giggle as he dunks his slice, Hilda looking stony-faced at them. Jack asks them how they are enjoying their break from school. There is clearly a lot they could say about the manner in which they are required to spend their days, Alex at Giffords and Dee in various church activities, but they are both, understandably, guarded. After they've politely asked about our holiday, and I've pleased Hilda with my praise of both Chantry and Ness, I take a chance.

'Uncle Leonard wondered if you'd like to read the poems he wrote at Hocton. They're in his study. He says you can sit up there, if you like.'

The girls' faces brighten at this prospect of private time together but they glance at Hilda, trying to temper the eagerness of their responses in case it should jeopardise the outcome. But Hilda is looking equable in the face of whatever Leonard's poems might have to offer in the way of education. She smiles her agreement, and the cousins make for the stairs.

'You'll find them on his desk,' I call to their backs, as the stair door shuts behind them. It's not all they'll find on Leonard's desk. Dee's little presents can be safely left there and collected another time, thereby avoiding any unwelcome questions from her mother about their implications. Phyllis has carved Dee's name in copperplate on a fresh new pencil, which reposes on top of a notebook I singled out at the stationers' a week ago. Its marbled cover swirls from shades of olive green into golden ochre and terracotta, reminding me of the light-filled colours in Italian landscape paintings we saw at the National Gallery. I could look at that cover for a long time. I hope Dee likes it, too.

After I've refilled our cups, Hilda says, 'I've been thinking, you two, about your trip to Hocton with Mother and Father.'

It is clear that she has further information to impart, but she's not going to surrender it without being petitioned to do so.

'We'd love to know whatever you have to tell us, wouldn't we, Jack?' I say, meaning it.

'Certainly would,' says Jack, only a shade less enthusiastically than me.

'You wanted to know what happened to the rest of us while you were away,' says Hilda, 'Well, we were at home, of course!'

'I wasn't,' says Phyllis.

But Hilda is not to be deterred. 'You see, Dot and I had to cook an evening meal for the boys.'

'But you'd only have been about – what – ten?' I begin.

'Dot was ten and I was nine,' says Hilda, as if explaining to a half-wit. 'We were perfectly capable of putting food on the table for Ted, Bob, Joe and Hubert when they came in from the fields. They were all working on the harvest that summer. Ralph had the dog with him at Grandma and Grandpa Clarke's, and Phyllis, yes, you were at Grandma and Grandpa Alleyn's. Fancy all that coming back to me!'

Hilda has a meeting to attend, so she leaves us, with strict instructions that Dee must return to the Vicarage by five o'clock 'at the outside.'

As soon as she has gone, Phyllis says, 'It's all coming back to me, too. I distinctly remember Granny Alleyn at the range. She let Hilda and Dot lay the table. But don't say anything,' she says to Jack, who taps the side of his nose. She rises. 'I must collect Jenny.'

Before she calls up to Dee and Alex, I act on an impulse. 'That lovely scene you described – in the workshop with Father and Mother – you wouldn't write it out for me, would you?'

Phyllis looks slightly startled, but not displeased, especially when Jack says, 'Oh yes.'

'All right, then,' she says, smiling. 'Oh.. and I'm expecting Florence and Beatrice back next week. I'll let you know when.'

The girls come down to say good-bye, Dee thanking Phyllis for her pencil and Jack and me for the notebook, whose cover she strokes tenderly, 'such beautiful colours,' and we all go outside to wave Phyllis off, as she wheels the motorcycle up the yard and under the arch. We hear her spur the engine into life and move away, its low roar fading as she heads out towards the factories and light industries off the London Road.

'We really liked all of Uncle Leonard's poems,' says Alex.

'The ones about the landscape were – lovely,' says Dee, 'and so vivid, it was as if we were there.'

'But we'd like to ask him about the one where he's talking to someone in the dining room and they're both keeping the conversation very – '

'Light,' says Dee.

Alex vigorously agrees. 'That one's the best.'

'He'll be very pleased you've understood exactly what he was aiming at,' I say with pride on behalf of my nieces' intelligent appreciation, 'and you know he always likes to talk to you about poems and writing, so come whenever you're able.'

'Pity he's not back from that valuation,' says Jack, 'you could have chatted with him now.'

This had passed through my mind, but I'm certainly not going to admit as much.

Another Place

It's a relief to turn my chair from talk
At my own table to the one behind me.
Hearing my honest but unwelcome answer
To the cleric telling us about the bishops,
A lady on my other side wants my views
On the much safer topic of the weather.

My wife hides her true feelings as she listens
To the expansive reminiscences
Of this servant of the Lord who visited
A place you and I remember all too well.
But he was there in a time quite different
From the one which, soft-spoken fellow diner,
You and I lived through, unlike so many
Stationed with us who were not so fortunate.
We might easily have met each other,
Far from our different countries, brought together
For a purpose neither you nor I ever
Would have chosen in other circumstances.

My wife's explaining to the erstwhile tourist,
Or pilgrim as he probably sees himself,
That you and I were stationed there in wartime,
And why we seem to have something in common.
She speaks with measured force, anger contained,
But her companion is oblivious.
You and I exchange a smile, which stands
For everything we had to see and suffer.
It's all we want to offer on that front.

You say that in the garden here you've seen
A plant you recognise. It's from Nepal,
And has, you tell me, spires of small white flowers
Which peep from sets of leaves on a hairy stem.
My wife, the granddaughter of a gardener,
Glad, like me, to turn from our own table,
Overhears you, and is in her element.
She smiles and says, 'That sounds like a bugle.'
For a moment, we are in that other place.

I'm up in the attic, re-reading Leonard's poem, which so impressed Alex and Dee. It's the last of his East Coast Sequence. I hear the front door open and the low rumble of the two men greeting each other, then the sound of Leonard bounding upstairs. I come down. We meet on the landing.

'They liked your poems,' I say by way of a sort of explanation, not that he'd require one, for my having been in his study.

He looks bewildered. Then, 'Oh! Did they? Excellent!' he says. He looks slightly unkempt, bursting with vitality. 'Dearest love,' he takes me in his arms, 'I'm sorry I'm so late. I ran from the station.' I have to smile. 'She wouldn't stop talking.'

'I know what that's like.'

'There's a lot to tell you.'

'Good, but we can't stand here all evening, or you'll never get fed.'

While I'm cooking sausages - quick, easy and they went down well last week - Leonard mashes the potatoes with as much vigour as he puts into questioning me about the detail of Dee's and Alex's response to his poems. I tell him exactly what each said, their love for his description of the landscape - seascape - their perceptiveness over the meaning of Another Place. 'They said they'd like to discuss it with you.'

'I'll take my lunch break at four o'clock next Monday,' he says emphatically, 'and come home so that I see them.'

'It's the school holidays,' I gently remind him, 'they're even less their own agents.'

'Ach!' He looks stricken, as the implications of his tardy return sink in.

I feel so sorry, but helpless, too. 'Some chance will turn up,' I offer, rather inadequately. 'Come on, let's eat.'

'Well, was it worth it?' asks Jack, after we're seated and tucking in.

'Oh, goodness, yes!' says Leonard, with a little, inward-looking laugh.

'So, you're going to make a lot of money out of this - what's-her-name - Linda Watson?'

This time, Leonard laughs out loud. 'I very much doubt it. No, it was an opportunity to dip into an absorbing collection of books - and have a stimulating intellectual exchange, a lot of it in Italian.'

'Blimey!' says Jack.

'That must have been' - nice? - lovely? I search for a suitable word which will rescue the mood after Jack's expostulation - 'a real tonic,' I say, meaning it.

'It certainly was. The fact is,' says Leonard, pausing with knife and fork in hand, 'the whole place may be up for auction - lock, stock and barrel. It's quite understandable that Teodolinda's state of mind - '

'I didn't quite catch that last bit,' says Jack.

'Teodolinda - that's Mrs. Watson's real name, in Italian. She shortens it to Linda here - '

'Just as well,' Jack chuckles, 'it's a bit of a mouthful.'

'I think it sounds rather splendid,' I say, rising to clear the plates.

'Well, apparently the original Teodolinda was a Lombard queen,' says Leonard, 'so, if queens are splendid...' He shrugs.

I come back with his Swiss bun, 'Oh, good,' he says, brightening visibly.

As the Madeira cake is making a return visit Jack, too, is satisfied.

'So, is Teodolinda,...' I try the name out the way Leonard pronounced it, Tayodolinda, 'thinking of going back to Italy?'

'She doesn't know,' says Leonard. 'She's not in touch with family there, but it is her homeland.'

'Poor thing,' I say.

'It was a bit of a waste of time, then, bothering to look at her books if she's not going to sell them to you?' says Jack.

'I was able to advise her,' says Leonard, 'which I consider to be part of my job - especially to someone in her position, with no other contacts. We could certainly sell for her if she doesn't wish to act independently. The books in Italian, beautiful and fascinating though they are, would require a collector with a special interest in the history and traditions of Italy. Those about its architecture and literature would, I think, be easier to place. I suggested approaching The London Library because they have a foreign language section and they're extending their premises substantially, so they might welcome them. I said I'd leave it with her. I was all ready to come home, but - '

'She insisted that you take tea.'

'I couldn't refuse,' says Leonard. 'The housekeeper brought it in. Teodolinda did ask me about my own poetry - which poets inspired me, but when I said Shelley and Keats - that was it, there was no stopping her. It was how she met Jeremy. He'd organised some lectures at the British Embassy - Byron, Shelley and Keats. Did she tell you all that?'

'Some of it. She told me it was love at first sight. She didn't go into the details of the talk on the night they met – and I didn't ask, as it was getting late.'

'Apparently, in his opening remarks he mentioned how Shelley had loved Dante. She just reached to a shelf behind her, pulled La Vita Nuova from it and started reading. Then, she passed it to me. That put me on my mettle, I can tell you, reading sight unseen and getting the meaning, the inflexion, the musicality...'

'But you obviously succeeded,' I say, looking at the light in his eyes from the recollection.

'Well, she did clap and say, Bravissimo!'

'I should think so.' My admiration is as much for the fact that Leonard could clearly tolerate that sharp, staccato sound like gunfire. I make a pretence of clapping.

'You've lost me,' says Jack.

Leonard seems not to have heard him. 'I started trying to extricate myself – I knew it was much later than I had intended leaving – but then she asked me if I would be prepared to take some poems with me and read them. They're in English, thank goodness, but were written by someone very close to her, she says.'

'Oh,' says Jack, 'so she's not completely on her own then, after all?'

'That person could have died,' I say, and gather the plates.

The rest of the evening seems to pass in no time, with clearing up and preparation for tomorrow.

In bed, Leonard reaches for me, and we embrace with a long and loving kiss, but we both hear the dull thud of Jack's weight, as his feet find the rug beside his bed, the muffled creak of the bedside cupboard door, the jug being dragged from within. We have to laugh.

Quietly, as we are both still awake, I ask Leonard what he thinks about the idea I've been contemplating. Stimulated by the accounts Jack and Phyllis have given of those two lovely moments in our parents' life together, I've been wondering whether to ask my brothers and sisters for similar memories of their happy times. 'I would keep them, and anyone who wanted to read them could.'

'Except your father, of course.'

'Well, if he wanted, one of us could do it. I'd be pleased to. But what do you think?'

'I'd say, it's a wonderful and worthwhile thing to do.'

We kiss and, in a little while, Leonard turns away. I hear his regular breathing. I lie and think about what I've taken on. Tomorrow, I shall write to my two brothers, Ted and Bob, living in America. They're always very busy, and this will give them time to respond. After that, I must steal myself and write to my brother Joe.

Chapter Eleven

Fairview
South Parade
York
22nd August 1920

Dear Rose,

In response to your letter of the 13th firstly, yes, we are in good health, thank the Lord.

Secondly, regarding your request for happy memories of our parents, whilst I understand your sentiments, I would make the following observation: why don't you ask Father directly? More to the point perhaps you should, in fact, seek his authorisation for this project which could, it has to be said, be viewed by a less charitable mind as going behind his back. This leads me to my final observation, namely, what is the point of the exercise?

I hope you will take this in the spirit in which it is intended if I say that I can understand perfectly that, without a family of your own, you must have time on your hands but I cannot, for the life of me, imagine what might be the purpose of this endeavour. After all, you have no one to whom you might hand the record on, and Father hardly needs a reminder of happier times, albeit that he has made the best of things with Cousin Grace.

On which note I have to remind you that I, too, have made a new life for myself with Jane. It is not the life I had envisaged. In view of this, I would be grateful if you do not contact me again unless I write to you. I have tried to put my life in Widdock, and for that matter Markly, behind me.

Our little Sidney gives us much joy.

Your brother,
Joe

I feel as if there is a stone in my stomach, a hand gripping my heart. This is exactly what I should have guessed would happen, rather than what I stupidly hoped for: that stepping back to childhood would give my brother a positive pleasure. I have alienated Joe, already-distant, by bringing Widdock before his eyes in the very fact of my residence here, thus reminding him of the scene of his former happiness which was so cruelly ended. I acted too impetuously in writing so quickly and now, instead of respecting his need for time to grieve in silence, I've blundered in and, effectively, put up a wall of ice between us.

In the still house, with Leonard already gone to work and Jack not yet up, I sink into my armchair and allow the anguish of remorse to spread inside me, reawakening my own heartache at the tragic circumstances of Joe's departure.

Poor Joe. I think back twenty years. When I came to Widdock, he had already done so well here in his job on the railway that he could ask the daughter of a respected local businessman to marry him. How he had cared for his family, his wife, Catherine and his two children. Robert was sixteen, Hannah fourteen in 1918, the year when Joe, who was based at Widdock North, gained a post in York as a Senior Controller of railways. While he was up there, working and looking for somewhere to house his family, if all three came to live there, Catherine wrote to him at his lodgings, telling him they were ill so, on his next days off, he should not come home. How he wished he had, regardless. They were dead within a week from Spanish 'flu, probably contracted by all three at Widdock North where Robert worked in the station, Catherine and Helen at the field canteen which fed returning wounded soldiers before admission to Widdock General Hospital. With his life in pieces, Joe remained in York. 'There's nothing to come back for,' he had said. During the course of the following year, he met Jane Barlby. They married and now, thank goodness, they have baby Sidney.

In times of tension, I find a way of relaxing in the simple act of tidying the books. Current fiction is always the most popular stock and likely to be disordered. I take solace from the gentle chock... chock... of spines coaxed, with the lightest middle finger hooked inside their top as its counterpart teases underneath, to the front of the shelf. Then comes the aesthetic pleasure of ensuring, with the merest touch from the back of the hand, that they are all lined flush. Older books are a joy of a different order, the scent of a leather binding, of parchment, the beauty of gold tooling.

By the time I open up, I feel more composed. Outside stands Mr. Longstaff, smiling. With his tufted white eyebrows and weathered face wreathed in whiskers, he reminds me of a kindly old ginger cat. Hearing his 'Good morning, dear Mrs. Pritchard. I trust I find you in bright spirits despite this dull day,' I am overcome, and have to let him lead me to my chair in the sitting room behind the shop, where he puts the kettle on and, propping open the door to the shop, tells me not to worry, 'I'll take care of any customers but, firstly, is there anything I can do for you?'

Mr. Longstaff is one of 'your gentlemen', as Leonard calls them, three retainers from the days of Auberon Quinn-Harper, who used to come in to discuss with him anything which took their fancy, sometimes books, much in the same way that Leonard's three friends, Messrs. Vance, Nash and Davison, have always done at Pritchard's Bookshop. I had never expected my three to continue their patronage once I was the proprietor, but I'm very touched to say that they have been some of my most steadfast customers. It is they who bring me flowers on my birthday.

I find myself telling Mr. Longstaff all about my brother's loss, 'Oh, I do remember, my dear,' and Joe's dampening response to what I have to admit was probably an ill-conceived idea.

'On the contrary,' says Mr. Longstaff, with some vehemence. 'As I understand it, this is a record of two lives brought together by love – and look what they achieved! Don't be thwarted by your brother. He's blinkered by his grief. Your parents should be honoured.'

'I couldn't have put it better,' says Leonard.

'And I certainly couldn't have,' says Jack.

We're between courses, catching up on each other's day, Jack's 'not so bad,' Leonard's predictably busy, accessioning new stock.

'I had a letter, too,' says Leonard, 'from Teodolinda Watson confirming Thursday.'

'Tay-odd-o-linda. I can't get over that name,' says Jack.

'Evidently,' says Leonard, with perfect equanimity. 'I hope she'll respond with pleasure when I suggest that her friend's poems are, in fact, her own.'

Leonard has already divulged this opinion to me.

'She should, shouldn't she?' I say. 'You think they're good.'

'Some of them, yes. So do you, don't you?'

'I only glanced at one or two,' I say. 'I found the foreign handwriting a little daunting.' Leonard nods. 'But yes, I liked what I read – the one about figs.'

'There are a few idiomatic discrepancies –'

'What are they?' Jack interrupts Leonard.

'Where she doesn't quite get the right expression – the way we would speak.'

'Ah,' says Jack. Then, 'It's a pity you can't just post them back to her, rather than flogging all the way over to Cottering.'

'Oh, I wouldn't do that,' says Leonard. 'I think it would seem too casual. I prefer to conclude my dealings with her on a courteous note.'

'And if you posted them back, you'd never know whether you got it right and she was the poet, this Tay –'

'That's not my primary motivation,' Leonard interrupts.

I stand up. 'How about some pudding?'

Real Figs

You tell me that you don't much care for figs.
If these are all you know, I'm not surprised.
Your greengrocer should have apologised.
Such travesties are only fit for pigs.
The desiccated fruit is fig disguised;
When fresh it is a glory to be prized.
So, come, dear English in-laws, Fortune rigs
My magic carpet's star-out-shooting flight
For Rome, this sunlit courtyard, a shady spot
And bowl of freshly-plucked, plump figs, which invite
Your tasting. Such sweet, rich flesh, dense as compote.
Feel skin, velvet soft, yielding to the bite.
A flavour more delicious there is not.

I come through to the kitchen with the shopping, which I start to put in the pantry. Jack is making his morning infusion of St. John's Wort. He performs this rather as a religious rite, using his special tea cup, an odd plain white one which neither Leonard nor I can remember buying. Into this he measures, from the brown paper packet, one tablespoon of the dried herb whose taste, he's told us, is difficult to describe 'sort of musty or metallic, but soothing.'

He pours on boiling water and, while the brew is steeping for five minutes, he shows me a note that Phyllis must have dropped in while I was out and he was still upstairs. It is addressed to both Jack and me on the outside. Inside, she has written, 'Do try to come this afternoon if you can, Rose.' [I had let her know I would if I could.] 'Apologies Jack. Too complicated to involve you, too. They are going back to Cornwall tomorrow! Love, Phyllis.'

'Good Lord! If I'd known it was going to be that short a visit I'd have tried to see them sooner,' I say, though how I don't know, when we had the chimney-sweep on Monday, and Lizzie and I spent the rest of the day, after putting out the wash, taking away the coverings and cleaning any suspect surfaces.

'Well, you'd better go today, then,' says Jack. 'Don't worry about me. If it cheers up, I'll sit on the bench out the back. You never know, old Hubert might turn up and sit next to me. We don't say anything. After a bit, he just gets up and goes off again.'

I walk under the spreading branches of the tree whose plump, shiny apples already bear a blush. The side of the house discloses its view of the lawn and borders, graced by regal spires of hollyhocks, reminding me of those at The Chantry, in glorious shades from darkest plum to pastel primrose. Under them, Japanese anemones add their blooms of white and delicate mauve-pink. In contrast, montbretias add a splash of fire and, filling any space between them, bold nasturtiums tumble in bright shades of orange and gold. I walk past the glorious scent of the climbing rose and into the vegetable garden where I find Phyllis harvesting her onions.

'Good, I'm glad you're early,' she says, striking her fork into the soil and dusting off her hands, 'I could do with a drink. It's made, I'll bring it out.'

There's a hint of sun behind the clouds, so I cross to the other side of the plot and sit on the bench by the south-facing wall which supports a joyful tangle of wild rose, honeysuckle and ivy. Phyllis brings out a tray with two glasses and a jug of clear liquid, straw-coloured with a glimmer of green. The honey-rich, intoxicating scent is unmistakable.

'Oh! Lime-flower cordial! How lovely!'

We chink glasses and simply savour the heavenly drink. Then, she takes a neat envelope from the tray and hands it to me. 'My recollections. I've simply written it down word for word as I told you.'

'That's exactly what I hoped.' I put the envelope safely in my little bag. I tell her about Joe's letter, but the encouragement I've had to carry on. 'What do you think, Phyl?'

She considers it. 'I agree with Jack. I'd like to hear everyone's memories – and I don't see why, despite our parents' hardships, they shouldn't be happy ones. That's not too strong a word for the childhood we had. I can't see it would do any harm. It might even do some good, I don't know how.'

I feel a great sense of relief. 'That's what I thought. I'll write to Ralph and Dot, then – and tell Hubert. In fact, I might write to Cousin Grace, so that she can tell Father – or not.'

'Yes, leave it to her discretion,' Phyllis says. 'I've been thinking about that time when you went away to the seaside, and suddenly I remembered something else. It was about then – give or take – that I found Mother's Dutch cap!'

'No!'

'That's what it must have been. Hilda was tidying the chest of drawers in our room. She told me I'd got to tidy Mother's drawer. In hindsight, I'm not sure she didn't hope I'd get into trouble for going into their bedroom. But I took her word for it, and soon I was absorbed in all the soft, lavender-scented woollens and pretty lace-trimmed handkerchiefs and whatnot. Then my little fingers closed round something very peculiar – round and made of rubber. I pulled it out. I still recall my puzzlement. I sat there for a while, then I trotted downstairs to where Mother was in the kitchen with Dot, making scones. I said, 'Mother, what's this, and may I have it as a helmet for Dolly Daisy?'

'Whatever did she say?'

'Well, you know how marvellous she was at handling a difficult situation. She just said, 'It's a silly old thing that doesn't suit me.' Then, she brushed her hands on her apron and came down to my level and said, 'And actually, Phyllis, I don't think it would suit Dolly Daisy either. It's too big, it would cover her eyes, and she might get frightened.' Dot agreed, of course. She'd been watching. So, Mother gently took it away, and then asked me if I'd like to cut out some scones, which I did.'

We agree it's probably better if I don't put all that in the memoir!

As we walk up to the house, Phyllis says, 'They're angry about last night's meeting. They'll tell you. I'd better go first, if we're going to drink more tea.' She nods towards the outside privy which we're approaching. I take my turn after her.

By the time I've washed and dried my hands in the scullery, Mrs. Fuller and Beatrice are seated at the kitchen table, agreeing with each other that it's just not nice enough to go to the effort of carting everything outside.

'Ah, dear Rose.'

'Don't stand up,' I say, hurrying round to squeeze her hand.

She leans up and we brush lips. I grip hands with Beatrice and move round to be out of Phyllis's way as she serves tea.

'So, you've taken on the responsibility of your sick brother since last we met,' says Mrs. Fuller. 'Phyllis tells me you're making an exemplary job of it, which doesn't surprise me, but how are you?'

I look into her bright green eyes with their gold flecks. 'I'm coping,' I say, finding it to be the truth. I give her a summary: his good and bad days; our holiday ('Ah, very good,' she says) and how Phyllis is my ally because she always makes him smile.

'Leonard is marvellous with him, welcoming him from the start.'

'Good, good,' she says, with what seems like genuine relief.

'But what of you?' I ask. 'How is Cornwall?'

'Cornwall is blissful.' Beatrice enters the conversation. 'That's why we're going back there. It's a vibrant, creative community.'

'Not that Widdock isn't, of course,' says Mrs. Fuller, loyally.

'Parts of it,' adds Beatrice.

'Am I right that you had a meeting of the War Memorials Committee last night?' I ask, bracing myself.

'We certainly did,' says Beatrice. 'Nearly three months since our last meeting and no further forward. Still dithering about whether it should be a cross, a wall or a bench. That was when Mother disgraced herself,' says Beatrice, proudly, 'by whispering rather too loudly in my ear.'

'I said it would have to be a bloody big bench. I was actually making a serious point. To get all the names of all the men from Widdock and the surrounding villages on it – but of course, they absolutely leapt on my 'unladylike' pronouncement.'

'Did anyone actually say that?' Phyllis asks.

'Not in so many words, but the Chairman asked us all to be restrained in our comments. So, I didn't go on to say, 'A bench, for God's sake. So who decides the names which are to be sat upon?"

'One of them even suggested we might wait until the unveiling of the permanent Cenotaph,' says Beatrice, and then in the voice of a committee member, ' "to see if it provides inspiration".'

'So we unveiled our suggestion. Honestly, we only took it along in case there was a dearth of talent. Ha! How long did it take us, darling, to think it up? A morning's intense consideration.'

'It would have been breath-taking,' says Beatrice. 'I could go and get the sketch – '

'Describe it to them,' says Mrs. Fuller.

'Well, imagine a hollowed globe and, receding back inside it, a series of flattened rectangles like dominoes. So, it stands for both the earth and the womb from which all these fallen men have come.' Beatrice's voice takes on the hard edge of passionate grief and anger restrained by imperative. 'But outside the globe, so considerably larger than the forms within, and slightly elevated, is a large rectangle, as if transcendent. On it are all the names of those men...'

At this point, the mother who is also grandmother rises, with tears in her own eyes, to comfort her daughter.

Phyllis pours more tea, adding a discreet spoonful of sugar.

'Frightened the life out of them,' says Mrs. Fuller, recovering first. 'No cake, Phyllis, thank you, just a ratafia. We've got all that bending to do with our packing.'

I don't refuse a slice of Phyllis's lemon sponge.

'So, we presented our back-up plan,' says Beatrice, who has no scruples about accepting a large slice of cake.

'You amaze me,' I say, full of admiration for their quick wits.

Mrs. Fuller makes a dismissive gesture. 'We suggested – no insisted – that they put the whole thing out to public competition. With minimal advertising in the right places – which we, heaven help us, said we'd organise – they will get first class entries from all over Britain. They can even charge a modest fee. The kudos for the competitor will be the prize of winning. They're going to put it forward to the next meeting of the Town Council.'

'Well, that sounds like an achievement,' I say, and Phyllis nods.

The women give their grudging assent.

It has become second nature with me as I reach our front door to take a step aside and glance in at the window to see whether Jack is sitting in what has become his chair. If he is, and he's awake, he raises a hand and smiles when he sees my silhouette darken the glass. Today, the chair is empty. In the tiny burst of emotion that this sight engenders, I'm disturbed to recognise both disappointment and relief. Soundlessly, I open the door, enter and flit straight through. That promise of sunlight in Phyllis's kitchen garden was not fulfilled, so it comes as no surprise to see that the garden bench is also empty. There is no sound from upstairs. The mad thought begins to cross my mind: could Jack have gone out for a walk? But even before it is concluded, I hear, above me, the slightest movement from the bed. He must be having one of his not-so-good days. I feel downcast. I'd foolishly entertained the idea that he might, just, be a little better since starting his medicinal infusion. I must remember that for every seeming progression, he tends to take a step back.

I go to pick beans and dead-head roses. After a visit to Apple Tree House, the ornamental part of our garden looks almost wild, with its unruly drifts of Michaelmas daisies vying with swathes of helenium, the understorey covered by glorious eruptions of erigeron or fleabane, its pink and white daisies like an embodiment of hope. Mrs. Fuller's gardener, another member of the redoubtable Munns family, would no doubt tut at my easy-going attitude, but I love it as it is. There are some wonderful blooms still in abundance. Before I go in, I will cut a deep red Rosa Gallica with a scent of myrrh, a yellow climber with a honey fragrance and a white rose with an almost lemony scent. These I shall place in my rose bowl on the table. First, though, I tour my namesakes, snapping off wilted flower heads and placing them in the basket so that their petals can be salvaged, spread out and, with stalks of the lavender which borders the path through Leonard's potager to our back gate, dried to make the most delicately scented pot pourri, reminding the heart in winter darkness of a summer's day.

Jack's in the kitchen, picking out cutlery. I have a sense of time having passed without me noticing. As he goes through to the dining table, he nods towards the clock on the mantelshelf. 'Not back yet.'

I can't trust myself to answer free of emotion, firstly, irritation with Jack for having voiced the manifestly obvious and, secondly, annoyance both with Leonard for giving him the opportunity to put me in this frame of mind and myself for allowing either to affect me.

Perhaps sensing my displeasure, Jack says, 'After you went out, I felt a bit anyhow,' which immediately makes me regret my lack of charity.

'Oh, dear,' I begin, as footsteps approach and Leonard opens the front door.

I read in his face, that split-second before he composes it to greet us, his natural exuberance at its peak, undergirded by exhaustion.

'Not quite as late as last time,' he says, as he hugs me, 'but I'm sorry.'

'What kept you this time?' asks Jack, looking slightly amused.

'Tell us over dinner,' I say, 'I'm about to serve.'

'All went according to plan to begin with,' says Leonard, opening his baked potato and mashing butter into its steaming bounty. 'I suggested that we should discuss three poems, have tea, then do the other three.'

'Did you tell her you thought she'd written them?' says Jack.

'I was coming to that. Once we were comfortable in her sitting room, I said that I was impressed with the writing and dared suggest it was she, not her friend, who was the author.'

'How did that go down?' says Jack.

I say, to allow Leonard a mouthful of food, 'Very well, I should think, wouldn't you?'

Leonard nods emphatically. When he's ready he says, 'We went through the first set of poems. I was quite expansive, trying to be helpful. We had tea, during which she told me that she's always written poetry, and over the last twenty odd years in English too, encouraged by Jeremy. She got a bit close to tears there, so I asked her if she still wrote in Italian. Yes, she does. She recovered and we went through the other three. I made some concluding remarks of a positive nature and said that all six, with the slight amendments we'd discussed, were of publishable standard. I did suggest, though, that in view of your difficulty with her handwriting – you being just as intelligent a reader as any poetry editor –'

'Goodness! What did she say to that?' I interject.

'She was smiling and nodding,' says Leonard. 'She guessed what I was going to say, and said she knows how to use Jeremy's Olivetti.'

'His what?' says Jack.

'Typewriter,' says Leonard. 'By this stage, I felt I'd helped her as much as I could, it was time to leave. I started to make a move. Then, she told me there were thirty more poems, and asked me if I would be prepared to help her edit those with a possible view to publication. I have to say, that hit me like a ton of bricks.'

'Well, yes,' I say. It has hit me too, but in a subtler way. 'She surely can't expect you to go over to Cottering all the time.'

'That's exactly what was passing through my head,' says Leonard, 'together with finding time for my own work - and running a bookshop.'

'What I can't understand,' says Jack, 'is why, if her husband thought she was so good, he didn't help her to get the right words.'

'Because he thought she was wonderful, I expect,' I say. 'He wouldn't have wanted to criticise her work. Besides, he may have loved poetry but, as I understand it, he wasn't himself a poet.'

'That's it exactly,' says Leonard. 'She wants someone to be ruthlessly honest.'

'I could do that,' says Jack, 'if she's looking for an audience.'

'Well, yes, she may be glad of your help when the time comes,' says Leonard, diplomatically. 'I said that I was immensely flattered to be asked, and it would be a very stimulating experience. I was about to say, but I couldn't do it now - the fact that this is my busiest time of year had already come up over tea - but she headed me off by making the suggestion that she could come here on Thursday afternoons. I had thought briefly about trying to combine a visit to Ash Manor with my talk to the Cotteringbury boys.'

'It would be too much,' I say.

'That's what I concluded,' says Leonard. 'I wouldn't want to short-change either party for lack of time, so I said that, provided you were happy with the arrangement, Rose, the sessions would start here on the twenty-first of October and run for six weeks.'

Almost without our noticing, for the trees are all still green, August shakes out her gorgeous skirts, patterned with glowing dahlias in crimson, flame and purple, and ushers in September, cloaked in bright chrysanthemums, trailing a breath of autumn.

School starts, and Dee and Alex resume their Monday afternoon meetings at our cottage. Leonard keeps his promise to himself and takes his lunch break in the afternoon to coincide with their visit. All the time that they are, between them, reading out loud, discussing Leonard's poems and talking generally, he gives them all his attention, as if he has nothing further in the world to do except, by this careful yet carefree interchange of intellects, help them into a nourishing adulthood.

> *Meadow Cottage*
> *Markly*
> *14th September 1920*
>
> *Dear Rose,*
>
> *Thank you for your enquiries. We are all as well as can be expected and George, over the past few weeks, a little better than we dared hope.*
>
> *Firstly, I'd like to set your mind at rest that I'm all for your idea of collecting happy memories of your parents. Your mother was the love of Robert's life and I think it would be a wonderful record of their happy years together. I had to choose my moment to broach your project to him but, once he was assured that I was comfortable with it, he said he was very touched and that he looks forward to its completion, when perhaps you will come and read it to him. I thought you might find it useful if I speak to Dot on your behalf next time I go there. If this doesn't suit you, let me know.*
>
> *We're glad that Jack has settled in with the two of you, and send you all our love,*
> *Grace*

Despite everyone else's encouragement to go ahead with my plan, that part of Joe's discouraging letter about seeking Father's approval has been a burr catching my conscience. I feel a great weight lift with Cousin Grace's kind words, not least her offer to speak to Dot for me. I will try to catch Hilda after Church on Sunday, and then write to my two brothers, Robert and Ted, in America and to Ralph in the north country.

I don't expect to hear from any of them very soon, which is why an envelope bearing a distinctly foreign hand gives me a bit of a jolt. It is, though, written by Ralph's wife, Delphine who,

French by birth, was a lady's maid at the grand house before being permitted to marry my brother. Inside is a sheet of fine notepaper with a printed heading, under which is Ralph's brief reply.

Ralph Alleyn
Head Gardener
GARDEN COTTAGE
GRYSWORTH
19th September 1920

Dear Rose,
How lovely to hear from you! We are all thriving. What an inspired idea of yours. I have to say, though, that the challenge of restoring the gardens with my band of ladies, and the demands of family life mean that I have precious little time. I fear I shall never finish my article on trying to resurrect his Lordship's orchidaceae, let alone have the capacity for reflection on our childhood, but I promise I'll try.
May the three of you prosper.
With much love from us all, especially little Rose,
Ralph

I feel a pang. I'm clearly asking my brother to take on what amounts to more work on top of the gargantuan task of reinstating the garden and grounds at Grysworth after the depredations of the War. All his team enlisted, some did not come back and, as in so many other areas, women stepped in, ably filling the breach. But Ralph's letter fills me with warmth and makes me think of all the times when I would patter round after him in Grandpa Clarke's garden, learning from them both. Ralph is the only one of us who has followed the precedent set by our parents in that he and Delphine have a brood of children, six so far, the last of whom, not yet one year old, bears my maiden name, Rose Alleyn. How I recall the utter joy, in December's darkness, of opening their card and reading this news. There could be no finer Christmas present. And how strange it feels to think there is another little me who will go on, up in that far northern place.

Chapter Twelve

Who would have thought that after so much time feeling as if we have been cheated of our rightful due of sunlight, we would be granted these perfect golden October days. Jack takes cushions and sits out on both benches, in the morning at the front, in the afternoon under the apple tree. When I can, I join him. One day, Hubert appears, so I sit on the rug. I tell him about my idea. He's sad to hear of Joe's response. They were always close, working together at Widdock East when it was simply Widdock, before the other station grew in status and became Widdock North. I see in his face love, sympathy and his own pain. Of all of us, Joe might have kept in touch with him. He says he will be glad to think of some special memory of our parents and put it down on paper. He's just not quite sure when that might be. Oh, dear. I sense Jack's impatience, but I mustn't let it infect me.

The glorious weather goes on. Leonard gives his reading and talk to a full quota of Sixth Formers at Cotteringbury School. It is well received and he's invited to return next year. At Quinn-Harper's, I keep all doors open for a gentle breeze to waft through. At break times, I take a chair outside, enjoying the chit-chat with passers-by, the more intense exchanges with those, such as my 'gentlemen' who care to stop. This mode of existence feels to me, somehow, continental.

The daylight hours seem longer, when they should be shortening. We manage to sit, two Sundays, in the garden after dinner. Leonard reads aloud a revised poem from his East Coast Sequence:

'Outside 'The Admiral Nelson'

From the west comes the murmur of voices
Rising and ebbing, clink of glass against glass.
My bench is the inn's easterly outpost
Nearest the sea, the cusp of this crescent bay.

I face north where sand stretches, compacted
As yellow dough, sprung, starred with washed pebbles.
Moored dinghies wait for the tide. Others lie beached
At angles. Tapering prows swell to hulls
Like gourds. I see again the maestro plucking
Elegant arabesques from the mellow strings
Of his Egyptian oud. I hear its deep voice.
But it fades, gives way to the high, fluting
Cry of sea birds, skuas or terns, their white wings
Flashing in sunlight. I turn east, where the shore
Is alive with dipping birds and where you,
In your bright dress, dip for glistening shells.'

I read the wonderful ode, 'To Autumn,' by John Keats. That marvellous first line: 'Season of mists and mellow fruitfulness' could not be more true of our experience now. In case we'd been hoodwinked – this must be July – the mornings have been wreathed in telling mists, sometimes almost fog and, after some cold nights, grass blades and leaves have been touched by frost. But then sunbeams brush aside the diaphanous curtain, melt the silver filigree, and the day is hot. The words on everyone's lips are: St. Luke's Summer, that last burst of clement warmth, which we all honour.

By the eighteenth, though, our prevailing easterly wind, never far away, is up again with an edge to it. This may be St. Luke's Feast Day, but our summer party is over.

I open our front door. The sitting room smells of smoke. Leonard turns from his position holding a newspaper across the fireplace. I can see from his strained smile that he's overcoming annoyance, as much as I'm overcoming dismay. I'd decided to save the coal in case the strike continues.

'I was trying to be helpful, Rose,' says Jack from his armchair. 'I thought I'd get it going before the two of you were home, but it just smoked, and that so-on-so wind blew it all back into the room.'

'If we can actually get it to draw properly,' Leonard says, more to the mantelpiece than us, 'then we can throw some orange peel on it or –'

'Careful! Careful!' I cry. 'I can see flames!'

Leonard steps back, folding the paper. 'Good.' He has a smear on his cheek, and hands black from coal and newsprint.

'You've got time for a wash if you're quick,' I say, as we both go through to the kitchen.

'I had to re-lay it,' he whispers to me, raising his eyes.

I let him take water from the kettle, reminding myself to refill it when he's finished at the sink. I put the ginger cake I've made on a pretty plate. The scent of it is mouth-watering.

'Mmmnn... Lovely!' says Leonard, drying himself quickly. He looks sparkling fresh and fully in control now. He goes back through to the sitting room. 'That's better,' he says to Jack. 'Well done with the peel.'

I fill the kettle and set out the crockery. Should I put out pastry forks? I do so. Then I ferret in the back of the dresser for some afternoon tea napkins.

The drub of hooves and creak of wheels in this quiet yard, where no one owns a horse, usually presage the milkman making his rounds. Now, the sound gives us time to prepare ourselves for the polite knock.

Leonard opens the door and then, suddenly, or so it seems, Teodolinda Watson is in the middle of our sitting room, making it look somehow smaller, more homespun. I manage to respond to her, 'Ah, Rose, how lovely to see you again,' as she clasps my hands.

The term 'widow's weeds' hardly does justice to what our guest is wearing. A black woollen coat in a bell line sweeps to touch her ankles, the shape echoed by its generous sleeves, which are decorated with two black bands in astrakhan, a motif followed around the skirt of the coat. The application of a subtly different texture at certain key points, together with the cut, create a stylish whole. I wonder whether I detect Lettie's hand in this choice of garment. I surely do when it comes to Teodolinda's hat. Sitting atop her piled up, honey-blonde hair, it is a tricorne, black with tiny jet studs around the three brims, rather like a cross between a Tudor lady and a highwayman, or so it seems to me. From one side of the crown depends a length of the finest black voile trimmed with exquisite tears of jet, an elegant screen if held across the face, a complete veil if placed over the head.

Leonard is introducing Jack, who takes the extended hand in its black net glove. 'Pleased to meet you,' he says, barely glancing up, blushing when our guest says, 'And I, you, Jack.'

I gather my wits and offer a hanger for that lovely coat, which I take, feeling its softness as I hang it on a peg by the door and catching from it Teodolina's scent, like some exotic bloom.

'What a delightful room,' she says, looking around her, 'and a fire, too.' She splays her hands out in a token gesture of warming.

'I'm afraid I haven't lit one in my study,' says Leonard. 'This time of year, it's still warm up there, but if you prefer to sit here, I'm sure Rose and Jack – '

'I would not dream of disturbing Rose and Jack,' she says. 'They will see quite enough of me when we break for tea.'

'I look forward to it,' I say.

'Well, shall we get started?' says Leonard, gallantly opening the door to the staircase. 'After you,' and closing it behind him.

We hear him giving directions and Teodolinda making appreciative comments about the character of the cottage. Then, the study door shuts behind them.

'Shall we have a look at Ralph's letter?' I say. This came today as I was about to leave for work. Thinking that it would provide an absorbing occupation for Jack and me, while mentor and mentee were working, I put the unopened envelope on the mantelpiece. Jack assents readily, and we both sit together on the sofa in front of the fire, now burning brightly.

Dear Rose,

Apologies again. The days pass too quickly. I was being hounded for that article I mentioned. [Before the War, Ralph was always writing pieces for horticultural magazines. Clearly, that side-line has started up again.]

The other reason for my delay in replying is that I've hesitated over the memory I'm about to share with you. It is an intimate one, but it keeps coming back to me as the most perfect representation of all that was good in our childhood family life. In the final copy, to be read to Father, you could cut the bit about the angel, but I have included it here because I think you'll understand my feeling that it completes the picture. ['What on earth's he going to tell us?' says Jack. 'You read it out.']

Your affectionate brother,
Ralph

Enclosed is a typewritten account:

> The scene is Mother and Father's bedroom, an afternoon in March, the room made darker not only by the fading natural light but by a curtain half drawn across the window. This was to protect my eyesight. I was about six years old, and had been off school with measles. Mother was in bed and I was lying next to her. The abiding feeling is one of utter peace.
>
> I can remember saying, 'Mother, are you still poorly?' 'I'm getting better, dear,' she said. 'Did you have measles, too?' I asked. 'No, dear.' Of course, I wouldn't let it rest at that. I must have asked, 'What illness did you have?' because she said – and I remember it very clearly – 'It wasn't really an illness, dear. I thought we were going to be visited by a little angel, but the angel went back to heaven and I felt sad. But now I feel glad because the angel is in the right place and happy.'
>
> The next thing I remember is Father coming home. He looked into the room and called me outside. When I

went to him, he was holding the glass bowl with my three hyacinthus bulbs which Grandpa Clarke had shown me how to grow in water. They were beautifully in bloom, a perfect gift for Mothering Sunday, but I had been too ill the day before to present them to Mother. Father must have fetched them from Grandpa on the way home from work. So he let me give them to her now. She held her nose to them to smell that gorgeous scent, then thanked me with a kiss and a cuddle. Father rumpled my hair and said that the blue of the flowers exactly matched the blue of Mother's eyes. To me, the memory is one of perfect harmony.

'Blimey,' says Jack, but there are tears in his eyes. By the time I've dabbed mine, Jack has recovered enough to comment, 'That's left you with a bit of a dilemma.'

'That's what I was thinking.'

'The trouble is, when we were young, Mother was laid up a lot of the time with - you know - '

'Miscarriages, Jack, and I do know. I worked it out - when I was older, of course - that she'd had five. That's not counting the one at Hocton, which I'd obviously blanked out, so that's six.' Jack whistles between his teeth. 'I used to think of that time as her troubled decade but really...' I can feel tears not far away again, 'it was more like a dozen years.'

'Poor Mother,' says Jack. Then, 'I don't understand. Why...?'

'Well, think about what Phyllis told us.'

'About finding the whatsit, the cap, you mean?'

'Exactly. And I once overheard dear Dr. Jepp being rather short with Father for his inability to take in what he'd told him 'on more than one occasion', I remember that phrase. They evidently tried to limit their family and failed. The fact is our parents were in love, and that's clear above all from this memory of Ralph's.'

'What I'd like to know,' says Jack, 'is where you and I were while Ralph had Mother to himself. If he was six, I must have been four and you were three, so we can't have been at school.'

We chew over the various possibilities in a companionable way. It's very pleasant in front of the fire whose glowing coals now give out perhaps a little too much soporific heat. I hear the slightest of movements two floors overhead, possibly that of chairs on polished floorboards.

'Oh, no!' I leap up and rush to put the kettle fully on.

Jack joins me. 'I don't know where I'm supposed to sit.'

'Let them decide. You can help me serve.'

Fortunately, the others must have gone on talking before coming down because Jack and I have everything ready on the table as Leonard opens the staircase door. 'Phew! It's hot down here. We've been freezing in my garret.'

'Nonsense,' says Teodolinda. 'It has been a perfect atmosphere in which to exercise the mental faculties.'

'Well, come in and sit by the fire now,' I say, offering her my chair and nodding to Jack who hovers by the sofa. He takes the end nearest Leonard's chair. I organise the nest of tables so that each of the others has one. I can use the dining table.

Leonard hands round the cake, which I know Jack will be wishing was down-to-earth Madeira.

'Ah! Zenzero – ginger. My favourite!' says our guest, inclining her head to take in the aroma.

I pour tea. I ask how they've got on. Leonard gestures that Teodolinda should answer.

'Very well. Your husband is such a considerate teacher. He praises me and then, very gently points out where I could do better, after which he adds further commendations.'

'I wouldn't if they weren't deserved,' Leonard says. 'You have a talent which just needs developing.'

'And you, Rose and Jack, what have you been doing?' She's smiling at both of us, trying to include Jack but he looks to me, so I give a brief answer about memories of our parents. I don't go into detail.

'That sounds a very good project,' she says.

I ask about her family background. 'Are you actually descended from the Lombard queen?'

'That's what my mother would have liked to think, but no. We come from Monza, which is where she reigned. Actually, she wasn't a Lombard herself. She was the daughter of the King of Bavaria, but she married two Lombard kings – not at the same time, you understand.'

'She was quite a force to be reckoned with, from what you've been telling me,' says Leonard. He turns to us. 'She managed to keep the peace between warring factions by uniting them behind building a church at Monza. That's right, isn't it?'

'It is,' says Teodolinda, accepting a top-up, 'and what I didn't tell you is that she was – we would say 'the flower in the buttonhole' of Pope Gregory the Magnificent, meaning...' She looks to Leonard for help.

'The apple of his eye,' says Leonard, smiling.

'Yes! Thank you, Leonard,' she says, her own eyes alight. 'She was the apple of his eye because she maintained papal authority at Monza. As a reward, the Pope gave her gifts, and treated her better than he did many bishops.'

'Quite a feat for a woman in the Middle Ages,' I say, 'or at any time, actually.'

'Exactly,' says Teodolinda. 'If I'm feeling faint-hearted – and I do, you understand,' I nod, 'I remind myself of my namesake and try to draw courage from her example.'

'That's wonderful,' I say.

There is the slightest pause, then Leonard says, 'Well, if you've got the courage now, Teodolinda, I suggest we address the three remaining poems, which I think need even less alteration. That's why I saved them for this second half.'

'I can't wait,' says Teodolinda. 'This intellectual discussion is just what I need.'

In the stillness after their departure, I ask Jack what he'd like to do next. He looks diminished, and I wonder whether all this

– Ralph's letter, our stimulating guest – has been too much for him.

'I'll help you clear,' he says, 'then I'll have a rest.'

In the kitchen, with all the crocks through, ready to be washed, we both stand looking out of the window. Although it is still light, the afternoon is drawing in its horns, ready to settle into an autumnal evening.

'Clocks go back Sunday night,' Jack says.

I nod. I can't begin to convey, nor would I want to, what this prospect feels like to me.

'This is the time of year when I go down,' my brother says.

It was kind of Leonard to let me sleep on till the last possible minute before bringing me tea, but I fear I shall be late for Church. Everything came together yesterday to wear me out: a busy day at work, bath night and then Leonard's caresses, 'let's have a cwtch', to which, of course, I responded. He has been rather invigorated since he began his role as poetry mentor, and although his earlier exuberance left him exhausted on Thursday night, so that he fell straight asleep beside me, he has been energised these past two nights. I feared that all this extra stimulation might produce one of his bad dreams, but so far this has not been the case. He knows, though, that however discreet our quiet coupling might be and however I might try to stop myself, I can't help listening for the slightest noise across the landing.

As I hurry to wash and dress I hear, above me, a desk drawer open and close. This is Leonard's most creative time of day. I hope that he's working on his own behalf and not dissipating that vitality on the next set of neatly typed poems which Teodolinda left for him.

In the kitchen, Jack is making his medicinal tea, being very accurate with the measurement. The packet is nearly empty. He knows that I must fly, so we barely do more than greet each other as I down my porridge. We have scarcely had a moment alone together since Thursday afternoon, but he's been rather quiet at meal times. I hope the season isn't affecting him already. In little more than a quarter of an hour, I'm fit to leave and pulling on my outdoor clothes. As I hasten across the churchyard, the bell stops ringing. I slip through the door just before the sides-man closes it, and slide into the back pew.

Afterwards, Hilda is not disposed to linger when I greet her but she does throw out, as she turns to go, 'I've nearly finished my piece about Mother and Father. I'll drop it round when I've gone over it and written it out in best.'

This leads me to believe that a late afternoon knock at the door will be her. Both men, who have been dozing in their armchairs, come to with a start, as I rise to let in, with pleasure, Meg and Winnie, who have come on to see us after First Day School, where they supervise the teaching.

'You can guess why we're here,' says Meg.

'I never like to take your kindness for granted,' I say although, at the back of my mind has been the hope to see them before the dark nights begin. I twist their arms to stay for tea and Madeira cake.

'Just cut that slice in half, that'll do for us,' says Winnie.

Jack positively beams at her as he dunks his large slice.

Declining seconds, Meg draws from her bag a familiar packet which I know contains a bottle. 'There you are, Rose, your usual.'

I thank both sisters from the bottom of my heart. Ever since my bad illness in 1900, Meg and Winnie have unfailingly supplied me, at this time of year, with Hallambury's famous tonic. It was a combination of the company's special nutrient food for patients, brought home by the sisters, and my own dear Phyllis's nursing, which brought me back to health.

'And how are you doing with the nerve tonic?' Winnie asks Leonard.

'I haven't needed it for months.' As he speaks, I realise how true this is. 'So, I've still got plenty, thank you.'

'Good... good... that's very good...' Both are saying.

'We haven't forgotten you either, Jack.' Winnie reaches inside her bag, retrieving a dark bottle, labelled in the sisters' neat hand: Hypericum: St. John's Wort Tincture. 'It's not the tea this time, Jack. This is a concentrated form of the herb, which is just right for this time of year.'

'One teaspoon, twice daily,' says Meg, 'three times, if you feel the need.'

'I've written the dosage on here,' says Winnie, handing Jack the bottle.

'Oh, I'll remember that,' he says. 'Nice and easy, too - easier than the tea.'

'And if it doesn't suit you, just stop,' says Meg.

'Oh, it will,' says Jack, 'thank you both, it will.'

And it does seem to suit him. He's lost that pinched look which he had at the end of last week and though, except for Monday, I only see him when I come in from work, he's cheerful enough. And is he moving around more easily? It's hard to say. But he's certainly not worse.

If Hilda had called with her contribution to the memoir before today, Thursday, Jack and I could have read it this afternoon.

Leonard and Teodolinda have just gone up to the study. There is an inevitability about the knock on the door. I should have known this would happen.

'Oh, good, you're not busy - oh!' says Hilda, stepping inside, her eye immediately caught by the tea things I've just set out on the table.

I say, 'Leonard's helping a friend with her poetry. She's a widow.'

'Well, that's very commendable of him.'

'Her name's Tay-od-o-linda,' says Jack.

'She's Italian,' I say, 'but you can call her Linda.'

'Goodness, first name terms - I suppose they're like that over there. Are she and Leonard likely to come in? - Only I thought I'd read my piece to you.'

'That'd be nice,' says Jack.

'They'll come down for tea at about quarter past,' I say, and then, in response to the emotions crossing Hilda's face, and trying not to sound resigned, 'You're very welcome to join us.'

'I'll just stay long enough to meet her,' says Hilda, 'but I've got a meeting. I suppose I can't persuade you to join the hassocks group, Rose? - No, you were never one for crewel work.'

I usher her to Leonard's chair. While she finds her spectacles and withdraws a sheet of notepaper from its envelope, I hang her serviceable coat next to Teodolinda's with its spicy, floral scent. I sit down on the sofa.

Hilda clears her throat. 'I've given it a title. I don't know whether that's what you wanted.'

'Lovely,' I say.

'I've called it 'Easter Saturday 1885' because I think I must have been six, and that would make it right. So, 'Easter Saturday 1885. I woke up early and slipped out of bed without waking Dot, Phyllis and Rose, who were next to me, or Joe, Hubert, Ralph and Jack, who were the other end. I crept downstairs and climbed into the bunk bed with Mother -' '

'Oh, I remember that - when she slept downstairs,' says Jack. 'Must be one of my earliest memories... And Father had Rob and Edward in with him. But I seem to think that didn't last long, did it...?'

Hilda removes her spectacles to sharpen her gaze on Jack. 'I wasn't going to mention all that. In fact,' she turns to me, 'I've been in two minds about saying that Mother was in the bunk bed. I could have said: 'Mother was up already', but getting in with her for a bit was part of the happiness of the memory for me. And it's the truth!'

'I think it will be fine,' I say. 'Just go on reading - from where you'd got to.'

' 'Mother pulled me to her and we cuddled for a while. Then, she said, - Will you help me make Grandpa Alleyn welcome, Hilda, dear? He's coming for his dinner.' That's what we called it then, wasn't it? He was such a poor old thing after the accident, and Granny Alleyn had gone to look after Great-Grandma. I think she was actually dying. I haven't put any of that in. Anyway,' she finds her place again, " '– I'd like to do that, I said.

'After everyone had got up and had breakfast, Mother asked me if I would like to lay the table for dinner. I asked if we could use the best napkins, and she said, yes. They had a sweetly-pretty garland of summer flowers in one corner, which Mother had embroidered. But, of course, we only had twelve, and there would be thirteen of us with Grandpa. I was sad about this but Mother said – Just wait a moment, dear – and she came back with one of Father's handkerchiefs. – You're a neat embroiderer – she said – Just copy the three daisies here – she pointed to part of the design on the napkins. She knew I'd be able to do that before Grandpa arrived.

'I sat on the bench outside with Mother's basket of embroidery silks. She threaded the needle for me and told me to call her when I needed the thread to be cut. I worked all morning in the sunshine without pricking myself once. Ralph was in the garden, too, picking sweet peas, with Rose toddling after him. Dot was making puddings with Mother, and the other boys and Phyllis were all with Father who was chopping wood for Grandpa, which they tied in bundles and took down to his cottage, bringing him back with them.

'We all sat down to a roast dinner together, and when Grandpa saw his napkin his face lit up. – I know which little miss has sewn this – he said, and kissed the top of my head. Everyone got on well and passed each other dishes without being greedy. Then, when we'd cleared up and Grandpa and the little ones had rested, we all played hide and seek until tea time and bed. There were many other lovely days in my childhood, but this one stands out for me as being one of the best."

In the pause, my sister removes her specs and blinks, with a hesitant smile.

'Well done, Hilda,' I say, 'Thank you.' Her smile broadens. 'That's just the kind of thing I'd hoped for.'

'Yes, jolly good,' says Jack, 'takes me right back there.'

We hear the faint sound of movement overhead. 'Hello, they're coming,' I say.

Hilda fetches her outdoor clothes. 'Mmm... Lovely scent,' she says, 'and what an expensive-looking coat.'

The staircase door opens and Leonard appears, followed by Teodolinda. I make the introductions.

'I'm so sorry for your loss...er...Linda.'

'Your sympathy is greatly appreciated,' says our guest.

I can see that Hilda is agog at the sight of the Anne Boleyn -cum-Dick Turpin hat bobbing up and down. She seems uncharacteristically at a loss for words.

'Hilda plays an important part in the life of the town,' I say. 'She's the vicar's wife.'

My sister dimples with pleasure. 'A vicar's wife.' She seems to have found her voice again. 'There is more than one church in Widdock. But I expect you're more familiar with St. Patrick's and Father Keogh.'

'Actually, no,' says Teodolinda. 'I am not a Catholic - or anything. I hope that does not offend you.'

'It's all right, Hilda's used to me being a complete atheist,' says Leonard. 'Her husband, Gerald, comes round here and we have some very lively discussions.'

'How enlightened,' says Teodolinda. 'And how the three of you - ' she includes Jack in her gesture - 'complement each other. What a charming family! Not forgetting you, of course, Leonard.'

They both laugh.

'Talking of church matters, I must be on my way,' says Hilda. It was lovely to meet you, Linda.'

'The pleasure is mine,' says Teodolinda.

'I'll start pouring,' says Leonard, as I see Hilda to the door.

Against the background noises of crockery and spoons, and Teodolinda offering my plate of shortbread to Jack, the remark which Hilda makes under her breath, prior to saying good-bye: -

'Not what I'd expected,' - is, I'm glad to say, lost to any ears but mine.

I just wish I could sit back and enjoy this evening rather than having the extra imperative of trying discreetly to catch Phyllis and ask her when we might have a chat. If only she'd been at home when I dashed up to Apple Tree House between wash day's hurried lunch and the arrival of Dee and Alex. I could have talked to her then.

By the time we reach the Quaker Meeting House a polite but expectant queue is forming to get in. We stand in the peaceful courtyard, savouring the burnt toffee scent of roasting barley from a nearby malting.

We are extremely lucky to have as our speaker tonight the socialist politician Ethel Snowden, admirable on so many fronts, from promoting temperance to women's suffrage and other rights. It was she who, during the War, founded the Women's Peace Crusade, which opposed the war and called for a negotiated peace. Whilst some of our members at the October meeting of the Fabian Society, in response to a reminder about November's influential guest, muttered that a debate on the worsening situation in Ireland and possible action by the Society might have been more useful, most of us are keen to hear Lady Snowden's account of the visit made in August by a team, of which she was part, to observe how socialism, or as we would probably call it communism, was working in the country of Georgia, whose neighbour is the Russian bear. She will undoubtedly compare and contrast this visit with the one she made in the spring as part of the T.U.C./Labour Party Delegation to Russia.

Inside, the room is warm with the press of people, the pungent smell of malt giving way to traces of coal smoke trapped in woollen coats and to ladies' perfumes. My eyes are immediately drawn to our speaker - for that is who the striking, dark-haired woman of about my age is bound to be - standing by the podium and chatting to our Chairman in a relaxed but entirely authoritative way. As I glance round, searching the room, my gaze locks with that of Fred Rawlins accompanied, of course, by his equally unsmiling wife. I look away.

'Two seats here,' says Leonard, and we have to take them, or we will be left standing. There is no possibility of saving a place for Phyllis and Jenny but, just before proceedings are about to start, they come in together with Meg and Winnie. They melt into the background, where someone seems to have found them a small bench from under a table.

From the moment of her introduction, Lady Snowden takes us on an inspirational journey to Georgia, describing the informal way that people, including little children, came up to her and the other team members, telling the stories of their happy lives, with no interference from or dread of an overarching state. We hear about princes who were glad to give up their titles and enter into this socialist enterprise, workers who were enthusiastic to do their best, knowing that everyone would be fairly and equally rewarded. How different an experience this was, she told us, from that of the impartial inquiry into the Bolshevik Revolution in Russia, where every move she and the other delegates made was choreographed by the state – and watched. 'Everyone I met in Russia outside the Communist Party goes in terror of his liberty or his life...' She brings us back to the stirring Georgian picture to close her talk by summing up their remarkable achievements: free and fair elections, with a number of parties, in which women are allowed to vote; agrarian reform which has not set city and countryside at loggerheads and caused suffering, as in Russia; independent trade unions. She doesn't have a crystal ball she says, when pressed during questions but, provided the 'Little Entente' signed this August and the Armistice of last month maintain stability in central Europe, and without interference from Russia, she is cautiously optimistic. Fred Rawlins says nothing. Perhaps this is a bitter pill, given his defence of the Bolshevik regime. The vote of thanks and applause is sincere. My mind flies for a moment to Alice Baker, my holiday friend. I wonder whether she has met Ethel Snowden.

I have managed to catch Phyllis's eye, but it's difficult to cross the room for all the people in between, standing about and discussing the talk in animated tones or simply trying to make their way to the door. Meg waves and mouths 'Good', miming applause, but Winnie points to her watch, I nod and we exchange good-byes. I see that the Chairman has introduced Leonard to Lady Snowden, but I'm already making my way towards Phyllis and Jenny. We three agree that the evening was very well worthwhile.

'We didn't think we'd make it,' says Jenny. 'Trust this evening to be one where my boss needed me to stay late. I swear he does it on purpose.'

I commiserate.

'Oh well,' says Phyllis, gathering herself.

'I wonder...' I begin. She stops. 'I'd like to talk about Jack. It's a bit – well – not urgent, exactly – '

'I could call at Quinn-Harper's,' Phyllis says. 'How about tomorrow, when you close at one? I'll bring my sandwich.'

Chapter Thirteen

Instead of relying on the paraffin heater to take the chill off the air for the few times I'm in the sitting room, I light a small fire at midday.

Phyllis arrives at the shop at ten to one, while I'm wrapping up a copy of Bliss and Other Stories by Katherine Mansfield, previously published in magazines, now in one collection. I did try to hint that the title might be misleading, but Mrs. Bledington says she is ready for anything, and I remind myself that one should never underestimate one's customers. She is the widow of a man who knew Leonard's father because they were both in the malting business. When Leonard first opened his bookshop, Mr. Bledington admonished him for doing this rather than taking over his inheritance, which the man wrongly assumed to be a profitable concern. He tried to cause a great deal of harm to both of us, but we managed to outwit him and make him feel remorse. I have to work hard, though, to convince myself that what happened to him was not Divine Retribution when, on that night in 1915, he rushed outside to view, passing overhead and caught in the searchlights, a Zeppelin which dropped a stick of bombs. Mrs. Bledington, in another new hat, this one a coal-scuttle with a monstrous clump of feathers, smiles goodbye and trips off with her purchase to take luncheon among her friends.

I close up and we go through to the back, now almost cosy. Phyllis takes one of the two ancient leather armchairs by the fire while I put the kettle on one of the two rings in a little stand next to the sink, which my benefactor asked the gas company to install when they were lighting the shop. I sit down opposite my sister, who looks enquiring.

'Yes, Jack,' I say. I suddenly feel quite embarrassed, and not only about discussing my brother behind his back. 'It's just that... when you were at Sawdens, did Jack ever... I mean, I know relationships were frowned on, but was there ever anyone – '

'No,' says Phyllis, 'and that's the long and the short of it. He got on well with everyone, women included, but he never seemed to be especially fond of any one girl. - Oh, and he doesn't prefer men, in case you're wondering.'

'Perhaps, he never met the right person,' I say.

'More than likely.'

'I had the feeling that you'd confirm my conclusions,' I say. 'Thank you for coming and telling me.' I get up and make the tea.

'But that's not all, is it?' says Phyllis, gently.

I sigh. 'No. It throws light on a situation. Do you mind if I tell you? It'll help me work out how I'm going to tackle it.'

'That's what I'm here for,' says Phyllis. 'Do you mind if I eat my sandwich?'

This may be my only opportunity to have a frank chat alone with my brother arising from the intense discussion I had with Phyllis yesterday, following her corroboration of my impression about his earlier life. I'm not looking forward to it but, equally, I'd rather get it over with.

Leonard has a Town Council meeting tonight. He was co-opted back in 1900, when it was just a Parish Council, because of his concern about providing sanitary, inexpensive homes for poor people. He jokes that he has become a victim of his own success because, before the Great War, the Council was carrying out an extensive house-building programme, so much so that any plans for flood relief, which would have benefitted all the shops in Holywell End, continually gets pushed to the back of the agenda. Although the Blaken threatens to flood every winter, and sometimes does breach its banks, there has never, thank goodness, been such a flood as the one in 1900. Tomorrow being Armistice Day, this evening's meeting will no doubt be dominated by a progress report on entries for the competition to design a war memorial.

I've boiled a piece of gammon to have with cabbage and mash. I chose this option rather than for example sausages, which are quick, to avoid the possibility that Leonard's clothes might, even if he kept out of the kitchen, pick up the taint of frying and carry it into the Council Chamber with him. Dinner, this evening, is not our usual leisurely, expansive exchange of the day's occurrences. It is a means to the end of getting Leonard fed and out of the door. This is just as well because my lack of conversation, therefore, goes unnoticed.

I realise, as I stand washing the dishes, with Jack beside me drying, I feel rather hot. Never mind.

Leonard comes to say good-bye. The front door shuts behind him. I thank Jack and tell him to go through. It's quicker if I put away the dishes alone. I hear him settle himself, with a satisfied sigh, in what is now his armchair.

I join him. 'Are we going to read Dot's letter, then?' he says, as I knew he would. It arrived this morning and is on the mantelshelf.

'Not at the moment.' Instead of sitting on the sofa, so that I'm looking obliquely at him, I sit in Leonard's chair, so we are face to face, the fire between us.

I feel the shock that this unprecedented action has caused emanating from him before he says, 'What's all this about, then?'

'I'd like to ask you something, please, Jack?'

'If it's about when I'm going to leave - if Leonard's getting -'

'It has nothing to do with you leaving. You know you are very welcome here for as long as you would like to stay.' The words seem to have spoken themselves. I feel light-headed, detached, marvelling at how they came out sounding as sincere as I would want them to. But I must get a grip before Jack speaks again. 'I'm just rather concerned that Thursday afternoons are too much for you - that they're making you ill. The week before last you seemed so agitated right from the start, and you had to go up to your room, and then last week, when you went up after lunch and didn't come down -'

'Right, I see where this is going,' Jack cuts across me. 'It's just a pity you can't, Rose. The fact is, I don't like the way they look at each other - Leonard and - Old Linda - laughing and jawing - quoting stuff. I can't bear to see'em and listen to'em. And yet I have to - to make sure nothing's happening up there. Because if it was, I swear I'd -'

'So, you've been going up to your room listening -'

'I care about you, Rose. I don't want you to get hurt.'

'Dear Jack, I'm very touched, I really am, but it's all right, honestly, I won't get hurt.' I'm not being very coherent.

I take some calming breaths as Jack mutters, 'Well, I'm glad you think so, but from where I am...'

This is my cue. 'But from where I am, I know Leonard's character pretty well by now. We'll have been married twenty years come next February.'

'That's as maybe,' says Jack, 'and granted she's older, but you've only got to look at her.'

'Looks mean nothing to Leonard,' I say, enunciating the words to drive them home.

'Well, that's not true for a start,' says Jack, 'he married you and you're a good-looking woman'.

I ignore this. 'Leonard is only interested in what's inside a person. That's what he fell in love with in me. That's what he likes and admires in you.'

Jack gives a dismissive snort.

'You know that to be true. Of course, he'd always be courteous, but you'd soon know if he couldn't stand you and was merely tolerating you.'

'So, wait a minute, you're telling me that he doesn't see what a glamorous woman she is, and how she might be after a bit of fun with him.'

'Jack,' I say, feeling very hot and tired, 'she lost her beloved husband four months ago. Every time she mentions him, she's close to tears. The mere fact that she's an elegant woman who takes the edge off her grief by doing something absorbing and worthwhile doesn't mean that that grief is any the less heartfelt.'

'If you say so,' says Jack.

This is going about as badly as it could. What did I expect Jack's reaction to be? He's got his fixed idea. Nothing I say is likely to change his mind. But I have to try. With Phyllis's unemotional endorsement of this course and her staunch support, I draw breath. I feel as if I'm bleeding inside, as if what I'm about to utter will wound all three of us, which is absurd when what I hope is that it will do the very opposite of harm, that it will heal. I regulate my breathing. 'I'm going to tell you something intimate about our marriage – no, it isn't sexual, it's the very opposite, actually. Leonard sees everything in me – all the best in me, as well as the worst, but he loves everything in me, as I do in him: the physical, the emotional, the mental or, to put it another way, the intellectual. That last is very important to him. It's what first brought us together, our love of the same poets. But he sees that in other people, too. He has a particular group of friends who visit the shop. He likes their discussions. Then, there's Gerald – '

'But that's understandable,' says Jack, 'they're men.'

I close my eyes and count to three. 'But there are brainy women, too. Why do you think he enjoys his work so much? He's surrounded by intelligent women from the teacher training college. Every year, there's a new supply of fresh young minds to engage with him on subjects which he loves. They keep his mind sharp. And yes, I've seen how, over the years, one or two of them have fallen for him – the dashing raven-haired bookshop owner with such dark blue eyes. It's hardly surprising. But the mind is as far as it goes. Do you understand me?' Jack nods, but I'm not sure he's convinced. 'If I were to tell Leonard what you've been suspecting – no, I'm not going to – he'd firstly look incredulous, blank even, because he'd have to think about Teodolinda's physical appearance and what you're suggesting, and then he'd probably chuckle. But he'd also be rather regretful that he'd feel he had to curb his natural spontaneity in case you were getting any further ideas – which is why I'm not going to mention this conversation to him. Does that allay your fears, Jack?'

'Well, you've given me a lot to think about,' says my brother.

'Good,' I start to rise, 'because I'm actually – ' I sneeze violently three times and scrabble for my handkerchief. After I've blown my nose, I tell Jack that, as I'm feeling rather feverish, I shall take my tonic and go up to bed.'

'Is there anything I can do?' says Jack, rising, his face a picture of anguished concern.

I assure him there isn't, and say good night. I sneeze again. In the old days, as I now think of them, if I'd thought myself to be infectious, I'd have gone and slept in the other room. No, there's nothing you can do to help me, Jack, though in a way you have just done so by simply letting me go. A different mind from yours might have had questions for me.

As it turns out, I am too ill to go to work. My customers will simply think I have elected, as some others have, to close all day it being both Armistice Day and Thursday. I get up for a short while in the morning to air the bedroom. Jack and I observe the Two Minutes' Silence. I think of Mrs. Fuller and Beatrice down in Cornwall doing the same thing, the three of us mourning dear Miles, who stands for all those others including the Unknown Warrior, whose funeral took place today at Westminster Abbey prior to the unveiling of the permanent Cenotaph.

This time it is I, puffed up with cold, who do not wish to encounter Teodolinda – or give her my illness, so I retreat to the sick bed leaving Leonard and Jack to serve tea in their break, along with a plate of the macaroons which Leonard bought at Askeys. As I drift, I can hear Jack's voice sounding normal, part of a general conversation, and Leonard mentions afterwards how amicable and helpful he had been.

But Jack is the next casualty of my wretched infection, keeping him confined to his bed for most of Friday, when I force myself back to work too early. Leonard succumbs on Saturday, letting Louisa Briggs take over in the afternoon and coming home to bath – the blessed relief of steam inhalation – and bed. I'm getting better, but will not be strong enough either to go to Church on Sunday or cycle up to the South Side to see Lettie on the morning of her birthday. Knowing this, I drop a card in at Giffords on my way home, shattered from work, on Saturday. 'You and my birthday,' says Lettie, 'you're always missing it!' This is entirely untrue, but she never forgets that time in 1900 when I was so ill I lost the complete month of November. I would have enjoyed seeing my brother Hubert and dear Tom and Alex – and Lettie herself. I find on the mat, that evening, a card which she must have delivered on her way home from work later than me: a rose garland encircling an open book upon whose pages are written: Get Well Soon.

An enclosure falls out of Dot's envelope when, eventually, Jack and I open it late on Sunday, Leonard still in bed with the papers.

Jack reads it out loud:

Recipe for Ten Happy Alleyns

Ingredients
10 heaped tablespoons of Mother's love
10 heaped tablespoons of Father's love

Method
Mix well.
Warm in a loving home over the years
When risen to full extent, turn out into the world
Yield: 10 Alleyns, Happy and Whole

'I like that,' he says.

I read Dot's letter:

Sawdens
9th November 1920

Dear Rose,

In haste, as ever. I don't suppose this is really what you wanted, but once I'd had the idea I couldn't get it out of my head. It doesn't include dear little Jim and Annie, who were also happy Alleyns while they were alive, God bless them – or the two that hardly got started, of course – Paul and Lucy, weren't they? And it doesn't apply to poor Joe, as he is now, but you did say 'happy childhood memories.' I hope it'll do.
With much love,
Dot
xxx

When I last saw this handsome Georgian house, the trees of its parkland were still opulent in late summer greenery. Now their tracery is a foil to the solidity of warm red brick, the pleasing symmetry of windows whose white-painted woodwork lifts the spirits. On this afternoon in late November, leaning towards dusk, all the ground floor windows are lamp-lit, enhancing their air of welcome.

Mrs. White greets us, taking our coats, and we step further into the hall where a fire leaps in the grate bringing to intermittent life, on the surrounding walls, the shadowy portraits of Watson ancestors in their gilt frames. Completely at one with them and their graceful setting, a smiling Teodolinda approaches in an elegant dark gown whose serrated hem, like delicate tongues, floats around her slender ankles. She leads us over to a trestle covered in a snowy linen cloth, at one end of which is a tea tray, at the other slender glasses and two large copper pans on tea lights. The pungency of blackcurrant and the delicious aroma of cloves, orange and mulled wine can already be detected.

'You are very welcome to join us in the library,' she says to Jack and me, 'but Leonard and I will be concentrating on the choice of poems to be submitted for publication and the accompanying letter. It might be rather boring. Feel free to roam.' She gestures towards the rest of the house.

'I'll just sit here and drink my tea,' says Jack.

When I've had mine, I wander into the adjacent room, a large salon with a beautifully moulded ceiling, more paintings, and French windows looking out to the garden. Over the fireplace is a large, gilt-framed mirror. Two candelabra have been placed on the mantelpiece, and another free-standing one has been set by a lectern, to one side of the fire. Two rows of spindly chairs form an intimate circle.

Through the doors on the other side is a drawing room, slightly masculine in its sensibility yet still comfortable. This room leads me out into the hall. As its grandfather clock chimes, the door to the library opens.

'Yes, we're all set,' says Leonard.

'As well as confirming our choice of English poems,' says Teodolinda, 'your husband has kindly helped me choose my six best Italian poems, which he suggests I send to a publication based in Rome.'

'But don't expect to hear from either, English or Italian, before Christmas,' Leonard says.

'That suits my plans very well,' says Teodolinda, but doesn't expand on this because we hear the crunch of hooves and carriage wheels on gravel.

Mr. White has been to the station to pick up Lettie, Hubert, Tom and Alex. Since the men of the family are not at work, it's a rare treat to see these Alleyns all together as they come through the door and surrender their outer clothes.

'This is very kind of you, inviting us,' says Hubert, when introduced.

'How could I not include you, especially when I believe you have something to read to us,' says Teodolinda - or Linda, as she is for the rest of the evening. Hubert has the original of his contribution to our childhood memories.

Lettie, of course, already has a relationship with Linda. She takes her hand and steps back gazing at her. 'Aaaah... the midnight blue mulberry silk,' she purrs. 'You suit it to a tee.'

And now I see that Linda's gown is the most exquisite shade of deepest blue, like Leonard's eyes.

Lettie, too, looks very striking in a crimson dress with deep-lapelled jacket bodice ending at a drop waist, skirt at mid-calf. I voice my admiration.

'And that was a good choice for you, the russet velvet,' she says to me with the satisfaction of a successful saleswoman.

I tell Alex, who looks rather down in the mouth, that her sage green dress is pretty, too.

'I think it's beastly,' she says, 'drab.'

'No, no it brings out the red in your hair,' I say, 'and it's stylish.'

'Very,' adds Linda.

'Do I look stylish?' Tom poses. Alex moves to clout him.

'Mind the table,' their father says.

While all this talk of clothing has been going on Leonard, who always manages to look stylish despite his lack of interest in appearance, has been chatting to Jack sitting by the fire. Now, he moves to the door behind Mrs. White at the sound of the next arrivals, Hilda, Gerald and Dee, getting out of Olly Bates's cab.

Hilda is statuesque in royal blue, which complements her eyes, as grey shows Dee's fairness to advantage. It also mollifies Alex to find her cousin likewise in a subtle shade. All the men, it should be said, have managed to find an approximation of evening wear, however old. Gerald, who gets round any such requirement by wearing clerical dress, thanks Linda for the invitation in similar terms to Hubert.

'I had to meet the rest of the family, having met your charming wife,' Linda says.

Hilda beams.

A now familiar din outside heralds the arrival of Phyllis and Jenny.

'These are smart,' I say of their leather coats, gauntlets and hats with earflaps.

'And practical,' says Jenny.

'Keeps the wind out – almost,' says Phyllis.

Linda, when introduced, takes the hand of each and gazes from one to the other with a warm smile. 'You even exceed my expectations.'

All who haven't a tapering glass of either vin brule or hot blackcurrant take one and move through to the salon. Phyllis and Jenny steal the fashion show, I think, in their straight, ankle-length tabards, Jenny's the colour of young green corn, Phyllis's the powder-blue of the sky above it for, as they move, the skirts split into four sections from the thigh, revealing glimpses of their slim leather breeches.

There is a flutter like birds settling for the night as the audience takes its seat in the beautiful room now bathed in candlelight. I'm relieved that, although all my brothers and sisters could have wanted to read their contributions to the memoir, they are happy simply for Hubert to represent us. More than this might have seemed indiscreet, when the evening is a celebration of Linda's work, with an acknowledgment of Leonard's.

I stand up and say how generous it is of Linda to invite us all – murmurs of 'yes' – and what a welcome diversion it is from recent sobering events. Everyone knows I mean the bloodshed in Ireland. More murmurs in solemn tones. 'But I'd like to say a special thank you to – Linda,' I've become so used to the longer name, 'because it's rare to have a gathering of Alleyns as there's rather a lot of us – '

'Leonard's birthday,' Jack intervenes, 'and that was back in May.'

Happy murmuring.

'Precisely,' I say, 'and thinking of Leonard, I'd like us all to express our thanks to Linda simply by holding our hands together as if clapping.'

Everyone understands immediately and does this.

'Well, thank you for coming,' says Linda. 'I can't wait to get to know you all better.'

I explain that Leonard will read a poem, followed by two from Linda, 'and then, given that in three days' time it'll be Advent – ' – muted exclamations about time flying – 'we'll conclude with a seasonal reminiscence from Hubert. Again, I'd ask you, please, to resist the urge to clap.'

'We've got it,' says Jack, 'we'll just do this.' He raises his hands, palms together.

I sit down, Leonard stands and, after a moment of hush, reads from his East Coast Sequence, much to the particular pleasure of Dee and Alex, the former looking quite transported. After we've all held our hands together, he introduces Linda, saying how we met at an earlier reading, and how helping her fine-tune her poetry has been a pleasure.

Linda thanks him and reads her 'Figs' poem. Then, she says, 'Leonard kindly did not mention my dear late husband, I'm sure for fear that the emotion would affect my ability to read – and perhaps it will – but I should like to say how I wish Jeremy could have met a like mind such as Leonard – and dear Rose and Jack – indeed you all.'

There is an audible sigh of sympathy.

Then, Linda gathers herself and reads a poem simply entitled For Jeremy.

> 'I would run to the Campo de' Fiore
> And buy up every bloom, place them in crystal,
> Displayed at every window, so the light
> Would catch them. The scent would fill every room.
>
> I would beg the mulberry worm to yield
> Its precious thread, and I would spin it into
> The finest cloth, which I would match with stitches
> So you would think that you were wearing clouds.
>
> I would sprinkle veal escalopes with lemon,
> Secure a slice of thin ham, prosciutto,
> Over each, rub them with fresh sage, and fry,
> Adding a dry Frascati. Three minutes more,
> And I would serve the dish, your favourite:
> Saltimbocca, which means: jump into the mouth,

It's so good. I'd do all these things to hear
That clear tenor voice singing an aria
From La Traviata, and see you, clad
In silk, stepping through the door, your dear face
Lighting up to see me and the food we'll share.'

She manages it all with only a tremor in the final two lines. As she sits down, I clasp her hand.

Everyone is moved. Leonard allows a moment of complete quiet before standing, thanking Linda and then introducing Hubert, 'who will bring a change of mood.'

'Well, I don't know whether I can follow that,' my brother says.

'Please,' says Linda, 'it's what we all want to hear,' which is, of course, the truth.

So Hubert stands and, summoning the authority of a station master, reads, with a good deal of background 'yes, yes', 'that's right', and laughter in the appropriate places during the course of it:

'Christmas 1881

We'd all woken up early, of course, in the dark. Joe and I were sharing one end of the bed with Rob and Ted. At the other were Dot, Hilda, Phyllis and Ralph. He was only a toddler, so he didn't count as a boy. We all found our stockings and sat peeling and eating our oranges. No one had been downstairs in the bunk bed that night because we'd been told that Father Christmas might need to have a rest in it – and we certainly didn't want to disturb him while he might be leaving presents, in case he got angry and decided to take them away again with him, but we couldn't keep very quiet because we were too excited. It wasn't long before we heard Mother and Father talking and moving, so we got up.

I can remember us all tip-toeing downstairs, and Mother putting her finger to her lips and saying, 'Sh...' because the bunk bed looked as though there was someone still asleep in it, all the bedclothes were piled as if round a body. So, we ate our porridge very quietly – and quickly. Then, Father said, 'Why don't you have a look and see if he's still there?' And, suddenly, I think we were all a bit scared, but Bob, being oldest, went and gingerly turned back the sheet – and there, instead of Father Christmas, was a wonderful trainset with an engine and tender, a carriage and a truck and a lot of track, all carved by Father. Bob and Ted seized the track and started putting it together, Joe and I both made a grab for the engine. While we were arguing over that the girls had taken the rest of the train and were filling it with the little dollies Father had carved for them, dressed by Mother. Joe was getting a bit rough with me, though I expect he'd say it was because I was being annoying, so that was the point where we were all told to stop, and we had to learn about sharing – having a certain amount of time with our favourite piece and then letting it go.

It was altogether a lovely Christmas Day, with enough turkey for everyone, even the old wayfarer – ('I remember him,' from Hilda) 'who used to come – until one year he didn't. I think I went to sleep that night clutching a bit of the train set. It might have been the engine.'

Hubert looks up with a smile to our profound mimed applause.

I give another vote of thanks to all concerned, then Linda tells us that supper will be served in the dining room. We cross the hall and enter another lovely room, bright with candles, silver and a good blaze in the hearth.

'A fire in every room,' comments Lettie. 'You're not worried there'll be another strike then, Linda?'

'Normally, my needs are modest,' our hostess answers, 'so why not enjoy some luxury amongst friends?'

We start to seat ourselves.

'Besides,' she adds, 'I'd rather burn my coal now than come back from Italy to find it has been stolen.'

'Oh,' says Leonard, sitting on her right, me next to him, 'you're going away then?'

'Next week,' she says. 'Please, gentlemen, perhaps you would pour the wine, while I organise the food. The Franciacorta is a sparkling white and, as you can see the Barolo is red. There is also cordial.'

She goes over to a dumb waiter in the corner, we women rise to help her and, very soon, everyone has been served and grace has been said by Gerald. We are eating gnocchi di polenta, corn meal dumplings with mushroom and ham sauce, which Linda explains is a dish from her region, Lombardy. A beef stew is also available, stufatino, a word whose lightly lengthened second vowel, between the f and the t causes so much amusement to Tom that he has to ask for seconds, deliberately lengthening the a still further, 'stu-fartino,' his father telling him to shut up. Linda graciously overcomes the situation by informing us that, as the rest of the title - all Romana - implies, the dish comes from Rome, where she has lived for many years and still has a house.

'Will you be back from Italy for Christmas?' Hilda leans past Gerald to ask. 'Because we'd be very pleased if you'd join us for the day at The Vicarage, wouldn't we, Gerald?'

'We certainly would,' says Gerald, perhaps a shade too eagerly, because he tones it down with the qualification, 'if you don't have other commitments, of course.'

'You are most kind,' says Linda, 'but I shall be away till after the New Year.'

The image of Linda alone here over the festive period has been gnawing at my conscience. Hilda's charitable words were, therefore, a reproach to me. But with Linda's answer, a weight lifts from inside me. I relax and enjoy the conversation which now seems to be flowing up, down, across between my dear family and the benign presiding presence at the head of the table.

The evening draws to a close in the most delightful way. Whilst coats and hats are being fetched, Clair de lune drifts out from the salon, where Jenny is playing the grand piano. Phyllis started to learn to read music as soon as they became friends.

She is now a faithful, trustworthy page-turner. They make an impressive couple.

Chapter Fourteen

Fairview
South Parade
York
11th December 1920

Dear Rose,

Further to my last, I have reconsidered your request for a contribution to your collection of our happy childhood memories. Given that one came to me unbidden, it would seem ungenerous not to share it. I hope it gives you pleasure.

What I remember chiefly, however, and have not, for obvious reasons, included is how the occasion described was the first time I'd seen Mother well in the morning for what seemed like a long time. I believe she was carrying Jack, so that would explain it. Also, I don't recall such presents again. We had to make do in subsequent years when there were even more of us.

Anyway, here it is. Let me know how Father takes it. You might be pleased to hear that I've written to Hubert.

Give my best wishes for the season to Leonard and Jack.

Your affectionate brother,
Joe

Christmas 1881

I was woken up by someone kicking me. It was early in the morning and we were all very excited. We got up and I managed to help Rob and Ted organise the others so that they didn't immediately rush into Mother and Father's room. We sat and ate our oranges but, inevitably, the little ones couldn't keep quiet and soon we heard voices. Mother came in to say we could go downstairs with her, but not to wake Father Christmas, who was asleep in our bunk bed. We could see his shape under the blankets. So, we ate our porridge very quietly. Then, Father told us we could give him a prod. We were slightly nervous about this in case we made him angry and he took our presents away with him but we, the boys that is, summoned our courage and pulled the covers back.

Father had made a superb toy engine. He said it was called The Rocket. Of course, it was nothing like it, but we didn't know that. Coupled to the engine were a tender, carriage and truck. There was also an excellent length of 1 gauge track, which could be formed to make a loop. I was torn between putting the track together and going for the engine, and in that moment of indecision, Rob and Ted grabbed the track and Hubert made a lunge for the engine. He was being quite dog in a manger about it, though he'd probably say I was being rough. Meanwhile, the girls were messing about, putting their dolls in the other parts of the train. It got a bit unruly. Father clapped his hands and said, 'Enough!' We all stopped. Mother told us to listen. When we were quiet, she gave us roles: crew; station staff, including guard and signalman; and passengers. Then, she improvised a shift system. At shift change time we had to swap, so we all had a go at being someone different. In that way, we settled down and enjoyed ourselves with no more cross words. A perfect Christmas Day.

St. Barnabas Vicarage
Greychapel
27th December 1920

Dear Rose,
Please forgive me, if you can, for not responding to the thoughtful note, full of news, enclosed with your Christmas card. I have been a little unwell over the last few months, but nothing to worry about – indeed, quite the opposite. I'm pleased to tell

you that I am pregnant. My baby will be due in June, which I seem to remember is your birthday month, and a lovely one. Sam walks on air!

I should very much have liked to hear Ethel Snowden. It sounds a fascinating evening. I met her briefly through Sylvia Pankhurst. One hopes so much for those people in Georgia.

I'm glad to hear that Jack is making steady progress.

Perhaps we might meet in the spring. It would be lovely to see you.

Do give Leonard our fondest wishes, and remember to look after yourself.

With much love from us both,
Alice

I write back straightaway. This is wonderful news for our friends.

Ash Manor
Cottering
18th January 1921

Dear Rose and Leonard,

I do hope that you had an enjoyable Christmas. Thank you for your note, Rose. I very much enjoyed having you and your family here, so it was no trouble. Indeed, it was like a little Christmas.

I'm sorry not to have been in touch since I returned from Italy. The truth is that I was rather dismayed to receive a rejection letter from the magazine you recommended, Leonard. They 'very much liked your poems, but not enough to publish them'. I delayed writing to tell you because I did not wish to burden you with this news with which I, myself, have come to terms.

I have plenty to keep me occupied here, so do not worry about me.

Con molto affetto,
Teodolinda

We write by return of post.

3 Blessings Yard
Widdock
19th January 1921

Cara Teodolinda,
We're both so sorry to hear that your poems didn't find favour with 'The Cut' – more fool them! Please do not be disheartened. This has happened to me countless times. One simply has to re-group and send them elsewhere. (See attached page of further possible magazines, with my comments – for what they are worth.)
Very best wishes,
Leonard

Dear Teodolinda,
I echo Leonard. I think you are very brave to send your work out, so I'm full of admiration. The poems of yours which I have heard are truly lovely. If those editors can't appreciate them, that is their loss.
Perhaps we could meet again in the spring, when the evenings are lighter.
With love,
Rose

This arrives next day...

Meadow Cottage
Riverdale
January 2nd 1921

Dear Rose,

We trust this finds you in good health and not champing at the bit too much for our contribution to your memoir of our parents. There was no time before Christmas as you'll understand, being yourself in retail. You'll see this is a joint effort. We found we both had fixed on a really early memory. It's not that there weren't many later heart-warming recollections, but this one spoke the loudest. Furthermore, Joe would only have been a baby and none of the rest of you were around at all, so maybe it contributes another strand which you will find interesting and, we hope, entertaining.

Just to let you know, we're planning a trip over later in the year. Will write again. Please give our regards to Leonard, Jack and the rest of the family.

Happy New Year!
Your loving brothers,
Rob x and Ted x

Recollections from around 1876-77

Ted says:
It has the feeling of a summer evening, the light falling on the diamond shapes of small wooden tiles – soft, dark oak, honeyed beech. Mother is showing me how to slot them together to make a perfect square with a balanced pattern.
Rob says:
Then, Father draws from his pocket more of these shapes, so we have enough each not to squabble. We start to make a wooden mat, if you will. Our creation has its own luster.
Ted says:
Above us now, at the table, Father sits with a book, Mother next to him. I can hear his voice stumbling over the words

his finger underlines. He has a pencil and the blue paper bag the sugar came in.

Rob says:

I seem to think he found it easier than white paper when he tried to write. It didn't hurt his eyes or make the letters jump.

Ted says:

What I remember, which I guess is why this evening sticks in my mind, is that suddenly the sense of tension, which built every time Mother tried to teach Father to read and write - even though she was the gentlest of teachers, and he was keen to learn, I get all of that impression still - suddenly the tension snapped.

Rob says:

My recollection is slightly different than Ted's, in that I'm pretty sure I had a board book open in my hands. I couldn't read, of course, but I was enjoying the shapes and colors. Mother gently put her hands over Father's and smiled into his eyes. She must have said something like 'let's quit.' In that moment, it was as if I looked into the book I was holding and could read it - as if the letters were grouping themselves into words which she had taught me at that very point rather than later when, of course, she did teach me. They both just laughed then, so happily.

Ted says:

And then they sat in their comfortable chairs, and Mother read the newspapers to Father. They were relaxed and enjoying themselves. That was one of Father's favorite pass times after work, wasn't it? I guess that happy feeling made us happy, too.

I let the papers fall on the kitchen table where I'm sitting alone, Leonard having gone to work, Jack not yet up. I quietly open the door into the garden, slip into my pattens and shawl and step outside. Last night's snow fall lies disconsolate in shrinking patches on lawn and borders. I hear the tiny drip of meltwater from the gutter.

I walk to the heart of the garden, by the apple tree. A mild, damp wind blows up from the south. I close my eyes and feel the earth's heartbeat, as I did when I blessed this tree with the Wassail Cup, as we always did at home. On Twelfth Night, I felt the earth turning in its sleep, now I sense it shaking, rousing. Although my project is at an end - I have all the recollections which my brothers and sisters have kindly and lovingly donated - this feels like a beginning. As I sniff the soft air whose droplets of moisture kiss my face and nestle in my loose hair, I realise the way in which, without intention, my parents' story has unfolded. I would not wish to change that order, only to complete it with the tale we have all heard told so many times that its music has become a part of our own history.

Summer 1873

Lydia hears the soft sounds of her mother moving about her bedroom, the click of the brush laid down on the dressing-table. She makes her way quietly downstairs and opens the kitchen door. Father's up already, of course, making the most of the one day when he can do the work he wants to, the work he loves.

It is a perfect summer morning, the sky already as blue as it must be in Heaven. He will have been up since first light deadheading roses, preparing his plants to go to Saturday market in the nearest town. Lydia can smell his pipe smoke coming from behind the rows of scarlet runners, can hear his gentle, tuneless crooning as he caresses leaves, checks his crop.

The smile between them speaks more than words, as she picks up a shallow basket and takes the path right down to the end of the garden, anticipating the delicate, scented joy of fresh raspberries.

Time must have passed, for she can hear Mother's gentle tones calling from the kitchen. She joins Father in hastening up the path. Her stomach growls. She's looking forward to her breakfast.

But before they reach the back step, where her mother is standing, Lydia can sense her agitation.

'He's come early,' Mother whispers. 'In the parlour.'

It must be the carpenter about the bookcase, her bookcase. Her heart expands with joy at the thought of her parents' generosity. How she will fill those shelves with all her favourites.

'You may go in and speak to him, Lydia,' Father says. 'You know exactly what you want. You can call us when you need us.'

So, she tries to walk confidently into the room, as a person might who is about to transact business. But it isn't old Mr. Alleyn. It's his son, Robert.

'Good Morning, Miss Clarke,' he says, smiling directly into her eyes.

And the warmth her heart felt earlier is as nothing compared to the leap it gives now, the heat of which suffuses her cheeks, her whole body. For a moment, she cannot speak.

I am shaking. I put down my pen. This is the start of everything.

Meadow Cottage
Markly
25th January 1921

Dear Rose,

Thank you so much for your letter. I'm glad to hear you're both well, and that Jack is improving. Thank you, too, for your kind invitation to join you and Leonard in your special celebration. We had to laugh at Leonard's quip: milestone, not millstone! He's very good with words. What a year of weddings 1901 was for our family!

It would certainly be lovely to come to Widdock and lunch with you both at The Railway Hotel, just as we did afterwards on the day. Tempting though the prospect is, however, your father says he would worry just as much as he did then about leaving the mare that long. Besides which, this one's had some problems with lameness. Thank goodness she's in her winter stable, not out on our field, so our grass can't be blamed for that! But we couldn't rely on her being roadworthy so, regretfully, I think we'll have to plump for the other option, the benefit of which is that we will see you sooner.

Either of the two dates in February you suggest would be convenient, so just let us know, when you know yourself, which it is to be. Weather permitting, it will be lovely to have your company for the day. We look forward to hearing all the recollections of your parents which you and your brothers and sisters have recorded.

With love from your father and me,
Grace

The two dates in contention for the visit arise because, even before I wrote with my invitation here, I guessed what Father's frame of mind would be. So, I'd already voiced my thoughts to Phyllis: would cycling to Markly be too much for me, did she think? Should I suggest to Leonard hiring a tandem? 'Leave it to me,' she said, and the next thing was Meg and Winnie, smiling at our door.

All we await now is the Sunday when Mrs. Fuller and Beatrice, back since Christmas and getting ready for an exhibition of their work in London, go out to Sunday lunch, thus leaving Phyllis free till five in the evening. 'And, honestly, Phyllis, if we can't boil ourselves an egg, we're as bad as the upper classes, so go with our blessing.' Phyllis and Jenny will lead to show the way, Winnie and Meg will follow. They'll make a day trip of it.

It turns out that Jack's got a leather jacket and gauntlets. They're both rather large on me, but as I shan't be required to do anything more than sit and observe my surroundings, this won't matter. In fact, it allows me to wear as many woollen layers underneath as I can pack in without discomfort.

'No, I don't envy you,' says Jack. 'I would if you were on the bike, but not bouncing along in that box.'

I hope he's wrong about the bouncing.

We pray that this fine, dry spell will hold.

'Pity you couldn't make an earlier start,' says Jack, 'you've got a perfect day for it.'

Both men are sitting in the living room, Leonard with the Sunday papers. The sun is streaming in through the window where I am standing, dressed in the leather coat and a woollen hat, looking down the yard for the first sight of Meg, Winnie and their vehicle. They will be coming straight from The Friends' Meeting House. I am holding two bags, one with the book of memories, the other with Jack's gauntlets and a jar of marmalade for Meg and Winnie, though I expect they'll have made their own. Since sugar went off ration in December, everyone's been baking and preserving. Still, my marmalade will taste different from theirs.

'Your trip should be very enjoyable,' Leonard says, a shade wistfully.

'Mmn...' Although I was profoundly relieved when I woke up to a fine morning, I'm feeling slightly queasy with nerves, so I can't manage a more enthusiastic assent.

'Actually,' Leonard says, 'I could cycle over to Cottering after lunch – see how Teodolinda is...'

'They're here!' I grab my shawl.

If I were any bigger, I would be packed into this snub-nosed bullet like a pea in a pod. As it is, I am secured with Meg and Winnie's rug wrapped round my legs and my shawl around my shoulders. I still feel very exposed though, as the sisters wheel the motorcycle up the yard. I turn and wave back at the two men in the cottage doorway. Then, we're under the arch and into East Street. Meg hops aboard the pillion seat and Winnie starts the machine which fires up at the first go. Now we're moving, and my nerves are right up in my mouth, as the familiar shops slide slowly past on either side, funnelling the din of the engine. I feel every vibration, and how close I am to the road beneath me. I'm holding my breath, as the whole elaborate contraption turns into New Road and the speed increases, held in check only by the need to slow when we come to the church half way up, from which members of the congregation spill in dribs and drabs, some crossing in front of us. I gaze through the tall windscreen - and there - yes - two figures on a motorcycle ease into view. The driver, inscrutable in goggles, turns and, as we come up the hill, waits till we are just behind, then lets the machine slide elegantly off.

We pass the cottages on either side at the top of the hill once, no doubt, a hamlet in its own right. There's the little public house, part of the terrace, and there's the cottage where Mrs. Munns lived, who used to clean for Mrs. Fuller at Apple Tree House. Now, we're out in open country on by-roads I don't know, bare tilled fields on either side of us, bounded by winter hedgerows and the stark tracery of trees against a clear blue sky. I feel every rut and pebble in the dirt road. We turn again. The sun is in our eyes, so we must be travelling due east - and yes, we've joined the Markly Road. On the off-side are riparian meadows, and that steely glimmer catching at the corner of my eye is our River Esh.

The speed increases along with the noise and vibration. I screw my eyes tight shut. The screen keeps the wind directly from my face, but cold air rushes around me. I feel in the grip of danger. The speed levels off. I open my eyes, determined to overcome my fear, to take in everything. I look up at the two monolithic figures beside me in their leathers and goggles. Meg must sense my gaze because she glances down with a smile, which I return.

Here, already, is Hadle Street, the village between Widdock and Markly. We pass gently through its sleepy high street and out into rolling countryside. The air is fresh and sweet. I take in great drafts of it, almost make myself dizzy.

As if in a dream, we have arrived in dear Markly, always smaller than I remember it. The Green Man is just about to open. We pass Father's workshop and the smithy and out the other side, with Dr. Jepp's house, the last in the village, the field between it and us, and now, Phyllis is turning off the road into the tree-lined lane running parallel with our meadow. I feel the difference under us from compacted dirt to leaf cover. She cuts the engine as we draw up level with the cottage, home.

'She doesn't let the grass grow under her feet, does she, our Phyllis?' says Father, as we wave the motor-cyclists off.

'They could all have stayed for dinner,' says Cousin Grace.

'They didn't want to impose,' I say. They are going to have a look round Stortree, a town even further east, and lunch at a coaching inn.

'H'mn,' says Father, as if he's deduced this and doesn't think much of it.

I ask if I may take a turn round the garden. I feel quite stiff and shaky after my adventure. Cousin Grace looks relieved that this allows her to go and get on. So, Father leads me to his rows of January Kings, and cuts one for us to have with the pot roast, which Grace wrote that we would have because it wouldn't spoil if I was delayed on the journey. This good sense inspired me to leave the same meal for Leonard and Jack, which they could eat when they were ready, with some of Leonard's leeks – if they remember in time to put them on. I feel the sweet stillness of this spot and would stay, musing amongst the gnarled winter perennials, but Father moves to go inside. As I turn to face the cottage, with the bench by the door and Mother's venerable rose next to it, which in summer would wreathe the whole front in fragrance, I am almost overcome.

While we are eating, I ask after George. It seems strange even to me for him not to be here, so what it must be like for the people who brought him up and have nursed him since his return from the War, I cannot think. But they're both smiling as Grace tells me that, yes, he really does seem on the mend – she touches wood – and he's settling in at Sawdons, where Master Hector has found a job for him in the Estate Office. He now lives under the same roof as his birth mother yet, truly, these are just as much his parents. My enquiry, inevitably, prompts one from them about Jack and – we all touch wood again – I tell them that he's taking short walks now and feels better in himself. In fact, I don't add this, he's told me he no longer needs to take his remedy. 'If he feels better, then he'd better start looking for a job,' says Father. I tell him Jack's already raised this proposition.

I help Grace clear away the dishes but she says, 'No, we'll just leave them in soak. I can do them afterwards,' so I don't argue. I wondered how she would feel about hearing our memories of the woman who was Father's wife before her, but both of them seem utterly composed, solid in their own love for each other. Father is sitting in his armchair. Grace perches on a chair next to him, insisting I take her rocking chair, formerly Mother's.

She and I take it in turns to read a recollection each, ending of course with mine, which I have practised so many times I now can read it without a wobble. I look up when I am done. Father has his wife's hand clasped in his lap. They both look slightly glassy eyed.

'I didn't see your mother often,' says Cousin Grace, 'but I always thought she was someone special - now I know it.'

Father clears his throat. 'When we were at school, I used to think about her, even when we were quite young. She always had a kind word for everyone. Then, when I got older, I realised she wasn't for the likes of me, a carpenter. After I left, I used to see her walking past, going to help the schoolmistress. I think she would have taken that job over, if I hadn't... I don't know what got into me that Saturday morning. Normally, my father would have gone to take any orders. It made sense. I mean, after his accident, he wasn't up to a great deal in the workshop. But that morning, I got up early and beat him to it before he'd even had his breakfast – or the Clarke's had had theirs.' He smiles to himself. 'I couldn't believe how... she seemed to like me. I kept thinking I'd imagined it, but when I went back with the bookcase... no, I hadn't. So, I plucked up my courage and asked if she would consider walking out with me and she said, if her parents agreed, then yes. They were good people, the Clarkes. They told us to make sure of how we felt about each other, so they made us wait six months, but they weren't like a lot of people when they heard about Father and the drink, even though he never touched a drop again. The Clarkes always accepted me.' The grandfather clock ticks, a coal shifts, and Father comes out of his reverie. 'I have been married to dear Grace, here, for almost as long as I was married to your mother, and I can honestly say I have never been happier,' with which announcement, he squeezes his wife's hand.

I think both Grace and I are rather taken aback by his heartfelt eloquence and demonstration of affection, but before there's time to be embarrassed, we hear the dull roar of approaching motorcycles. Father thanks me for organising the recollections, and for the copy I've made of them. 'Would you put it in Mother's bookcase, please?'

Yes, they will come in for a cup of tea. All are in high spirits.

'They thought Phyl was a man,' Jenny giggles.

'A table for four, certainly sir,' Phyllis mimics. 'May we take sir's coat?'

'They didn't want us going into the dining room in leathers,' says Meg.

'But they had quite a shock when we turned out to be women,' says Winnie.

They're all giggling, but Phyllis says, 'It would be interesting to know whether they'd have been willing to serve us if they'd grasped we were four females on our own.'

Father asks about Mrs. Fuller, for whom he's always had a great deal of respect. Phyllis says that she and Beatrice were disgusted with the Council's boring choice of winning entry for the War Memorial competition last month: a plain wall. 'The cheapest option,' she says.

Jenny tells them about next month's London exhibition of their Cornish work. 'Then, they'll be back down there for the summer.'

'It strikes me,' Father says, 'you might do well to start looking for another home.'

Although his pronouncement doesn't exactly cast a shadow, it heralds the sense of it being time to go. As always, it is a wrench to leave my former home.

It's getting colder, and the motorcyclists think I should have the hood up. This fits to the windscreen, so I'm in a box with only the view straight ahead. As we bowl along, I turn over what Father said, which seemed to come as no surprise to Phyllis and Jenny. I know they love The Byre. The thought of them not living there fills me with sadness. These reflections are interrupted by the fact that it really is very cold now. The closer we get to Widdock, the more I'm overtaken by an urgent need, not helped by the vibration and jolts I receive every time a wheel hits stones in the road.

I can hardly think of another thing as we coast into East Street, and am getting myself out of the rug as the engine dies and the sisters hop off the motorcycle, Winnie to wheel it under the arch, Meg to push back the hood.

'I'm so sorry, I'm busting,' I blurt as I clamber out. I push the jar of marmalade at my delighted friends. 'Thank you so much both of you.'

'Go!' They chorus.

I run down the passage by the side of No.1, along the alley past their garden, fling open our back gate and hurtle down the path to the privy. I race inside and find relief.

Nudging the kitchen door open, I let my bag and shawl fall soundlessly on the table. I can hear the men's low voices in the sitting room. I quietly rinse my hands. There is something serious about their tones. I step closer to the closed door between us, wondering whether I should interrupt them.

'...Oh, well, apart from sunstroke, malaria and flies - you know all about that lot,' Leonard is saying, clearly in answer to a question, 'the noise, undoubtedly. We had the Royal Navy guns shelling over our heads from the Red Sea. Ear-splitting, the bombardment.'

I put a hand to my mouth. I feel as if I'm weeping inside for him. He's never told me this before.

'But they'd gone when you went in?'

'Thankfully, yes. I was dreading what we'd find - and have to deal with, but they'd all evacuated.' He's talking about Gaza, that much I do know - from his nightmares, which take a different turn. 'Whereas you... must have had some very nasty moments of another sort.'

I'm frozen to the spot.

'You're right about that,' says Jack. 'Forcing the enemy's retreat through the mountain passes was no fun. We'd find pockets of 'em. Hand to hand, some of it.'

Hand to hand... face to face... I creep away out into the garden, where I take deep gulps of air. I find I'm shaking with anger. No wonder these two men have, in their own ways, been ill, mentally ill. Who could be expected to survive such ordeals as theirs unscathed?

I have to find my equilibrium again before I can declare my presence. Besides, it might be good for them to go on talking about what they have been through. I'm cold and stiff, so I go for a brisk walk up and down the High Street.

I'm welcomed as if I, not they, were the returning hero. Over tea and toast in front of the fire, I answer their interested enquiries about my day. Jack says he'll go up early, during which procedure Leonard and I, sitting opposite each other as in the old days, read our books, Leonard's Some Contemporary Poets, a new anthology edited by Harold Monro, whose own work Leonard respects, mine The Lost Girl, D.H. Lawrence's latest novel. I am at the point where the heroine marries an Italian and goes with him to Naples. That reminds me to ask, when we close our books to prepare for bed, whether or not, since he hasn't mentioned it, Leonard cycled over to Cottering.

'No, I didn't,' he says, a shade tersely. 'Jack had chest pains. He was quite upset, so I felt I couldn't go. Later, he said it was only wind.'

Chapter Fifteen

I have been married twenty years to this day which falls, coincidentally, as that one did on a Saturday. Since most of our friends and relatives would, like us, be working on the day, we kept our wedding very simple, which suited us. This also laid to rest any fears, on Hilda's part, of upstaging hers, due to take place after Easter. So, we shall do exactly what we did then, the only exception being that we shan't go to Church first at nine o'clock. Leonard humoured me with a religious ceremony. Then we went on to work all morning, had luncheon at The Railway Hotel and returned to work. But there was a feeling of celebration, with champagne and a splendid cake from Askey's. Afterwards, I joined Leonard as his wife for my first night at 3 Blessings Yard. Goodness, what a night that was. I blush even now to think of our pent up, innocent pleasure in each other's bodies.

We've asked Jack whether he wants to come to luncheon with us at one o'clock. He says he'll think about it. I believe he doesn't want to intrude and, forgive me, I rather hope he decides not to come. I'm looking forward to the rare treat of having my husband all to myself for stimulating conversation in fairly elegant surroundings.

My customers seem to have absorbed, from the notice I hung over my 'Open' sign, that I shall be closing today at ten minutes to one. By five to, the shop is empty. I step outside and lock up.

I hurry through the closing market, not looking to right or left as I might normally, my eye caught by a pretty dress at a bargain price. I plough along the High Street, busy, too, with Saturday shoppers. In Gifford's, I glimpse Lettie, working as ever, advising a customer on her choice of hat. I cross the river, scarcely noticing what a picture of industry it presents this fine morning with its barges carrying sacks of coal or barley, the roasting scent of which drifts from the many riverside maltings.

Haring down Holywell End, I am surprised to see not Leonard waiting for me outside Pritchard's, but Louisa Briggs.

'A friend of yours turned up unexpectedly at half past twelve – a foreign lady.' My stomach drops as Louisa goes on, 'I told them to go early and I'd wait for you. She seemed to have something to celebrate.'

I manage to thank her with a smile, but my mind is a blur of selfish disappointment as I hasten to The Railway Hotel, a former coaching inn with vestiges of grandeur in the form of its ornate dining room upstairs. This is my destination but, in order to get there, I have to pass through the bar room first, saloon on one side, tap room on the other. I am not best pleased about this. I push open the door and find myself surrounded on every side by men, drinking, arguing, raising a hand in demonstration of some point. The noise of all their voices is like the baying of deep-throated hounds. They spill across what should be a thoroughfare. I have to say, 'Excuse me,' more than once in order to make them notice me and step aside to let me pass.

A hand touches my arm. I jump.

'He went upstairs with his friend.' I know that voice. I swing round to see Fred Rawlins, on his way back from the facilities outside. 'Would you like me to escort you, Mrs. Pritchard?'

My face must give him his answer, but before I've time to speak Leonard's voice, coming from the stairs behind Fred Rawlins, makes me turn again. 'That won't be necessary, thank you.' Leonard comes down and takes my arm, leading me back up with him. 'I'm really sorry about this, dearest. Teodolinda suggested luncheon. I said I was lunching with you anyway, and she looked so pleased at the prospect of seeing you, I had to say we'd love her to join us. And I couldn't leave her here on her own while I waited for you at the shop.'

'Of course not. It's all right.'

As we rise above the bar, I see that Mr. Rawlins has joined a group of men wearing, albeit discreetly tucked inside their collars, red kerchiefs.

At a charming table in the bay window, Teodolinda sits studying the menu. She rises with a broad smile as soon as she sees us. No longer in mourning, she is stylish in dove grey and amethyst. Her hat, in a shade of darker grey, is a cylinder with a wide, flat brim which suits her oval face. My navy woollen suit, its jacket with a neat cream border to the lapels and cuffs, now feel less smart.

'Ah, Rose, I am honoured to join you on this special occasion,' she says. We clasp hands. 'Since there will be no Italian equivalent available, let me order champagne – my treat.'

'We'd better address the menu, then you can tell Rose your good news, Teodolinda,' says Leonard. 'We had the Dover sole on the day, didn't we, my love?'

But before we can order, who should appear but Jack! I find I'm pleased to see him. He seems to complete what is now a small party. He is followed by Fred Rawlins and his comrades, who seat themselves at a large, less attractive table by the door.

We three plump for the fish, Jack steak and kidney pie.

'Wait till you hear what Teodolinda omitted from her letter,' says Leonard. He turns to her, ' – what you did in Rome.'

'Well,' says our friend, 'while I was there I thought I'd pay a visit to the publishers to whom I'd sent my six poems. They couldn't even locate them under all the piles of paperwork. Anticipating this, I had made copies of them – and of my letter. I asked the rather naïve young man who seemed to be on duty whether I could have a few words with his master and, as luck would have it, he was free. So I took my poems and presented them to him, and said that I also had a complete collection, should he be interested. We had a very civilised, cultural discussion. I gave him my address in Rome. Then, a few days later a letter came, yes, I could submit the complete collection – which I also had with me, of course, so I hand-delivered it that day.'

'Why didn't you tell us this, when you wrote in January?' I ask.

Teodolinda makes a dismissive gesture. 'They promised nothing at the time. Then, when I had the rejection from the English publishers, I thought: well, that's it, I was foolish to dream. A rejection from Italy is bound to follow.'

'Whereas...' Leonard prompts.

'Bondoni Press have just written to say that they will publish three of my poems in their magazine due out next month, and they would like to publish my entire collection in June.'

We all clink champagne saucers.

'And let us raise a toast to John Keats,' says Teodolinda. 'As you will know, it was the centenary of his death in Rome last Wednesday.'

We do it again.

'And here's to Rose and Leonard,' says Jack, 'twenty happy years.'

And a third time. Teodolinda wants to know how we met, so we tell her.

Our meal arrives. I can't help noticing that every time I glance up from my plate or away from our little group, Fred Rawlins seems to be looking at me. Perhaps the champagne has made me reckless, but I find I can ignore him.

'I have had the most wonderful idea,' says Teodolinda, when we're on our sherry trifle – more alcohol – oh dear, so much for Lent. 'As I told you, Leonard, I have regained contact with old friends at the British Embassy in Rome. With their help, I could arrange a reading for you to coincide with the launch of my collection – say, late June?'

'Our birthday,' comments Jack. 'Rose and I were born on the same day a year apart – the twenty-first.'

'How wonderful!' says Teodolinda. 'Perhaps the three of you would like an Italian holiday...'

'No thank you,' says Jack, quickly. 'I've done enough foreign travelling for a lifetime.'

Leonard is clearly taken with the idea. 'Late June or early July would be very suitable, wouldn't it, Rose?'

For you, I feel like saying. His busy time will be over with school ending. My summer holiday trade will have just begun.

Luckily, Teodolinda doesn't wait for my answer. 'It will be hot in Rome, of course, but after the launch and reading we could head for Lake Como via Monza. I should like to show you the freschi of Teodolinda in the chapel there. They really are superb.'

'It all sounds irresistible,' says Leonard also, I suspect, somewhat affected by the champagne.

'Lovely...' I say, and I'm sure it would be.

It's time for us to go – just as Fred Rawlins's table rises, too. On the way to the stairs, he says to Leonard, 'I'm waiting for you to say, I told you so.' He means the Russian invasion and fighting going on in Georgia at this minute.

'I'm sure there are many topics on which you and I are in agreement,' says Leonard, equably. 'Stalin's Bolshevism might not be one of them, but I certainly don't propose to argue with you now over its most egregious example.'

We help Teodolinda locate Mr. White in the tap room, and say good-bye, promising to keep in touch about our tentative plans.

Leonard leaves us at Pritchard's. Jack and I walk up Holywell End, over the bridge in silence, and turn into the High Street. About to cross for home, he pauses. 'All starting up again,' he says.

I merely say, 'See you later,' choosing to ignore his observation which has irritated me chiefly, I have to own, because that strange and unworthy thought had crossed my own mind.

After work, I find Leonard already home and scrabbling around in the dresser drawer for an Alka-Seltzer. 'The champagne and sherry,' he says, by way of explanation.

March opens as fair and dry as February. Jack goes for ever longer walks, pushing himself to be well enough to work. Sometimes, I think he over-exerts himself, for he comes back breathless, but he's determined not 'to be a burden' to us for much longer which description we, of course, dispute, especially as he has been contributing from his savings towards the cost of food from the start. We won't take more than this.

Now, he's talking about taking the first steps towards finding a job. I devoutly hope he won't be disappointed. Periodically, former veterans will approach us at Pritchard's and Quinn-Harper's. These are men, probably with a family to support, worn down with trying to find employment at any menial level. It's all we can do to pay the wages of Louisa Briggs, let alone try to support another. But it breaks my heart to have to turn such men away.

'You could try Hallambury's,' I suggest to Jack. 'On your walks, you must have seen their fleet of vans.'

'Oh, yes,' says Jack. 'Before the War, they won prizes for their De Dion-Boutons at the Annual Parade in London. I went with Master Greville. A grand day out. I met a lot of his friends, all motoring enthusiasts. The King was there - the old King, that is - he gave out the prizes. In our class, we got £2.10 for the Lanchester Landaulette.'

He dresses in his smartest clothes, but comes back deflated. 'No vacancies at present. Yes, I think they thought I was all right. They've kept my name, but I can't wait around, can I?'

The trouble is, though I have not articulated this to Jack, his set of skills, groom-cum-coachman/chauffeur and mechanic, though impressive, is not wide-ranging. That's before we even broach the ticklish question of his lack of references. I really don't know how he's going to get round that one.

We have received and, of course, accepted our invitation to the Preview Evening of the exhibition of Cornish paintings. This will take place on Thursday, 17th March, a date which Mrs. Fuller agreed with her gallery so that most of us former housemates, plus Leonard and Hubert, could attend without too much difficulty. Hubert's invitation is really just a courtesy - he says he is working - as, sadly, is the invitation to Meg and Winnie, whose winter shift pattern, which doesn't change until the clocks go forward on the 3rd April, makes it impossible. They say they will go up to London on Saturday afternoon, as the show is on for a week.

'You know who would really enjoy the occasion and the paintings?' says Leonard.

I do, but nothing would induce me to beg an invitation from Mrs. Fuller for someone she hasn't even met. I feel privileged enough myself to be included in such a prestigious event.

I trot up to see Phyllis on the previous Thursday afternoon to find out how she and Jenny are proposing to travel. The house's eponymous apple tree is now in blossom and, as I walk down the path to the Byre, the garden is glad with daffodils and white narcissi. I find the place thriving, Mrs. Fuller in her studio and Beatrice in hers, on the other side of the partition from Phyllis and Jenny's home. Phyllis knocks on it to let them know that tea is ready.

'We'll go on the bike,' she tells me, while we wait for the two artists to appear. 'The timing's tight for Jenny after work, but we should be travelling into London when everyone else is coming out.' And yes, they can leave the bike in a locked outbuilding at the back.

Mrs. Fuller enters with Beatrice following. She looks almost her old self, face full of animation. I tell her how much we are looking forward to the exhibition.

On the Monday before school breaks up for Easter, Alex and Dee arrive with Swiss buns from Askeys. These are back to their pre-War splendour, dripping with icing. The girls have each, at their respective institutions, won a writing competition, Alex for an article which could be sent to a newspaper, Dee for a poem which, when he reads it later, Leonard says she should submit to a magazine. They did not collaborate, because the pieces were written and refined at school, but the subject both have chosen is The Plumage Bill which, having failed to pass through Parliament last summer, still rumbles on with no greater likelihood of a successful outcome.

Alex's article discusses why the Bill did not go on to become law. This, in short, was due to vested interests in the millinery industry in Britain. Masquerading as concern for the livelihoods of all the workers here, mostly women and girls, who turn the dead birds and/or their feathers into hat trimmings – and who, by the way, she adds, are very poorly paid, so what does that say about their masters' caring attitude – the industrialists' real motive was, in fact, wanting to keep out unregulated competition from Europe which would corner the market. Alex begins by quoting the editor of The Nation on the Bill's fate: 'But what do women care? Look at Regent Street this morning.' She follows this, however, by another quotation, this one from Virginia Woolf, observing that discussion of the Bill had not even gathered enough members of the Standing Committee devoted to it to make a quorum, concluding, 'The Plumage Bill is for all practical purposes dead. But what do men care?' Alex manages, though, to link the implicit discussion of women's role as decorative objects to her personal experience as a part-time shop assistant in ladies' fashions by expressing the dichotomy between her remit of trying to convince a customer how elegant she looks with a dead bird on top of her head and her revulsion for an object which she can hardly bear to handle not only in itself but also, and more importantly, because of what it symbolises. She concludes with a plea to Parliament to outlaw a morally indefensible trade.

Dee's poem is no less heartfelt. She takes as her starting point the fact that thousands upon thousands of birds are shot during the breeding season. She writes, therefore, from the point of view of the little egret chick who witnesses the arrival of grim, upright figures who slaughter his mother and all the adult birds he knows. She conveys graphically his total fear and grief and his ultimate realisation that from his hunger he, too, will die.

If confirmation were needed that either girl would have a bright path ahead in continuing her education, then here it is.

But there is another implication which doesn't escape Alex's mother. As Lettie and I settle into our First Class seats (by courtesy of Hubert) from Widdock East to Liverpool Street, she continues on the subject, 'I told her, if that's how you feel about working at Gifford's, you'd better stay on at school as long as you can. Me, I've always been thankful for the job. I've had to put my scruples to one side, but you - you could go on to all sorts of clever things.'

At the thought of travelling to London with the two of us - well, one of us - chatting non-stop, Leonard has gone ahead and will spend an afternoon walking round the capital, 'or I might pop into the National Gallery,' he adds, mindful of the possibility, recently aired, of an admission fee being introduced. So, Lettie and I are alone to enjoy the thrill of the escalator down to the 'Tuppenny Tube', though we are travelling further than the two stops which this fare buys. The Central London Railway, to give it its proper name, has electric trains and powerful electric lighting which reflects from the white tiles cladding the tunnel walls of the stations. Even interspersed with large boards of advertisements the effect is uncompromising. 'Tell me I don't really look like death warmed up,' says Lettie, grimacing into her compact mirror, 'which means I must,' I giggle, borrowing it to peer at my strangely drained face. I assure her she looks altogether magnificent, which she does in her crimson outfit and a wide-brimmed hat without avian adornment. We zip along to Oxford Circus, amused at the sight of our reflections in the carriage glass.

Like Leonard, we also spend our afternoon walking, but in our case up and down Oxford Street. We are surrounded by people, some strolling as we are, others purposeful, making their way to the underground. All are poised and self-possessed. I feel quite a country bumpkin. I have to drag Lettie away from Marshal and Snelgrove's window, 'you see, shorter skirts - they're coming, Rose,' in order to get to the gallery in Mayfair. We find Mrs. Fuller dazzling in a cocktail of bright colours not seen since she went into mourning. Beatrice, too, has shed her black in favour of warm earth tones but, once again, Phyllis and Jenny steal the sartorial show in their tabards, which seem to complement the white walls and bold paintings on them. We accept a glass of champagne, which I only sip. There are dainty pastries, rapidly disappearing as the room fills up with people, some of whom I can guess, from their assured manner, are the art critics. I spot Fred Rawlins, no doubt here on behalf of The Greenfield Argus. 'Very impressive,' he says, when we coincide in front of a painting by Beatrice, 'less bourgeois than her earlier work. I must come back with Gladys.'

Leonard arrives, and joins us looking at one of Mrs. Fuller's landscapes.

'They're very modern, aren't they?' says Lettie.

She's right. The glowing colours which are a hallmark of the artist's work are still there in the turquoise and purples of the sea, the patchwork slabs of brown and orange in what must be the local stone of cottages, but there is a new angularity, a sort of hard edge to the style. The same can be said of Beatrice's portraits of local people, fishermen, and women at market. Perhaps this is how both have to work, their response to what they went through.

Even if I hadn't guessed it already, I know first-hand from Hilda that the Easter weekend, almost upon us, is the busiest for vicars. It would be unreasonable, therefore, to propose to Alice Baker any part of it that we could manage for a meeting between the four of us, a suggestion I had, of course, meant to take her up on before now. But what with work, Jack's health, and now the anxiety about his failure so far to get a job, I've been distracted. So I write, full of apologies and wondering whether a Thursday afternoon in April would suit them.

The other person on my conscience concerning the social implications of Easter is Teodolinda. We're working on Saturday, of course. On Sunday, after Church, I always linger to chat, enjoying the celebratory occasion, with Hilda, Gerald and Dee. In the afternoon, I cycle over to the south side where, it being a holiday, I can count on seeing Hubert and Tom, as well as Lettie and Alex. This leaves only Monday free. Once again,

Lizzie Munns has volunteered, Bank Holiday notwithstanding, to come and help me with the wash, so I really can't turn down that valuable offer. And in the afternoon, frankly, I'd like to put my feet up and read a new novel, The Story of Jenny, written as the diary of a twelve-year-old mill girl which, so far, is compelling.

I get a swift reply from Alice whose warmth radiates from the page, telling me how glad she is to hear from me but that I mustn't feel at all guilty, 'you've got enough on your plate. And I've been advised to rest until the baby's born – nothing serious, but I must take it easy, which I shan't mind at all. I've just started a new book, William Morris and the Early Days of the Socialist Movement. That should keep me occupied! Do write and tell me what you're reading.' She signs with love from both of them to both of us.

Teodolinda replies, in response to an apologetic letter written by Leonard and signed by both of us, saying that we must not worry about her at all, she is very busy. She has been writing poetry. (She doesn't say in which language, but I could make a guess, given that there are no poems enclosed for Leonard's consideration.) Soon, she will be in touch about our trip to Italy.

Ironically, as Mrs. Fuller commented, the light here in the east has apparently been better, during the tail end of March, than it has been in the west. The artists' friends have told them of low cloud, showers, rain and hail, even thunder. 'Stay away!' they counselled, so mother and daughter have gone on working in their own studios here. But they have been poised, with everything but the bare essentials packed, ready for spring to declare itself in Cornwall – and now it has.

Phyllis calls in at Blessings Yard to tell us that a letter arrived yesterday. There are clear blue skies in St. Ives, 'and the seaweed's set fair,' so they leave tomorrow, Friday.

'Oh – so you'll have the house to yourselves for your birthday?'

'If all goes according to plan,' says my sister. 'I'll go back with her on the bike. Leonard, who has only just come in, will walk up after he's had a sandwich. Both of us want to say goodbye.

'What's happening to the house?' I ask, my insides knotted with anxiety.

'They're not selling it.'

'Phew,' says Jack.

'They had words about it. That's the impression I get from Florence. She won. But,' says Phyllis, 'she had to compromise, too. They want to rent it out.'

'Oh, no!' I'm almost as dismayed. 'How will that work?'

'We could take their room - we can afford that. Yes - I know The Byre's lovely, Rose, but in winter - well, thinking ahead. Anyway, we've got that option. It's the other two rooms that are the problem.'

'So, they're prepared to let Miles's room?' says Leonard, coming through to the sitting room where Jack is sitting and I'm standing ready to go. He sits down with his sandwich.

Phyllis rubs her thumb against her first two fingers. 'They've got to pay rent down there, haven't they? We might just about have stumped up the extra for the little room, but not for the other big room as well. We'll have to advertise. Florence would like to give us the whole of May to resolve it. Beatrice would like people in by the first.'

In the kitchen at Apple Tree House, Phyllis has already laid out, at one end of the table, the national press reviews of the painting exhibition. As with the glowing article in The Widdock Courier, which I've read in our copy at home, each one is complimentary. My sister even 'tootled down to Greenfield' and picked up the Argus, which has a gracious comment by its editor. Well, good for Fred Rawlins.

Mrs. Fuller appears before Beatrice, who is still packing. Seated at the head of the table, she is bathed in afternoon sunlight. 'Yes,' she says, in answer to my question, 'our friends have found us what sounds like a lovely house with a sea view. We can take it for six months starting from tomorrow. So, we travel on April Fools' Day - makes perfect sense.'

'It sounds idyllic,' I say. 'I hope you will be very happy.'

Mrs. Fuller laughs. 'So do we!' She leans towards me. 'And what of you, Rose, dear? Phyllis tells me that you plan to go to Italy with your new friend. How do you feel about that?'

How do I feel? 'I suppose everyone has an idea of what Italy is like,' I say, slowly, '...beautiful old buildings, sunshine. But in another, strange way it's unimaginable. It's so outside anything I've ever had to contend with - such as coming to Widdock from Markly. That felt intimidating. So did going to London for the first time, of course, but this is on a grander scale of... apprehension - excitement, I suppose I should say.'

'Apprehension is more accurate, I think.' Mrs. Fuller is looking at me very intently. 'What I'd want to do in advance would be to define exactly which elements of the trip were making me apprehensive and why. In focusing my attention on each - assuming there was more than one - I might find that I was worrying about something which I could, in fact, sort out beforehand. As you know, given how first class you are at it, there is very little that can't be managed one way or another.'

As I'm giving her my blushing, heartfelt thanks - she's helped me resolve something, I tell her - Leonard appears, coming round the side of the house.

'I'll write to you from Cornwall with my address,' she says. 'Do keep in touch.'

Leonard and I walk home down New Road. In some of the grander gardens at the top, stately magnolias unfurl their delicate white petals flushed with pink, and joyous camellias sport their crimson pom-poms. Lower down the smaller gardens are, like their bigger counterparts in this spring sunlight, bright with tulips.

'I've been thinking about the opening arrangements for the shops while we're away,' I say, and before Leonard can answer more than, 'oh yes,' I go on, 'Don't you think Louisa ought to be based at Quinn-Harper's most of the time? It's my busy period. She could always go to Pritchard's on Mondays – or close Quinn-Harper's early and go up to catch your returning season-ticket holders.'

'Jolly good idea,' says Leonard. 'It's rather thrilling, isn't it, the thought of Italy?'

Clearly, this fair, warm weather is encouraging people from their houses. Some of the cafes have brought out their summer chairs and tables. I put a chair in front of the shop, as I always do when it's fine enough, and chat to passers-by. By closing time, I've had a rather good day for sales, especially of the novel, Not Known Here, by Mrs. Wilfred Ward, set during the War. The hero is a man who believes he may be the son of a German. It plucks at the heartstrings in no uncertain terms.

I cross the square past others, like myself, in lighter clothing. Daylight Saving Time starts at two o'clock on Sunday morning but it truly feels as if summer is already here. As I walk up the yard, I'm thinking about the lovely piece of cod I'm going to poach and serve with Leonard's leeks and some crusty rolls and butter. I pause to smell our heavenly rose by the door. It opens to let me in.

'Hello,' says Jack. 'Had a good day, Rose?'

He must be feeling well to ask after me. I step inside and tell him that I have. 'Oh!' He's laid the table.

'I thought I could do that to help you. Not that I've been in long. I've been on the bike.' He follows me through to the kitchen.

'Goodness! Wasn't Phyllis working?'

'She was working.' He's grinning now. 'I went on my own.'

'My word!'

'She didn't mind. I only went as far as the turnpike. It was good.'

'And how's your back?'

He touches wood. I follow suit. 'Seems all right. I had something to discuss with her. I'll tell you both when we've finished dinner.'

It turns out that in his will Master Greville left a very small legacy to Jack. 'I said I wanted it in cash – in case those bas – the family had some way of claiming it back. So, I've got it here under the mattress. I've said to Phyllis that I could afford to rent one of their rooms – she showed them to me – for two months at what the ladies are asking. If they can't find another person, I could manage the sum they want for two rooms, but only for one month. But I'm bound to have got a job by then. I'm going to go out looking on the bike.'

Chapter Sixteen

'We moved in over the weekend,' says Phyllis, 'so on Monday morning Jenny could simply walk along the corridor and use an indoor lavatory and wash basin. Untold luxury.'

We were supposed to be having afternoon tea with Hilda to celebrate her birthday today, with an acknowledgement of Phyllis's, last Saturday, as she doesn't go in for parties. Unusually, though, Hilda has cancelled due to 'a minor ailment' according to her note. So Phyllis dropped in at the shop and invited me to hers, and now we're sitting in strong sunshine on the bench in her kitchen garden. The arbour's dense twisting honeysuckle almost shelters us from a keen north-easterly breeze.

'You won't miss the dear old Byre, then?'

'Of course, we will.'

She doesn't elaborate, so I say, 'It must have been a bit of a shock, Jack turning up here with his plan to become your fellow lodger.'

'I discussed it with Jenny, obviously, and she doesn't mind. If it comes to anything, I can tell you, he's got his eye on this place.' She nods across at the Byre, '– with the option of Miles' little room in winter. That would suit us down to the ground. And it's time we took some of the strain off you, now that we're free. I said to him, 'If you come here, you behave yourself.' He liked that.'

I say, 'I'm glad he only went out once on the motorcycle. I was surprised you'd agreed to lend it to him.'

Phyllis groans. 'You know how persuasive he can be. I had to keep telling myself that he is, after all, a driver. But I must say I was relieved when both came back safe and sound.'

'Me, too. I did wonder...'

We exchange tight, knowing smiles.

'I checked the bike after he'd gone, and there was no damage to it, so whatever happened must have been an incident rather than an accident, but he was definitely rattled – and out of breath.'

'That's what I thought. But he seemed to get over it. He's been out the rest of the week looking for work in town again. The very fact that he tells us nothing about it suggests to me he's had no luck.'

'You know he twisted my arm not to put in the advert for lodgers until tomorrow week's paper?'

'I didn't know that.'

'Well, he'd better pull something out of the hat on the job front before then, hadn't he?'

Our routine is that Leonard picks up a copy of The Widdock Courier when he buys his paper on Friday morning. He reads it during his lunch break, then offers it for general use when he gets home, having it back if there are still items in it which he hasn't fully absorbed. He usually leaves it on the sofa, where I'm the first to pick it up. I do this today, after dinner, only to find that it has been eviscerated. All of the advertisement section has been removed. I'm glad. Jack's footwork around the town has been humiliating. Any businesses who employ a driver, mostly of carts, have such a person already well ensconced. Olly Bates runs a family firm, as does the motor car salesman who, therefore, has no need of another mechanic. Jack's studying the paper for posts vacant is a sensible idea.

Even though I'm early, Jack's out before me this morning. I stop at the market to buy kippers from the fish stall. On my way to the shop, I spot Tom, browsing at the stall which sells games and novelties. He sees me and we pass the time of day.

'Uncle Jack was at the station bookstall,' he says. 'I made him jump when I came up behind him. He was looking at local maps. He almost seemed cross that I'd said hello.'

It being bath night, we change our beds before eating, so we don't get indigestion afterwards. The men bring the sheets down and put them in the basket in the wash house. I can hear them chatting beneath me in the kitchen, as I start tucking in Jack's top sheet. On his bedside cabinet is the advertisement section of The Courier, much folded and with one item ringed. My eye is caught by the heading:

Night Soil Collector

In frozen horror, I can't help reading on:

> Widdock Town and Extra
> Mon–Sat inc. Horse & cart provided.
> Apply Widdock T.C. Offices. 9-5, Mon-Fri.

The pay is pitiful for what's involved. I shudder at the thought of my brother having to contend with this.

I hear Jack's tread on the stairs, coming to help me finish making up the bed with hospital/military corners. I shake myself out of my numbness, but say nothing. This is not unusual. We both want to finish the task and go downstairs to eat. But he must have grasped the shock in my silence.

'I'd get to work with the horse without the responsibility of its upkeep,' he says, gently. 'And I'd be my own boss, after a fashion. It might be quite nice going out into the countryside round Widdock.'

And who am I to contradict him? It's a vital job, which certainly deserves respect. What a shame the wage doesn't reflect a similar respect.

It's another glorious morning, just like yesterday, with the promise of heat to come. Lizzie and I are pegging out the sheets when Jack comes out of the open back door, heading for the privvy. Everything about him bespeaks dejection. When he reappears, I ask him what happened.

'Job had gone already. I must buy my own paper first thing Friday morning.' He sounds almost angry, and certainly looks red in the face. 'I went asking round the town again, but it was no good. I'm going to have a wash and a lie down.'

Phyllis calls by Quinn-Harper's this morning, Tuesday. I confirm that, as she and I both hoped would not be the case, Jack is still without a job. She leaves to place the advertisement for a lodger, which will be in Friday's paper.

Without the cold nor-easter accompanying the earlier sunny spell, these days of heat would have us believe this to be summer. I am not the only woman out and about in muslin and straw hat. Café chairs and tables are gracing the square and, when I've finished what I need to do inside, I take up my position on a chair in front of the shop, which seems to encourage customers – so there's my justification, if I needed one.

Yesterday, Jack went round as many of the maltings as he could. Although there must be many repetitive aspects to this employment, it is not a trade he knows – and this is the wrong time of the year for managers to hire more men, when maltings will be closing at the end of their season. They told him he'd be better off waiting for the brickfields, Widdock's summer work.

Today, Wednesday – my heart aches for him – he set out as I was getting up, the sun already high in a clear sky, to walk a good half hour or more to the factories and light engineering workshops just off the London Road, situated by the Blaken at Swan Mead. With few trees amongst those industrial buildings, it must be sweltering.

Janus faced, April turns its inclement cheek. Thursday's torrential rain, which we read covered the whole of England, yesterday turned to hail and even snow. The emotional climate at 3 Blessings Yard is no less temperamental. Donning his greatcoat and armed with an umbrella, Jack left the house with me to buy his paper.

A day later, his evident sense of betrayal, arising from his discovery of Phyllis's advertisement, still permeates the atmosphere. We go through our Saturday night routine as normal but he retires to bed an hour early, saying that the kippers, this week, have given him indigestion.

Rain and thunderstorms throughout the week confine Jack largely to the cottage. From what I see of him, in these gloomy days, he shuffles from kitchen to chair and up to his bedroom as if, like the weather, his health had regressed. I ask him if he needs his tonic, but he says he doesn't.

I am not surprised to learn from Phyllis, calling by the shop on Friday, that they have not received a single enquiry about their rooms. Who would venture far from their own fireside unless they were about to be turned out from it that very instant?

A letter drops on the mat just as I am about to leave the house today, Saturday. I recognise the foreign handwriting. Leonard has already gone out, so I put it on the mantelpiece for later. Grabbing an umbrella, I head off with my basket for the market. Perhaps smoked haddock, simply served with bread and butter... Invalid food... I try to dismiss the disturbing thought.

A busy day takes over but I am dismayed to notice, after dinner this evening, how Jack is bravely masking discomfort. He retires early again, sucking a sliver of the crystallised ginger I keep for cakes, biscuits and puddings.

In the garish flicker of lightning, with thunder growling ever closer, Leonard reads Teodolinda's letter, asking us which we would prefer: 'Menaggio, which is bigger and has a train service or, Bellagio, if you prefer peace and quiet...'

'Rose... you're not really taking this in, are you?' says Leonard, gently. 'You look tired.'

I apologise. Both facts are true. I am tired, and it all feels so remote, as if it has nothing to do with me. I pull myself together. 'I really don't mind either place. You choose – or leave it up to her.'

Another wash day, cloudy, but at least it's dry. Lizzie and I are mangling the sheets. Jack is not yet down, which does concern me.

'You go back in and see if he's all right. I can carry on here,' says my trusty helper.

I stand in the kitchen, ears cocked – and hear a knock at the front door.

I'm astonished to find Louisa Briggs. She's holding a folded copy of The Courier, and looks anxious.

'Come in, come in.' I'm always pleased to see Louisa.

Leonard has sent her post-haste. She tells me that she's had a letter this morning, out of the blue, from her odious landlord. He's selling up and wants his tenants out.

'Oh, then I know why you're here,' I say.

We arrange that Louisa will come back at one o'clock. Phyllis is likely to be taking a break then.

The two women get on well from the start. Louisa exclaims at the room. 'It's huge, and lovely. I bet it catches the evening sun.'

'It was once my bedroom,' I say. It feels so long ago – and is.

They agree that Louisa will come back in the evening to meet Jenny. Both are smiling broadly as we leave.

I look in the window at No 3. Jack is nodding in his chair.

My three old gentlemen favour Thursday mornings at Quinn-Harper's Bookshop because these are usually quiet, and they can browse my antiquarian stock as well as glancing at any new titles without the risk of other customers getting in the way. They also like to start their weekly exchange of news and general discussion here. This will continue when they leave my premises at twelve o'clock for a pint of ale at The Fox and Hounds which also offers an economical luncheon aimed especially at elderly bachelors or widowers of modest means and capabilities in the kitchen.

I see Phyllis outside the shop, pretending to be studying my window display in order to give them the time and space to bid me goodbye and leave in their gracious way.

'I won't stay,' she says. 'You'll know Louisa's moving in this afternoon.' I did. 'I just thought I'd tell you that the three of us had a talk about Jack. He can move in when he likes from Sunday onwards – just to give Louisa a chance to settle in first.'

'Are you sure?' In many ways, I should feel pleased, but I find that I'm quite anxious. 'It's a responsibility.'

Phyllis takes my remark a different way. 'Yes, quite sure. Now we've got Louisa's contribution it does make all the difference. His money should last till August. If he hasn't got a job by then, we'll have to think again.'

Leonard has his annual meeting, this afternoon, at the training college, to discuss the textual requirements of next year's curriculum. Jack is out, which does not surprise me. What does, though, is the evidence of a scratch meal hurriedly tidied away, crumbs on the table and – I find this later when I am clearing up – a slice of bread and butter barely touched, discarded in the bin. This all means he must have gone out unusually late. Perhaps he simply came back in to eat, but found he wasn't hungry after all...

I don't question him. He comes in having walked once more to Hallambury's, just in case the situation's changed regarding their need – or lack of – for drivers. He looks shattered, but brightens when I tell him what Phyllis said. 'It'll take some getting used to, mind, not living here.'

Over dinner, he says he will be out early to buy his own copy of The Courier. I broach the possibility of an office job.

'Pen pushing?' He says, but then seems to be considering it.

Jack isn't down when I leave for work today. What can I do to help him – besides pray?

'If I'd got out yesterday and bought the paper, I could have gone for it, there and then.'

Jack's been pouring over The Courier bought by Leonard. The night soil job appears to be back. Even in the midst of Jack's anguish, I can't help reflecting that the turnover of operatives is, due to the uncongenial nature of the work, likely to be high.

'Well, it's still worth going first thing on Monday, isn't it?' I say trying, without success, to calm his agitation. I leave for work.

When I come in, he's shuffling through with cutlery. I can hear effort in his breathing. I say hello and go into the kitchen. I come out again.

'Jack, you're not well, are you?'

'It's just a bit of gyp.'

'But it isn't, is it? I think you're getting worse.' I hate to say the words, but know them to be true. 'Perhaps you ought to see a doctor.'

'No! Not that bloody bugger!'

'We'll find another one.'

'I'll be all right.'

Leonard makes his own assessment as soon as he looks at Jack.

'I'll go on Monday,' Jack mutters.

It comes as no surprise that he declines a bath and goes up early - very slowly. Leonard comes and holds me. I find I'm crying.

'We're doing all we can,' he says. 'We can't force him.'

I dry my eyes. We try to carry on as normal and take our baths.

Last things for the night. I'm making our breakfast porridge, Leonard's checking that we're locked and bolted. He joins me with a letter he's just opened, which both of us had forgotten earlier. I recall seeing Teodolinda's writing on the envelope.

'She wants to know whether we'd prefer a hotel room or something simple, a pensione - that's like a B & B.'

My mind can't switch to that other life.

Leonard says, in my silence, 'This isn't the right moment.'

I feel a kind of clarity, heavy and cool. 'I think you'll have to go to Italy without me. Jack's too ill. I'd be worrying about him all the time.'

We stand looking at each other in the kitchen's uncompromising lamplight.

'I hoped it wouldn't come to this,' says Leonard, sighing. 'I don't have to go, of course.'

'But I'd feel bad if you didn't because of me and my family. The reading's all set up. Who knows what opportunities it might lead to?' That sense of detachment returns, as if everything is pre-ordained.

'I won't enjoy it half as much without you.'

'You'll just enjoy it differently,' I say, with a certainty which is almost light now that I have nothing to do with all this.

'I don't know what to think.'

'You'd better write and tell her I might not come,' I say, and then, as an afterthought, 'but you'll still need a room, won't you?'

I wake to sunlight. 'White rabbits,' I whisper, to bless this month with luck. I let myself drift, wondering how many May poles I shall see, it being Sunday and the times still recovering from the long shadow of the war.

And now I remember my dream, Jack and I riding together on old Sable but not, as in the dream I sometimes used to have, a grotesque revisiting of the occasion when Master Greville's dog upset the mare and, instead of Jack bringing her under control, the mare rearing till I am falling... falling... No, this was the most glorious ride we had in the meadows around Markly at Easter in 1900 when Jack, who had been suffering from melancholia, regained his healthy state of mind. I lie back and recall my dream, Jack on Sable and I riding Jack's horse, Iolo... the soft scent of earth turned under cantering hooves, the jingle of harness, the song of skylarks all around us... When I open my eyes again, they are moist. There is a cup of tea beside me, and

I can't be sure I didn't feel, instead of a low branch touching the top of my head, Leonard's hand caressing it.

I wash and get dressed in the quiet house, Leonard having gone to get the papers. There is no sound from Jack's room, but that is probably good. Let him wake refreshed. Leonard comes back and sits down on the bench out front in the strengthening sunshine. It's going to be a lovely day. Perhaps that summery weather we had before the hail and snow is back to stay.

Casting a final glance around the kitchen at all my preparations for the Sunday roast, I hear Jack moving in his room and am filled with relief. I go through to the front and step outside, unprepared for the warmth which greets me. 'It's going to be hot later,' I say, looking at the cloudless sky.

'Yes,' says Leonard. 'As soon as Jack's down, I'll go out on the bike while it's not too much of an effort. I thought I'd cycle over to Ash Manor – explain what's happened.'

Today, I am in Church before Hilda who, looking slightly pale, joins the end of the choir just in time to reach the chancel step with them.

Afterwards, she doesn't want to linger. Nor do I. I'm afraid my concentration wasn't at its best during the service, my thoughts divided not between the two apostles, Saints Philip and James, whose Holy Day this is, but between my husband and my brother.

The sky is a clear blue, the sun high and remorseless, beating down on the shuttered shop fronts in the High Street. I take a shaded alley, cross sunny East Street and step under the cool arch into Blessings Yard, itself baking.

I had thought Jack might be sitting on the bench but, when I look through the window, I see him in his chair.

A greeting falters upon my lips. His blond hair is damp with sweat. As he tries to respond to me, pain creases his face.

Fear leaps from my stomach to my throat. 'Tell me what's wrong,' I say, 'and what I can do.'

'It's my arm,' he says, 'and it's going right down my back.' He grimaces again. 'I feel a bit sick, too.'

'I'll get you water,' I say, doing so and bringing a bowl. It gives me time to think. I go to feed the water to him, but he takes the glass with his right hand. 'You must see a doctor,' wishing Leonard was here to run for one or offer some other magic cure.

'All right.' He must be feeling bad. 'Will he come?' The final word is a yelp of pain.

'I don't know, but I can try. I hate to leave you. I'd better go.'

'Go. I'll be here...' he whispers.

I step out of the door, my head exploding with indecision. Do doctors come out on Sundays? Would a man like Doctor Warnish do so? My mind flits to Meg and Winnie. They are probably still in the Meeting House. I can hardly interrupt their silence - well, of course I can, but what could they do now? I hesitate in silent East Street. Perhaps it would be better to run the other way, down Holywell End to Station Road, and summon Olly Bates or whoever else has an available cab which could take us to the hospital. But will they receive us without referral from a doctor? Will they grasp the emergency? If only Warnish were our dear Doctor Jepp, who cared so well for Mother and was so keen to see me make a life for myself in Widdock, so full of enthusiasm, giving me Charles Darwin's book on worms... Instinctively, I look east towards Markly.

Rounding the corner into East Street, a figure wheels a bicycle. It is not Leonard, the man who, until this moment, was the one I most wanted to see... It can't be, I must have conjured him from my imagination... He raises a hand. He smiles broadly. It is. I start running towards him.

He understands instantly, as he did that terrible morning of Mother's death when he cycled as fast as he could - but too late. Please, please, let him not be too late this time. He runs the bike down the yard, leaning it against the bench.

Inside, he takes one look at Jack, whose symptoms I've already gasped out as I ran beside him.

'We'll soon put you right, Jack,' he says. 'Rose, have you any aspirin?'

'I think so.' I run through to the dresser. 'We've got Alka-Seltzer.' – Leonard's preference, these days, for his occasional headaches. I start rummaging. There was a packet.

'That would do, but aspirin's better.'

Yes! I bring it through with more water.

Dr. Jepp is taking Jack's pulse. 'Right, let's see if you can get a couple of these down,' he says, handing Jack the pills. I give him the fresh glass of water.

'It was such a lovely day,' says the doctor, conversationally, but not taking his eyes off Jack for a moment, 'I found myself cycling over here, and then I thought, 'Well, I could just see if Rose is at home.''

'Thank goodness you did,' I say.

After a while, Jack looks a better colour and says he is in no more pain. Dr. Jepp puts his hand to his forehead and cheeks. 'Good, temperature feels normal.' He sits down again. 'Now, Jack, I must tell you, I think you've had a minor heart attack.' I try not to show my shock. 'But without my instruments, I can't make further checks, so I'd like to refer you to the hospital for them to do that – and just keep you overnight.'

'To make sure I'm all right,' says Jack.

'Exactly so. You haven't a history of heart trouble? No, I thought I didn't recall your being prone, though your mother and her father were, of course. It does run in families.'

'I only started feeling odd this last month,' says Jack. 'I was a bit dizzy – you know, Rose, that day I went out on the bike.'

'If I were you,' says Dr. Jepp, mildly, 'I'd avoid being on the roads for about – oh – a month or so, just to be on the safe side.'

'All right,' says Jack, meek as a lamb.

'Do you have notepaper, Rose?'

I go to fetch it. In my bedroom, I'm sure I hear the door and Leonard's voice – thank heavens – but there's no sign of him when I come down.

'Your husband was here,' says Dr. Jepp, 'but he's gone to summon a cab.'

I place a glass of lemonade next to the doctor, but he doesn't touch it until he's written his letter and addressed the envelope, by which time Leonard is back with news that Mr. Randle, the car salesman, was just about to give one of his vehicles a run, so he will take us to the hospital. We hear the engine as Leonard finishes speaking. I bring him lemonade and take our roast out of the oven. Who knows when we'll be back?

We surrender Jack to the professionals and are told that all being well, if he's on a ward, we may see him at three o'clock, visiting time. Dr. Jepp, who kindly accompanied us to deliver his letter and see Jack admitted, says goodbye and cycles off.

So, we walk down to the water meadows and find shade under a willow by the river, where we eat the heel of loaf and slab of cheese I grabbed and put in my bag when we left. All around us is intense heat, the flickering of light through leaves, the gentle sigh of the breeze and a low buzz of insects which sometimes dart across our line of vision. I doze. I think we both do.

In the distance, the strains of Widdock Brass drift from the bandstand in the park where there will, no doubt, be young people dancing round a May Pole. It's time for us to move.

We find Jack, appropriately, on Markly Ward – they're all named after local places. He's had lunch and a nap. Yes, a minor heart attack but, thanks to Dr. Jepp's prompt action, the danger has been averted.

'I think they just want to make sure I don't have another one,' says Jack, cheerfully.

We tell him where we've been.

'Nice,' he says. 'So, Leonard, how was Tay-od-o-linda?'

I'd forgotten completely about the trip to Ash Manor.

Jack and I both wait for Leonard to speak.

'It was a very funny thing,' he says, slowly, 'but I was about half way and – I can't explain it rationally, I had an overwhelming feeling that I must turn round and come back.'

The tow path is heady with the scent of may, its white, sometimes red, blossoms festooning the hedgerows. We pass Hallambury's mill and a couple of maltings. Sunday afternoon stillness is intensified by the torpor of heat. In the park, bright spots of colour are people basking in the unaccustomed sunshine. If we continue on the towpath, we hug the welcome shade but if we cut across the park, we keep greenery beside us longer. Our choice is made for us. As we round a bend, the towpath is blocked by people queuing for the first summer boat trips on the Blaken.

We cross the High Street to take the smaller, cooler streets, West and East, running parallel with it. Under the arch, Blessings Yard is now in warm shade.

We are trying to get used to our strangely empty home – that first sight of the chair, which even I have now begun to think of as Jack's, the two places I have set for dinner.

I put the roast and potatoes back in the oven. Both were all but cooked when we left so, to make a passible if not ideal meal, they only need re-heating.

The garden door stands open, letting in the scents of almost evening. Leonard comes in with stems of broccoli, from which he rinses any soil. He leaves them to drain and dries his hands.

'How long?'

'About an hour.'

In the sunlit kitchen, he tenderly cups my face and kisses me. 'That should be long enough,' he says.

I run my fingers through his silvered black hair and gaze into those eyes of darkest blue, which still melt me. As our lips close, I kiss him in the strongest, most loving way I know.

Upstairs, the house to ourselves, we celebrate our union without restraint.

Lizzie Munns gently presses me into a chair at the kitchen table, giving me a glass of water. Jack stands with his back to us at the dresser taking his daily heart remedy, a tincture made from the meadowsweet – spirea – in Meg and Winnie's physic garden.

Testing the firmness of the stopper, he picks up the bottle ready to pack it. 'I'll bring my sheets down,' he says, going upstairs.

'Just to finish what we were talking about,' Lizzie says in a circumspect voice, 'it can start as early as four weeks.'

'That's it, then,' I say, trying to take in the enormity of what she's told me.

We hear Jack on the stairs. I take his bedlinen and, feeling better now, follow Lizzie through to the wash house. Jack is up and down, removing his few belongings from his room. We have left the door open to let out the steam from the copper, so Lizzie speaks quietly, 'Just as well you're not going to Italy.'

I agree. Leonard wrote immediately to Teodolinda telling her what had happened with Jack, and saying that he would not want to leave me to cope with the consequences on my own. I added my regret, and we both signed the letter.

We did not hear from her for a while, and then a reply came from Rome. Teodolinda understood entirely. She had some news for us. She would not be coming back to England as she'd sold Ash Manor. She was sorry she'd had to leave without saying a personal good-bye but matters had moved quickly. She had become re-acquainted with an old friend in Rome, had added new ones through her publishers and had re-established contact with relatives in Monza. She hoped we would understand and might be able to visit her another time. She asked us to keep in touch, and wished us and our family well, signing with affection.

Jack starts to gather his possessions by the front door.

Lizzie says, for my ears only, 'I bet you can't believe he's really going.'

I smile, but I'm actually finding that his departure, now it's finally here, brings a mixture of emotions on top of everything else I'm trying to digest.

We expected that Jack would want to convalesce with us, and so he did, but just when he was fit again and set to leave, Phyllis had to tell him that they'd had an infestation of mice in the Byre. 'It happens sometimes,' she said. 'They remember it once had a lovely hayloft.' But that's all dealt with now. We will walk up this afternoon to settle him in.

With the wash on, and Lizzie prodding it with the dolly, I go back inside the cottage for a sip of water. I see Jack out in the yard, smiling and talking animatedly with a stranger, standing by his car. I join them and he immediately introduces himself as Mungo Topping – 'Toppers' – a friend of the late Master Greville. He and Jack have met several times at motoring events.

'It's been quite a mission finding your brother,' says Toppers. 'I went straight to Sawdons, thinking he'd be there, but Hector told me he'd moved here with his sister – more's the pity from their point of view, his services are sorely missed, I gather. Still, their loss, my gain. Hector told me to go to Pritchard's Bookshop, and your husband directed me here. I'm so pleased your brother is willing to come in with me on my madcap project.'

'What's that?' I ask, warily.

'Since before the war, I've had a yen to design and build a flexible car which could accelerate from virtual standstill to top gear – with sporting performance. Couldn't think of a better man than your brother to work on the mechanics.'

Jack is grinning from ear to ear.

'I don't know this town, but I like the look of it,' Jack's future employer continues, 'so I've rented an empty workshop on Swan Mead. Should be ready to start by the middle of next month. That suit you, Alleyn?'

It turns out that he's offering Jack a lift up to Apple Tree House. We say a hurried goodbye. Feeling the pang of it, I say, 'I'll come up later.'

Today being Leonard's birthday, I've roasted a chicken for a treat. We're sitting eating this with potatoes and peas. I've already asked him about his day, and learned that several people besides Louisa Briggs, seemed to know of its significance, and have been in to express suitable good wishes. These, of course, included his dear stalwarts Messrs Davison, Nash and Vance, the latter of the farcical yet auspicious poetry reading last July, another age.

'It does feel strange, just the two of us,' Leonard says, 'not that I'm complaining.'

I smile to myself, but he's asking how the move went. So, I tell him all about Mungo Topping.

'Well, well,' he says, 'that is good news. What a relief.'

'I went up to the Byre this afternoon, and Jack said that he and Toppers were following Phyllis up New Road. It turned out she'd been to drop Jenny off at work and fill up the tank with fuel. So, Jack introduced the two of them and Toppers stayed long enough to admire the motorcycle - and Phyllis, Jack rather thought.'

Leonard laughs. 'He's going to be unlucky there.'

'That's not the only news,' I say, allowing him dispensation on plate-clearing, and bringing in his birthday cake in the form of a frangipane tart each from Askey's, heaped with halves of cherries. I gesture to him to help himself to cream. 'I learned from Lizzie Munns that Hilda's pregnant.'

'Good Lord!' He nearly drops the jug.

'Yes - apparently, that's what Gerald said. She's rather embarrassed - or was, but he's as pleased as punch, and so is Dee.'

'That's going to cramp Hilda's style a bit, isn't it?' says Leonard. 'Mmm... this tart's divine.'

'I shouldn't think so. Lizzie looked after her first two children, and she's said she'll do it again.' I pause a fraction, hardly able to contain myself, but wanting to savour every moment. 'She likes looking after babies.'

I take in with love my dear, big-hearted husband being glad for the Armstrong family. 'Splendid,' he says.

My own heart is beating faster in its skipping way. 'And being an old hand, Lizzie told me I was right about myself - and how I've been feeling these last couple of mornings.'

I see my own astonished joy reflected in his, suffusing his face with light.

Phenomena

The 2nd of February 1922

Wanting to make your tiny presence felt,
You called up a squall line to travel east.
Tracking across a sky as blue as your eyes,
A string of storms, black as your abundant hair,
Were the bunting you ordered to adorn
Your day. Sweet pet, your mother did not need
Such proclamation of your arrival.
Nor was it necessary to invoke,
For a wider audience, town and gown,
As I later learned you did at Oxford,
A parhelion - two bright spots flanking
The sun. Dear daughter, we three are our own
Shared trinity of dazzle, refracting
Through life's ice crystals, high in the atmosphere,
Perfect love. As for me, I paced downstairs
While the gale tossed rain and hail against the pane.
Lightning electrified the room, thunder rolled.
Above all this cacophony, I heard
Your line squall - your little local storm
As you greeted the world. Now, I hold you,
Feel you steady as the one small flame which burns
Beside your tired but radiant mother.
She tells me that today is Candlemass.
The dark is gone, we're bathed in mellow light.

Leonard Pritchard

Commenced on the 3rd February and completed on the 4th when snow fell in eastern England.

Acknowledgements

I am hugely grateful to my husband, the poet John Freeman, for his editorial advice and encouragement. Great thanks are due to my daughter, Nell Dawson, for her cover art work, and to Ben Miller for his advice about classic motorbikes and sidecars. Heartfelt thanks also to my publisher, Stuart Gaskell of 186 Publishing, for his enthusiasm and hard work. Warm thanks to my son, Trevor Dawson, and to all my friends and family for their steadfast support.

I have made extensive use of the archives of the Imperial War Museum, of the Meteorological Office, and of the Fabian Society, and am grateful to all these organisations. Among other sources I have drawn on, I should particularly like to acknowledge three books: Weeds in the Heart by Nathaniel Hughes and Fiona Owen (Aeon Books and Quintessence Press, 2018); Hertford's Past in Pictures by Len Green (The Rockingham Press, 1993) and At the Sign of the Plough by Geoffrey Tweedale (John Murray, 1990).

Available from: All good bookshops; Amazon.com; Amazon.co.uk; www.186publishing.co.uk:

The Testing of Rose Alleyn by Vivien Freeman

England in the year 1900. A vibrant young woman must take control of her destiny. Vivien Freeman's atmospheric novel brings late Victorian England hauntingly to life in the mind of the reader. In this beautifully written romance, Vivien Freeman explores the choices facing an independent-minded woman at a time when women struggled for self-determination.

'Full of gorgeous detail... I'd definitely recommend it' - Jennifer C. Wilson

'The writing has a poetic, almost haunting feel to it' - PRDGreads

'I loved the warming and comforting feeling I got when reading this story, words can be very powerful when used by those who know how. 5 Stars' - The Bookish Hermit

'An atmospheric read' - C L Tustin

A Distant Voice in the Darkness by Leela Dutt

A chance meeting at university leads to a relationship that spans marriages, the world and the decades in this sweeping and fulfilling novel from acclaimed author Leela Dutt.

Turtle Crawl   Chris Mason

When her marriage implodes, Rose Summer must leave behind everything she loved: her husband, her home, her shop, even her dog. With nowhere else to go, she returns to the only other place she ever felt happy: Key West, a bawdy tourist town at the tip of the Florida Keys. Working as a waitress in the same busy restaurant she served when she was young, and living with two other women—a stolid bistro manager and a rowdy singer/songwriter—her once joyful life has grown small and bleak. Then she meets Kurt, a wanderer with a tragic past of his own. Following an instinct she can't explain, Rose tries to draw him out of his shell and back into the world. Overcoming mistakes, misunderstandings, and the unwanted attentions of a potentially dangerous stalker, Rose opens her heart to Kurt and convinces him that life could be better.

Together, these two wounded souls can find happiness again, but only if they can overcome the obstacles that life throws at them. Like a turtle on the beach, they must navigate off the rocks and take one slow, careful step at a time across the sands toward fulfillment.

'In a culture where stories of finding all-encompassing love often are viewed through the lens of the rich and beautiful, Mason has created a romance between two seemingly unremarkable people, whose caring for one another creates a pleasing, fast-paced love story' - Publisher's Weekly

'Chris Mason hits all the right places in terms of humour, romance, sorrow and loss' - booksweverreadandloved.blogspot

Milton Keynes UK
Ingram Content Group UK Ltd.
UKHW021535101023
430299UK00014B/558